HAVEN CROSS

OTHER BOOKS AND AUDIO BOOKS
BY JULIE DAINES

A Blind Eye

Eleanor and the Iron King

Unraveled

Willowkeep

HAVEN CROSS

a regency romance

No regrets!

—Julie

JULIE DAINES

Covenant Communications, Inc.

Cover image © Ilina Simeonova / Trevillion Images

Cover design copyright © 2017 by Covenant Communications, Inc.

Published by Covenant Communications, Inc.
American Fork, Utah

Printed in the United States of America
First Printing: August 2017

23 22 21 20 19 18 17   10 9 8 7 6 5 4 3 2 1

ISBN 978-1-52440-332-4

For my parents

Thank you for showing me the world, teaching me what is important in life, and helping me see wonder.

If you wake at midnight, and hear a horse's feet,
Don't go drawing back the blind, or looking in the street.
Them that ask no questions isn't told a lie.
Watch the wall, my darling, while the Gentlemen go by!

"A Smuggler's Song"
Rudyard Kipling

CHAPTER ONE

Elaine

Two hundred fifty miles into this journey and not a word spoken. Elaine's body swayed as the carriage made its way over the rough track. She sat beside her mother and across from her father—though not one of them acknowledged the other.

Her mother had not stopped knitting since they'd left London. Her needles flew in a blur, and the pale-green lap rug she'd been working on was now big enough to cover the king's bed. This was how she coped. After John's death, she'd knitted enough shawls and blankets and stockings to keep the entire parish warm all winter long.

When her mother wasn't knitting, she stared out the window through teary eyes. Her father hadn't turned away from the opposite window's view.

Both of them there, her mother and father, squashed into the space of a cupboard, and each of them pretending the other didn't exist. Elaine wanted to scream into the silence, but what good would that do? It would serve only to hasten the saltwater drips falling onto her mother's enormous knitting project.

Ruined, her mother had whispered as they'd boarded their coach to escape London. *He has ruined us all.*

Elaine agreed. But all her mother's lamentations would not make amends.

Certainly her father was not the first fellow to be caught in an indiscretion. Unfortunately, they were commonplace among the *ton*. But when her own family became the target, well, she'd never been more humiliated in her life.

And when the woman's husband had come pounding on their door with pistol loaded, threatening her father that if he showed his face in London again, he'd blow it off, the decision to leave was rather easy. One did not press one's luck with General Forton.

However pointless her mother's complaints, they were all too true. Her father's folly left all their lives in a pile of tumbled-down ruin—like the rubble of the old abbeys and castles scattered across the ground. The best Elaine could do was gather as many stones as she could and try to rebuild. It would never be the grand edifice of her old life, but perhaps she could construct a respectable sort of cottage.

The countryside turned from rolling fields and gentle gardens to rocky tors and wild moorland. The air changed also, to the unmistakable dampness of Cornwall.

Elaine hadn't been to their family home in over five years—not since the death of her brother, John. She and her family had fled that memory, leaving it in the West Country and choosing instead to live in London. Now, with rumors of her father's indiscretion spreading through town like fire, they returned in disgrace. Not the reentrance into country life Elaine had hoped for.

In truth, she'd hoped never to make a reentry into her life at Havencross at all. She'd made a clean escape for good reason. Ending up back in Cornwall was not part of her plan to forget everything about John's death.

Her plan was to find a man to marry. A man who would take her far away from Cornwall, where she'd never have to face her past again. She'd thought perhaps she'd found one—in Edmund Crawley, Earl of Chiverton.

Now she'd likely never see him again. For every mile they traveled from London, Lord Chiverton's absence pulled tighter and tighter against her heart. She could look forward to life as a spinster, nursing her mother's broken heart and her father's gout. No decent man would connect his family to such a fallen lot. And the Earl of Chiverton was a fine and decent man.

The carriage rolled through the village of Camelford in the late afternoon. With any luck, news of her father hadn't reached this far. But judging by the looks from the villagers as they recognized the Cardinham ensign on the carriage door, she was out of luck.

Elaine leaned back into her seat as far out of view as possible until they crossed the River Camel, passed Market Place, and headed out west in the direction of the coast.

The ancient elm tree flashed past, signaling the turn-off toward Havencross. Its branches had been reaching to the sky for over a hundred years. Now it seemed too tired, and the tips drooped back toward earth.

Next came the weathered stone cross put up centuries ago by the monks—the mark that gave Havencross its name. A quarter of an hour later, the carriage slowed and the gray stones of her childhood home came into view.

They rolled to a stop, and a footman opened the carriage door. Her father dove for the exit, trampling Elaine's foot as he made his escape. She swallowed down an oath because, unlike her father, she had learned to control her impulses.

Her mother sniffed. Elaine handed her a clean handkerchief, and her mother blew her nose into it. She handed it back to Elaine, then stepped out of the carriage and shook out her skirts. Elaine followed, taking a moment to gaze up at the ancient stones of her childhood home.

Her mother hooked her thin hand through Elaine's arm. She had always been a beauty, but since John's death, she seemed to be wilting little by little.

She leaned close to Elaine. "I doubt Lord Chiverton will have you now."

"No," Elaine answered. Her father's ruination had assured her of that.

"If only John were here," her mother said. "I'm sure none of this would have happened."

Indeed. If only John were here. Five years gone and her mother continued to mourn him, blaming every ill that befell them on his absence. As if adding past pain to the new would cancel out the previous agonies. If her mother knew the truth, all her blame would turn on Elaine. And she deserved every bit of it. For this time, her mother was right; none of this would have happened if John were still here.

John's loss was the beginning of the end for the Cardinhams. None of them had been the same since. Her mother had turned to knitting, stabbing her needles through the air like she was crossing swords with her demons. Her father had lost a part of himself that had never returned, drifting silently away. Her family torn apart. All because of her.

She did not want to be back in Cornwall.

"And did you see the faces of the townsfolk as we drove through?" her mother asked.

Elaine nodded.

"The smirk on young Mr. Kemp's face. You must have seen that?"

"No, mother. I did not." Thank heaven.

To avoid Gareth Kemp was her top priority. He had been John's closest friend. His was a long-standing family in the community, freely owning the land they skillfully farmed, the elder Mr. Kemp foreman at the local mine.

Gareth had made her an offer of marriage when she'd been but seventeen. She refused him. Then, two days later, John had disappeared, and her whole life had changed. She'd left for London with her family, where she'd hoped to remain and never have to face Gareth or Havencross ever again.

Her mother squeezed her arm as if that was all she had left to offer her daughter. She dabbed at her eyes with her damp handkerchief.

The moment they crossed the threshold, the butler held out a silver salver with a single letter on it. "Mrs. Cardinham, a letter has arrived."

"Thank you, Mr. Winkleigh." Elaine took the letter and turned it over. "'Tis from Aunt Rose."

That brought a glimmer of cheer to her mother's eyes, but it faded almost as soon as it appeared.

Elaine broke the seal and skimmed the words. Her mother would not be interested in its contents verbatim. Not in her present state.

"She extends her love and sympathy," Elaine said. "She is outraged at what has happened and expresses her disappointment that we had to leave London so suddenly. Oh! And hear this. She and Uncle Charles are coming for a visit. To bolster your spirits. They shall arrive by week's end."

At last, some good news. If anyone could drag her mother out of the gloom, it would be her sister. It had been ages since they'd seen Aunt Rose and Uncle Charles. The Beafords never went to London. Not since the accident that had left Aunt Rose confined to a chair.

Elaine saw her mother to her room, then slipped out the back door, desperate for a moment alone.

Tomorrow the place would be flooded with neighbors coming to call. Always under the pretense of friendship, but all their excuses would be thinly veiled whisperings of scandal.

Mrs. Kemp, Gareth's mother, could very well be one of them. Elaine had no idea whether his mother knew about Gareth's failed marriage proposal. Just because Elaine chose to tell no one did not mean Gareth had made the same choice.

Thinking back on it stirred up the writhing coils that always accompanied such memories.

She pushed those thoughts away and crossed the garden courtyard. Havencross had been built on a rise, giving view to most of its surroundings. Elaine gazed out over the fields. The air was sweet with lengthening grass and blossoming blackthorn from the hedges. By summer's end, the hedges would be bursting with brambles and her fingers stained blue from picking and eating them.

The breeze shifted and a whiff of dung drifted past. Not the awful, acrid smell like the mews and stables of the crowded city but a rich and fertile smell as field workers churned it into the rows of freshly plowed earth.

She wound her way through the garden and out into the heath leading up to the sea. The whole landscape dropped away down steep, rocky cliffs to the water below. The waves crashed fearlessly against the black rocks, spraying in all directions.

Elaine turned her face up to the sky. The clouds moved so quickly it made her dizzy. So unlike the heavy clouds of London that snagged on the steeples and spires, keeping the city under perpetual haze.

Up the coastline a few miles to the north jutted the island-like headland of Tintagel, covered with the remains of the old castle. Between here and there, Lowentop, home of the Kemp family. Their nearest neighbors.

Two hundred fifty miles behind her, Lord Chiverton. What a mess her life had become.

The wind followed hard on the heels of the clouds. Her skirts whipped against her legs, and her bonnet tugged on its ties. She untied it and took it off, pulling the pins from her hair. The breeze caught her locks, and she shook her head, letting the strands fly like so many kite-tails trailing behind her.

She closed her eyes, facing the cliffs and the gusts from the sea. Tonight, there would be a storm, but just now, after three days trapped in the coach with her parents, it was a welcome zephyr. Perhaps some time at Havencross wouldn't be so bad after all.

"Miss Elowen Cardinham." She jumped at the voice from behind her.

Only one person in the world called her by the Cornish version of her name.

Gareth Kemp.

She turned around. The last person she wanted to see. Not that she could see him exactly. With the wind to her back, her entire view consisted of tangled copper hair. She grabbed a handful and pulled it away.

He stood before her, his hands on the reins of a horse.

He had not escaped the wind either, and his dark hair fluttered about his head. His hazel eyes matched the cloudy glow of the sun. He held a top hat under his arm and looked undeniably handsome in buckskin breeches and a dark coat. Not that she was paying attention.

"Mr. Kemp." She dipped her head.

CHAPTER TWO

Gareth

GARETH HADN'T SEEN ELAINE FOR five years. No, that wasn't entirely true. He had noticed the Cardinham carriage roll past The Black Hart Inn with Elaine inside trying desperately to hide her face.

His horse had thrown a shoe about a half mile back. It saved him a good mile or so to cut across the back of Havencross and take the coastal lane.

When he saw her perched on the edge of the cliff with the wind swirling her hair, he couldn't help himself. He'd never been good at resisting a chance to see her squirm. And squirm she would, for she was five years past due with an explanation.

She floundered with her hair again, trying to keep it out of her face.

"How was London?" he asked.

Her eyes flicked to his, then back to the ground, unable to hide her blush at seeing him again. He hadn't planned on it being quite so easy for him to accomplish his task, for with that single question, she undoubtedly squirmed.

She pulled the hair from her face again, though the wind only blew more to replace it. "Good day, Mr. Kemp."

And that was that. She hurried past him, back toward Havencross, smacking her bonnet on her leg as she marched away.

All right, then. Now he knew where he stood. Still no explanation as to why she'd turned him down five years ago. He was unworthy, no doubt. The son of a miner—even though his father had been the foreman. But a Kemp was no match for a Cardinham. Gareth had convinced himself she loved him. Wasn't the first time he'd been wrong. Just the most painful.

He shouldn't have come. It had been an impulsive move and had only told him what he'd already known: she never wanted to see him again.

Just as well. He need not entangle himself in that mess anew.

Gareth turned back along the path that led home. The sun barely drifted above the heavy waves to the west. Any moment, the clouds would open and drench the earth. The freshly planted fields needed the moisture, but he would be soaked through.

Served him right.

He veered off course and took the wide, graveled path to the church. With a flip of the reins, he tethered his horse, then dug into his saddlebag and removed a small stack of papers rolled and tied in a leather cover. He pushed the old iron gate, and it squeaked open.

In the back corner of the churchyard rested his father's grave. Six months to the day. Seemed like yesterday. But also like years since his father had been killed.

He'd been walking home from Polkreath Mine along the clifftop path—just like Gareth had today—when he'd stumbled upon the smugglers.

They crawled along these coasts like moles, with their tunnels and hidey-holes. Places like Penzance and Lizard down south got the worst of the smugglers. Regular people, most of them, fishermen and the like, living a secret life of lawlessness in the underbelly of Cornwall.

Those blackguards were not the only ones to blame for the sad state of affairs. If the crown did not tax the import of foreign goods so heavily, there'd be no need for smugglers. Every cup of tea was taxed beyond what any decent man should have to pay. If a person wanted brandy or lace, the choice was buy from smugglers or sell your soul to the devil to pay for it.

Gareth had made his share of purchases from the so-called *free traders*. Everyone did. Until they killed his father. Then no more. He'd dive headfirst off Peak Point rather than give a farthing for any goods smugglers touched.

The grass round his father's tombstone had been lately trimmed, and loose blades were caught in the chiseled lettering. Gareth brushed them out.

His father had been quite fond of Elaine. It was he who had given Gareth the courage to ask for her hand. Gareth had fooled himself into thinking his friendship with Elaine had grown into something more. Or perhaps he'd been deceived altogether, believing Elaine might look past the gap in their stations and situations. As it turned out, she could not.

Yet he was not so low as Elaine must think.

He knelt on one knee and unrolled the papers, lifting the top one from the bundle. It had a large red seal in the upper corner. "I wish you could have been here for this, Father." It was the deed and title to Polkreath Mine.

His father had worked his whole life at Polkreath as the foreman. He'd done well in the eyes of the owner, Mr. Penhurst. It was mostly due to his father's smart management that Mr. Penhurst had become so rich. Old Mr. Penhurst had never married and so had no son to pass the mine to. Gareth's father had had little difficulty convincing him to sell. Then his father had been killed before the deed was finalized. Today, Gareth realized his father's dream.

He was now the sole owner of Polkreath Mine. A laborer no more. A gentleman.

He laughed out loud at the sound of it. Not a soul in these parts would ever consider him a gentleman. Leastways not yet, but perhaps with time. Still, it was the beginning of a new life.

He rolled the deed back into its calfskin cover and placed it on his father's grave to let him get the feel of it.

"Miss Cardinham is back," he told his father. "Though I don't know for how long." He shook his head. "Do not worry. I'll not be making that mistake again. I shall avoid her at all costs. By mutual agreement, I believe."

After she'd left for London, he had honestly wished her well. Now she was back, still without her wealthy knight in shining armor that would carry her off to a castle in Surrey. Or Kent. Or wherever it was the fashionable gentlemen lived. It was not here in the West Country; of that he was sure.

A few raindrops landed on his father's gravestone, spattering dark flecks across the slate. He snatched up the deed and tucked it safely into his coat. His horsed whinnied from where he was tied in front of the church. Blasted beast hated the rain.

He hurried back through the churchyard and loosened the reins just as the clouds became waterfalls. Galahad looked more miserable than ever as he limped along soaked to the skin, his mane clumped and dripping.

"Sorry, old boy. We'll get you home and to the farrier."

Galahad leaned his shoulder into Gareth, and Gareth leapt to the side to avoid being trod upon.

"Oaf." He pushed the horse away. "Ungrateful beast. 'Tis not my fault it's raining."

By the time they reached the house, both man and animal had not a dry spot on them.

"Holy Saint Piran!" Gareth's mother burst out the door with an umbrella. "You're wet through. You'll be sick come morning, mark my words."

She held the umbrella over Gareth's head as if ten more feet under its cover might be the difference between life and death.

"Thank you, Mother. I'm sure you have saved me." Gareth handed the reins to Tomas. "He's thrown a shoe. See to it." He started toward the house but then called back. "And mind your feet. Remember, he gets grumpy in the rain."

Tomas nodded and headed off to the stable in the back.

Gareth ducked into the house behind his mother.

"Straight to the kitchen," she said. "I'll not have you dripping all over my clean floors. Remember when Violet Maddern's husband slipped on a wet floor? He hasn't been right in the head since. And all because Violet let him lolly about dripping all over the front hall."

She called to Martha for a towel, then pushed Gareth toward the back of the house. "Mrs. Penmoor has a nice pot of tetty-rattle for you. Well, don't stand there. Get."

Gareth strode off to the kitchen, leaving a trail of water down the hall, with poor Martha wiping a towel along behind him.

His mother followed, stepping here and there to avoid the wet. Gareth smiled as his short, stout mother maneuvered gracefully on feet too small for her size.

The kitchen fire blazed, making the housekeeper's face bright red as she stirred the large pot of stew.

His mother moved a chair nearer to the hearth and nearly pushed him into it. "How did it go in Camelford?"

Gareth laid the deed in his mother's hands. "'Tis done."

She smoothed her fingers over the calfskin cover. "You've made your father proud."

"This was his doing," Gareth said. "He is the one who worked and saved and arranged for the purchase. I only finished his business."

"And Polkreath? Will it be good?"

Gareth tugged off his coat, pulling hard as it clung to him, wet and heavy. "Aye. Quite good. They finished sinking the new shaft, and I believe we're right on top of a lucrative lode."

His mother beamed at him. "All his life he dreamt of owning that place. No longer a foreman. Breaks my heart he's not here for this." Her eyes turned down, and her lips pressed together as they always did when she dwelt on his father. She might never recover from the shock of her husband's violent death. Now she clung to Gareth like he was made of porcelain.

Martha knelt on the floor and tugged on Gareth's boots. "I'll get these dried right away, sir."

Thus far, all his efforts to track down the blackguards responsible for his father's death had been fruitless. They lurked in the shadows and underground, known only to each other and the man they called the operator, who organized the schemes. It was this operator Gareth wanted to get his hands on, for he doubted the others would have dared kill his father without authorization.

He also wanted to get his hands on the gentleman who paid for the smuggling runs. There was always some wealthy gentleman backing the ventures. If Gareth stopped him, he might end the whole ring. Problem was, only the operator could identify the gentleman. They kept it all separate so people like Gareth or the Landguard could prove nothing.

Such violence was rare for smugglers. Most of them moved their goods from land to sea and kept to their own business. But this band had turned on his father so quickly. Gareth wondered again what cargo they'd had worth killing over.

He'd already asked these questions a thousand times and was no closer to the truth. He would get there. Eventually. Then he'd rally the Landguard and get rid of these smugglers once and for all—or at least for a few weeks until a new batch came along and took their place.

With Elaine back, he had even more reason to clean up the shores. Heaven forbid she meet up with the moles.

"Gareth?" His mother tapped his shoulder.

He blinked. His mother was speaking to him, and Mrs. Penmoor held out a mug of warm mead.

"You *are* ill," his mother said. "I knew it. You come home drenched, and you're getting sick already. Martha, fetch Dr. Woodbury."

Gareth took the mead. "Martha, don't fetch Dr. Woodbury. I'm not ill. I was just . . . distracted." This was meant to be a happy day. The fulfillment of all they'd wanted for their family. His dwelling on the past only distressed his mother more.

He handed the mug back to Mrs. Penmoor untouched. "Ready our best bottle. 'Tis a day of celebration."

His mother smiled at him. Mine owner or not, all she really cared about was her family.

"Now, off you go. Get out of those wet clothes, and rest up a bit. You've been going twenty to the dozen these past months and have worn yourself right out. I'll have Mrs. Penmoor prepare you a draught of elderflower and a fine meal." His mother tottered off toward the pantry muttering about colds and chills and certain death. "Oh." She turned back. "Did you hear the news?"

He had learned that question was not meant to be answered no matter how much news he might have heard. Gareth would never deny her the telling of news. He shook his head.

"The Cardinhams are returned. Back from London with some sort of scandal hanging over their heads."

"Oh?"

"Likely that daughter of theirs got herself into some kind of trouble."

His mother did not know about his previous dealings with Elaine. Even so, he didn't want the tongue-tabbis spreading untruths about her. "Now that you mention it, I did hear something of the matter in Camelford. Seems it was to do with the father and not Miss Cardinham."

His mother frowned. "Poor Mrs. Cardinham. Her spirits must be so low. We shall invite them to dinner." Her eyes lit up, at last chasing away the glum brought on by all the talk of his father.

"Well, now. I'm not sure that is such a good idea." They'd never accept. The Cardinhams hadn't come to Lowentop since Mr. Cardinham had married Mrs. Cardinham's ten thousand pounds.

Now they were far too good for the Kemps. Mostly in the Cardinhams' mind, but so often one's own mind became the only truth one lived by.

CHAPTER THREE

Elaine

ELAINE DID NOT COME DOWN for dinner that night. Nor did her mother or her father, Betsy told her. Each took their meal in their own chambers. Elaine had promised herself all would be as it should be, that she'd not give the servants reason to chatter. She'd not even made it through the first evening.

She spent the night lying in her bed, listening to the rain as it pattered against the roof slates, the wind as it whistled through her windowpanes.

When the bell rang in the late morning with the first visitor, Elaine slunk down the stairs. She'd rather be anywhere besides trapped in the drawing room with a flock of curious women. But she couldn't leave her mother alone to attend to the neighbors.

From the smell of pipe smoke leaking under the door, her father was shut up in his library. She paused in front of it and lifted her hand. She could knock and go in. Confront him. Blame him for ruining them all. For putting a moat between her and Lord Chiverton and then filling it with burning oil.

But the truth was she didn't know exactly what her father had done. There had been a flood of rumors but a famine of facts. She lowered her hand. Not today. If he had anything to say to defend himself, let him say it on his own.

A footman she'd never seen before kept his post by the drawing room door. With the family gone for so long and only her father returning for occasional business, Mr. Winkleigh had let much of the staff go. He must have scrambled to find these new servants on such short notice.

"I'm Miss Cardinham," she said. There should have been some sort of formal introduction between the new staff and the family. Perhaps Mr. Winkleigh had assumed that in this case, the family might wish to forgo it.

The footman bowed.

"And you are?" He clearly hadn't been long in this position.

"Brixton, miss."

He couldn't have been a day over twenty, and he eyed Elaine with an appraising grin. It was entirely improper. A reprimand was in order, but on this day of bad to worse, she soaked up the compliment and savored it.

"How bad is it in there?"

He raised one eyebrow. "Full of clackers, miss."

Just as she'd suspected. A room full of wagging tongues in pretty dresses. She gave him a nod.

He pulled on the handle, revealing a congregation of ladies dressed in day gowns far from the London styles she was accustomed to. Her mother sat in the middle of them, handing out knit shawls to any woman who would have one, her eyes still ringed in red. So busy were they fluttering over her mother that Elaine went unnoticed.

"Oh, you poor thing," a woman said. Mrs. Dawlish, perhaps? It had been so long, and Elaine had never been one for sitting in parlors.

"And your poor daughter. What will become of her now?"

"Bal maiden, no doubt. Workin' out o' the mines," another woman Elaine did not know said. Several other hens clucked in agreement.

For heaven's sake. As if Elaine would need to stoop so low as to take up work hammering tin ore. She was still a gentleman's daughter. Her family was scandalized and humiliated, not impoverished.

Elaine made her way across the room toward a young woman who appeared to be her own age.

"Here's your daughter now." This from a woman with feathers in her bonnet dyed every color of the rainbow.

Each face in the room swung in Elaine's direction. She gave them all a sort of general curtsey.

"You poor dear. I'm sure you'll remember me?" the feathery one said.

Elaine shook her head.

"Mrs. Swallowford. From Brakenmill Farm."

The name sounded vaguely familiar, but Elaine did not recognize the face. "Oh, yes. Of course."

"How unfortunate for you that your seasons in London didn't work out." This came from a different woman with graying hair and a missing tooth. "You poor little thing."

"Thank you," Elaine said. What else could she say? Though the woman's sympathy grated, the sentiment remained true. Elaine's seasons hadn't worked out. She'd fled to London to get away from memories of John. To find a new life where his loss did not weigh on her like a burden she could never shed. Now here she was, back again and worse off than before.

Elaine pried herself away from the older women and managed a seat by the younger one. The girl's gown was simple and more worn than new, but it suited her.

"Hello," Elaine said, sitting in the chair. "I don't believe we've met."

The woman shook her head. "I've been in the neighborhood a few months, but I still feel like I don't know anyone. I'm Miss Tippet." She had glimmering auburn hair done up in a pretty knot. Her eyes were a soft blue.

"Well, I was born and raised here, but I've been gone so long I feel like I don't know anyone either."

Miss Tippet laughed heartily. Perhaps a little too heartily, for all heads turned in her direction again. Clearly the hens found any form of gaiety inappropriate under such dreadful circumstances.

"Where are you from, Miss Tippet?" By her accent, it was not the West Country. Perhaps somewhere north.

"I'm from Wrexbury. Up by Liverpool. And please call me Ambrosia."

Her parents certainly had a great deal of confidence in their daughter. "Food of the gods," Elaine said with a smile.

The girl shook her head. "No, thank you. I'm stuffed."

Elaine stared at her for a moment. "I mean your name."

She laughed again, edging once more on excessive. "I'm named after my father, Mr. Tippet. I think he wanted a boy. His name is Ambrose."

Elaine stared again. Who was this girl? "What I meant to say was that your name, Ambrosia, is the Greek word for the food of the gods." She could not have gone her whole life and never learned this. Elaine couldn't possibly have been the first one to notice.

"Oh, yes." She nodded. "I see what you mean. Zeus and Athena and so on."

Elaine nodded.

"And if you eat it, you get immortality."

So she did know something. That was encouraging.

"But I've eaten my whole life, and I'm not immortal." She laughed again, and it made her pretty face even more beautiful. Perhaps she was Ambrosia after all.

Elaine moved on, avoiding any more talk that might cause another outburst of merriment. "What has brought your family to Camelford?"

"Not my family. Just me and my father. Well, I mean we two are the whole family." She took a sip of tea from the old rosebud tea set. "My father was in the militia up in Wrexbury. But now he's taken a post here as head of the Landguard."

The smuggling must be getting worse for the crown to put preventive men in Camelford. Hopefully they were better behaved than the militia. She'd seen enough of their depravity to have no confidence at all in their abilities to keep the peace. Rather, they were destroyers of inns, builders of debts, and ruiners of daughters.

"The Landguard," Elaine said. "That sounds interesting. I hope you are settling in well."

"The people here are very nice. Mrs. Swallowford has had us out for dinner several times." She gestured toward the rainbow of feathers. "She brought me here today. And the Kemps have been especially kind. Do you know the Kemps?"

"Yes. Mrs. Kemp is very kind."

A faint blush colored Miss Tippet's cheeks. "Do you know her son, Mr. Kemp?"

Elaine preferred the topic of the Landguard—or even the Greeks. "Um, yes. A little. He's . . . very kind."

"He has been particularly attentive. My father enjoys his conversation greatly, and we've been to Lowentop more than once for an evening meal."

"How nice for you." Ambrosia, food of the gods. How could a mortal man resist? Elaine should never have come down the stairs.

She sat for another quarter of an hour, until Mrs. Swallowford stood and took her leave, dragging Miss Tippet along with her.

Elaine slipped from the drawing room and out the back door. The rain from the night before had left the earth damp but clean. Clouds dotted the sky, empty and pale, not unlike Miss Tippet's eyes.

Elaine had dutifully spent the last few days making visits with her mother. She'd yet to see or speak with her father, who kept himself tucked away in his library or outside riding his horse. She was determined to make the most of this day, her last before the arrival of Aunt Rose and Uncle Charles.

With her shawl pulled tight around her shoulders, she cut through the kitchen and out the back door. Just as she turned to close it, Brixton was there.

"Going out, miss?"

She nodded, not that it was any of his business.

"Shall I accompany you, miss?" He bowed as he made his inquiry.

Had she been in London, stepping out to do some shopping, she would have been glad for a footman. But this was her home, and she knew the ways well. The last thing she wanted was a stranger hovering around. Perhaps her father had put him up to this. *Keep an eye on my daughter, and don't let her get into trouble.* What a sham coming from him, of all people.

"No. I'll be keeping to the garden today." She turned and left him there.

As soon as she was out of sight of the house, she set off, following the rocky clifftop northward for the better part of an hour. This had always been one of her favorite places, with the rushing of the water as it broke upon the shore below her. The mouse-ear buds bulging as they were days from bursting their blooms.

She'd traveled this path many times with John and Gareth, but this was her first time going alone. The wind came off the sea, gusting up the cliffs and blowing inland. It always blew, and the stunted, bowed trees were testaments of it. In Camelford, these same trees grew tall and straight. Here, their wispy branches all reached inward as if desperate to escape the rocky coast. Just as she had been. And in the end, she'd gotten about as far.

Sheep grazed in the fields, skinny and pink from spring shearing. A half a dozen or so choughs followed behind them. The crow-like birds snatched up insects with their red beaks as the foraging sheep stirred up the ground.

She passed the ancient Trevanna parish church, St. Materiana's, and came to the ruined castle of Tintagel clinging to the side of the cliffs, built out of the same grayish stone so it almost looked like a natural feature. People came from all parts of the country to see it—the fabled place where King Arthur was born.

She'd climbed these rocks many times, always with John and Gareth. If she closed her eyes, she could hear them laughing. But no, it was only the gulls. The larger part of the ruins was out on a small headland connected by a narrow bridge of rock, making it more like an island than anything.

The place seemed deserted today. Too early in the season, perhaps, and those with leisure time to feed their follies were all still in London. Probably discussing the great scandal her family had left in its wake. Just as well. If word got back to her father that she'd ventured here on her own, she would be severely chastised. That was, if he ever came out of his library.

She crossed the treacherous stretch of land that connected the main coast to the headland. It was nearly straight down, then straight back up again. Walls made of crumbling shale and moorstone left outlines of a once-magnificent place. She wandered about the remains, running her hands along the rocks, trying to imagine the people who had lived here.

The scholars claimed the largest site was built nearly six hundred years ago by Richard, Earl of Cornwall, the king's brother. Before that, King Arthur. And before that, people she knew nothing about.

Must have been an ungoverned life so far away from the London court. How did they live in such dark, forgotten times?

Or perhaps those were the enlightened times.

After all, Arthur and his knights were famous for their chivalry. From what she'd seen of the men in London—including her own father—chivalry had all died out.

She left the castle ruins and stood atop the ridge overlooking the rocky beach below. The tide was out, making Merlin's Cave accessible. When the water rose, it flooded the cave, filling it with a dangerous pull.

Another steep, winding path descended from the ruins to the small beach and cave below. Checking again that she was alone, she lifted the hem of her dress and started down, setting her feet carefully. If she took a fall, there was no one for miles to carry her limp body back to Havencross.

This was where they'd played as children, acting out stories of knights and kings and wizards. From sunup to sundown, the three of them here, scrambling the cliff sides. An idyllic childhood. Just along the ridge was the clump of sea thrift where Gareth had picked her a bouquet of round pink flowers on the day he'd asked her to marry him.

She'd thought nothing of it, for he'd often picked her handfuls of whatever happened to be in bloom. She had tucked the thrift into her hair, making herself a crown of pink. Lady Elowen, he'd called her, then had beckoned her to come with him to the cave.

Walking here today was like treading in the footsteps of her own ghost. Elaine made it down the steep slope without loss of life or limb and crossed the sand to the mouth of Merlin's Cave. It was said the enchanter's body was still here somewhere, entombed inside the rock, awaiting the return of the king.

She left the warmth of the sun and stepped inside. It opened into a large cavern with a tunnel of light at the far end, where it let out again on the other side. The water churned and sloshed as the receding waves fought with the incoming tide.

This was Gareth's favorite place. He loved it for the copper deposits. Always practical.

On that last day, Gareth had stood before her, where she stood now, and told her he loved her. That she was the most valiant and the fairest in all the land. Just a boy of nineteen, working in the tin mine where his father was the foreman and managing the fields of Lowentop.

She'd been so young, completely unready to make such a decision. He'd taken both of her hands in his rough ones. If she closed her eyes, she could hear his voice whispering in her ears. See the devastation in his eyes. Feel the crush of the beach pebbles beneath her feet when she ran away.

She'd left a trail of pink sea thrift from here all the way back to Havencross. A trail of flowers and tears.

Mostly she'd been overwhelmed by the suddenness of it. Then it was too late. At first, she'd thought she'd made a mistake to refuse him. Then two days later, John had died and everything had changed.

Except the cave. It had not changed at all—the rock and sand timeless. If she could go back to that day, she would do it all so differently. And John would still be alive, and she would not be carrying his grave across her shoulders.

His empty grave, for his body was never found. She had sent him out into the night, and he had never returned.

"Merlin," she whispered. Not that she believed the legend now that she was fully grown. That would be nonsense. But she spoke to him anyway because she had nowhere else to turn. "If you can hear me, I beg your help. Our family has fallen apart, and it is all my fault. My folly. I wish I could go back and . . ."

But there was no point in stating her wish. She could not go back in time and undo all that had been done. The best she could hope for was a life far away from here where she could leave her troubles behind.

A noise came from the depths of the cave. Like someone moaning.

Elaine spun around, but all was silent again. She took a few steps in. "Hello?"

Another groan and the clatter of stones came from deeper inside. Elaine peered into the darkness and glimpsed a silhouette of someone lying on the ground about twenty paces in.

She picked her way across the stony floor. “Hello?”

As Elaine drew closer, the figure slowly came into view. Judging by her size, it was a young woman. The whites of her eyes stared at Elaine, following her as she approached. She looked stricken with fear. And wounded.

“Hello, there.” Elaine knelt beside her.

Upon seeing her face, it was clear she was older, perhaps closer to thirty, but small of stature. She lay in a patch of sand, clutching at her midriff. A dark liquid seeped from beneath her and left a rivulet of red through the sand.

“Are you hurt?” The question seemed obvious, but she didn’t know how else to bridge the silence between them.

The woman did not answer. She wore a dark dress, the green of a forest at twilight, and in a fashion Elaine had not seen here in Cornwall nor in London. The fabric was heavy wool but finely woven. At first she thought a miner’s wife or a tenant farmer’s. Or a vagrant. But then she noticed the circlet of gold on her brow. It was small and dainty and held a single emerald in the center. Far too fine a piece for someone of lower circumstances.

“Let me see.” Elaine reached out to lift the woman’s hand and examine the extent of the wound.

The woman slowly removed her hand, revealing the source of the blood.

“What happened to you?” This lady needed a surgeon. Or at least something besides a sandy cave floor—a cave that would be flooded in only a short time.

She did not answer.

“Do you speak English?”

Shipwrecks were not uncommon on these rugged shores. She may not be from England—which would explain her silence and odd dress.

“Can you walk?” Elaine motioned toward the entrance, a gesture she hoped conveyed *Let’s get out of here*.

The woman made an attempt to sit up, but the effort left her gasping. Elaine tried to assist, but it was no use. She helped the woman lay back down.

Elaine needed help. She couldn’t move her out of the cave alone. Not without doing more damage to the injury. Suddenly, having a footman trailing her did not seem like such a bad idea, but she’d left Brixton back at the house. She’d have to go back to Havencross to fetch help.

She did what she could to slow the bleeding, pressing her shawl against the wound. “Hold this here.” She put the woman’s hand over the shawl. “My name is Elaine." She pointed at herself. "Elaine." She then pointed at the woman. "What's your name?"

"Gwen," she said with a gasp.

"Gwen." Elaine gave a reassuring smile. "I'm going to go get help."

The fear entered her eyes again.

"I'll be back. I promise."

At last, the woman nodded.

Elaine hurried out of the cave. The water was already a few feet closer than it had been when she'd entered. She didn't have much time.

Hefting her skirts, she scrambled up the steep path. At the top, she turned south, back toward Havencross. Then she paused.

Gareth's home was much closer. Much, much closer. He'd think her a lunatic if she came rapping at his door, but she had little choice. Gwen would either bleed out or drown if she delayed a moment longer.

She ran off, cutting across the fields and along the hedgerows toward Gareth's house. Every few minutes, she had to pause to catch her breath. She'd gone soft during her time in London. The Minuet and the Cotillion were no replacement for a good run across the heath.

Gareth's slate-covered house loomed in the distance. A pretty two-story structure settled in a quaint situation with a lovely woodland behind. Woodlands were scarce things in this landscape of water and wind and rocks.

She ran the last few yards to the door. This would be her second encounter with him since her return, and both times, she'd looked a windblown mess. She made an attempt to smooth her hair and straighten her dress, then gave five raps at the door.

A woman answered, his housekeeper, Mrs. Penmoor. Elaine remembered her, though her hair was now threaded with gray.

"Miss Cardinham." The housekeeper curtseyed.

Elaine put her hand to her chest as if it might help her draw air. "Is Mr. Gareth Kemp in?" she gasped.

Before Mrs. Penmoor could answer, Gareth came into view behind the housekeeper, peering over her shoulder.

CHAPTER FOUR

Gareth

"Miss Cardinham?" Gareth couldn't believe his eyes. He was sure she'd rather swim the channel in naught but her dancing slippers and white kid gloves than show her face at his door.

Her hair tumbled loose over her shoulders, and a flush of pink tinged her cheeks and nose. A look he preferred far more than the tidy and perfect aspect she'd taken on before leaving for London. Her eyes, though, held an edge of something troubling.

"Are you well?"

"Perfectly well, thank you," she said in a formal tone she must have perfected in London. Then she bent forward, and her shoulders rose and fell as she panted. She'd come in a hurry.

Mrs. Penmoor slipped away. Elaine took a few more moments to recover her breath, then she straightened.

"Will you come in?" he asked.

Elaine shook her head; her eyes wandered behind him as though searching for something. Or someone. She did not look at him. He leaned against the door, waiting for her reason for being here. It was not a social call, else he had no doubt she'd have arrived in the carriage with bonnet intact and wearing something trimmed in gold.

"Are you looking for someone?"

She shook her head again.

He waited longer this time for her to speak. Still she did not. "Much as I enjoy a good guessing game, perhaps you might simply tell me why you are here."

That seemed to pull her out of her silence, and a sense of urgency crossed her face. "I need your help. Down in the cave."

Merlin's Cave? He'd not been there in ages. Not since he'd taken her there and asked for her hand—which she'd then used to slap him. Perhaps it wasn't a physical slap, but he had felt the sting nonetheless.

She must have followed his thoughts. A flush colored her cheeks. She glanced around and then said, "I found an injured woman in the cave. I believe she is in danger else I would have never dared impose. I could not move her, and the tide is coming in."

This sounded rather far-fetched. But Elaine did look serious. And there was the whole swimming of the channel thing. She must be in earnest else she'd have never come knocking on his door.

"Will you come?" she asked, at last meeting his eyes.

It was then he glimpsed the real Elaine. Elowen, though she hated that name.

"Of course."

He closed the door behind him. They hurried along in silence until the discomfort of not speaking became worse than the discomfort of speaking. "I hope your family is settled in."

"Thank you, but I'm afraid we will never be settled again."

He glanced over at her. That was quite a candid sentiment coming from this woman who never shared her true feelings with anyone.

"I'm sorry to hear that."

"You are?" She was not taking her family's fall well at all; that much was clear.

"Of course I am." However much she had wronged him, he would never wish this kind of ill on her family. Perhaps a different subject might be better. "Tell me about the woman."

Elaine described what she'd found in the cave, all the while urging him to move faster.

They reached the steep path leading down from the castle to the small beach below, the only patch of sand in the cove. The water lapped at the entrance to the cave.

"Hurry," Elaine said as she started down the cliffside. A gust of wind shook her off balance, and she flung her hand out behind her.

He caught it by reflex, steadying her. Another sign that she was not herself; she could scale these slopes better than anyone. Gareth paused, caught off guard at the familiar warmth that spread from her touch. After all this time he'd spent determined to forget about her, he was betrayed by his own body.

As soon as she got her balance, he let go, and she rushed down to the cave. She didn't even stop to remove her boots.

"In here," she called as if he didn't know where to go.

He followed her in. She went deeper and deeper and then stopped, glancing around. The opening on the other end glimmered beyond the bend.

Gareth saw nothing but shining black rocks and sand. "Where is she?" he asked.

Elaine looked toward the rear, then toward the mouth. "Hello?" she called once, then again. "Hello?"

She bent down and studied the ground. "She was right here."

Gareth leaned over. The sand was undisturbed. No footprints. No bumps. Not even the trailings of crabs.

"She was here, bleeding into the sand. I told her I'd be back with help. I promised." Elaine looked up at him with troubled eyes. "Why didn't she wait?"

Gareth found no evidence that anyone besides themselves had been in the cave for some time. If this mysterious girl had been bleeding, as Elaine said, no trace of blood remained. He raked the sand. Nothing.

Perhaps Elaine remembered the location wrong. He stood and paced, searching for any evidence that someone had lain here bleeding, as Elaine had described.

"I'm going farther. Wait here." Gareth jogged into the depths. Nothing. But this end of the cavern was rough rock and shallow water. Unlikely anyone would come to rest here.

Was she lying? Shamming it for some kind of practical joke? He returned to Elaine, who stood staring at the blank sand as if it had personally wronged her.

"Nothing," he said. "The place is empty."

"I don't understand." Elaine couldn't seem to take her eyes off the spot where the supposed lady had been. "She was right here. She couldn't have left by herself; she could not even sit. Someone else must have come for her."

"Then we would have seen footprints." His suspicions about Elaine's motives were growing, and it must have shown on his face.

"I swear it. She said her name was Gwen, and she was right here."

"Gwen?" Now he knew she was playing him. "As in Gwenevere. And we are standing in Merlin's Cave." He started back toward the entrance. "Nice try, Elaine."

"Don't be ridiculous. I don't believe in that childish nonsense anymore."

He stopped and stared at her. "Childish nonsense?"

Of all the strange things that had happened today, this was the hardest to believe. And the saddest. Elaine had been the greatest believer of them all. The legends of King Arthur were the roots from which she'd grown. To lose her faith in that seemed dangerous indeed. London had taken a harder toll on her than he'd suspected.

She shrugged and looked away.

"Whatever you say, Miss Cardinham." He set off again toward the entrance, the water sloshing around his ankles. There went another pair of boots. He would have to set these aside for when he was needed down in the mine. Elaine splashed along behind him as she waded through the incoming tide.

There was a time he would have turned back and carried her out. But no more. She wanted nothing to do with him. She'd made that very clear when she'd turned her nose up at him and his small house and his even smaller income.

A loud splash came from behind him. He turned to find her sprawled in the water. She'd tripped and fallen. And now he felt like an imbecile. Some gentleman he was to leave a lady to fend for herself in a cave with the tide rushing in.

He lifted her from the water. The wet caused her dress to cling to her figure. Whatever damage London may have done to her attitudes, she'd lost none of her beauty.

She pushed away, brushing the sand off her frock. Then she looked up to find him staring at her.

He was a fool and more for thinking he could return with her to this place and feel nothing. He removed his coat and draped it around her shoulders.

"Thank you," she said, pulling it tight across her front.

"Come. We'd better hurry unless you want another swim." He offered his arm, she put her hand on it, and they balanced each other across the rocky ground whilst the waves pushed and pulled against their legs.

When they cleared the swells, she made as if to shrug off the coat, but he stopped her.

"Keep it. You'll need it for your walk home."

"I had a shawl," she said. "I brought one. But I gave it to Gwen to staunch the blood." Her mind had gone back to the mysterious woman. Or perhaps it had always been there. Perhaps his was the only one that strayed.

"Gwenevere?"

She pursed her lips. "'Tis the truth. She was right here."

Maybe she was telling the truth. She looked a wreck, and the frenzy in her eyes was real enough. He had to be the one person she never wanted to be with inside that cave ever again, so something very real must have brought her to his door.

Whoever she was, the woman was gone now. For all he knew, she could have been part of a trap for unsuspecting wanderers. Smugglers weren't the only vermin along these coasts. They got a batch of pirates every now and then.

If pirates were involved, it was lucky Elaine had gotten away so easily instead of being held for ransom. He made a note to check with the Landguard and ask if there was any news of marauders in these parts. He'd also talk to the magistrate, Squire Stroud. Any excuse to spur on the squire's investigation into the death of his father. So far, the squire had turned up nothing. Not surprising considering the way these men melted away into nothing.

Gareth followed Elaine up the path. They reached the top and journeyed through the castle ruins in silence.

"Perhaps she was part of a ploy," Gareth suggested.

Elaine shrugged. "Perhaps. If she was, something went terribly wrong, because she was dying."

"Terribly wrong?" He almost spat but thought better of it. "We're talking about smugglers. They care not at all about who they put six feet under." This he knew too well. "Nor would it be the first time a person has disappeared in these parts without a trace."

She spun around and glared at him.

Blast. He was an idiot. Of course she would go straight to John. "I didn't mean him. Elaine—" He'd lost his closest friend when John had died. He'd been devastated. But no one had taken the loss harder than Elaine.

"Sorry to have bothered you," she said and turned away, hurrying across the heath.

Gareth watched her until she disappeared behind a hedgerow, then he followed after, keeping just out of sight. At the very least, he would see her safely home.

CHAPTER FIVE

Elaine

Elaine broke into a run. Of course Gareth would bring up John.

Maybe he suspected it was because of her John had been killed. No. He couldn't. She'd never told a soul about Gareth's proposal and her refusal and then her sending John out into the night. Even John had not known about Gareth's offer.

She never should have gone to Gareth for help.

Not to mention that he thought she'd lost her mind, leading him down to Merlin's Cave for apparently no purpose whatsoever.

She slowed to a walk. Her day of pleasure had quickly turned sour. She'd accomplished nothing more than proving herself the lackwit Gareth already considered her to be. Though she hadn't missed the way he'd looked at her with her gown wet. Nor the way his coat smelled of him.

She slipped in through the back door. Even with the coat on, she shivered from the cold.

When she reached the bottom of the stairs, she paused. A voice came from the drawing room. A man's voice. Perhaps her father had at last decided to come out of his library.

She crept across the hall and pressed her ear against the door. Her mother's voice came through, going on about how nice of him to visit and should she call for tea.

Then she heard a voice she thought she'd never hear again.

Lord Chiverton.

What on earth could he be doing here?

At that moment, the drawing room door opened and her mother nearly ran her over.

"Elaine!"

Elaine had a clear enough view over her mother's shoulder to see Lord Chiverton stand. If it had been King George himself, she could not have been more surprised. She stood there, in the open door, gaping at him like a startled fawn.

"Close your mouth, dear. You'll let the flies in," her mother whispered.

She tried, but it was not so easily done. She'd thought he would be done with her after the scandal. Now he was here. And she looking like a ratty polecat.

Her mother smiled at Lord Chiverton. There was no escape now.

"Here she is," her mother said. She stepped aside and motioned Elaine into the room.

He bowed to her, and she curtseyed back.

"Lord Chiverton."

He smiled as his eyes traveled from her disheveled hair to her dripping and muddy boots. "That is a very fine coat you are wearing," he said.

Appearing in another man's coat would not better his opinion of her. Quite the contrary. She would have taken it off, but her dress underneath was still wet through. She'd not forgotten the reason Gareth had lent it to her in the first place.

And now that Lord Chiverton mentioned it, it was a very fine coat. Finer than she'd expected Gareth to be able to afford.

The room waited in silence for her to explain the gentleman's coat and water seeping from her shoes.

She smiled at Lord Chiverton. "It is so good to see you, sir. And good of you to come. And I am . . . If you just . . . Please excuse me a moment while I tidy up." Elaine left the drawing room before she could make herself into a greater fool. Already she wanted to crawl under the floorboards and hide. She called for her maid as she ascended the stairs.

Betsy appeared in Elaine's room.

"I must change immediately," Elaine said, throwing Gareth's coat onto her bed.

Betsy sprang into action, helping Elaine out of her wet and ruined dress and into a pretty little green-sprigged muslin that would bring out the color of her eyes. It was a dress made for London, not the West Coast, where the wind howled and the air chilled, but she looked splendid in it. What did it matter if she froze when Lord Chiverton was here. Perhaps all was not lost.

Half the girls in London had their eyes on the handsome Lord Chiverton. The other half had their eyes on his money. She had come to appreciate him for more than that.

It was at the Wilmslows' ball that she had first met him. He'd smiled at her from across the dance floor and made his way toward her through the crush of people, much to the dismay of at least a dozen other young ladies. And much to Elaine's surprise, for she was nobody and Lord Chiverton could have anyone.

Since that time, they'd danced together frequently. Played cards at his house. Even taken a turn around Hyde Park. He owned a large estate in Warwickshire, right in the heart of England and far away from Cornwall. A perfect situation.

Her cheeks were too pink from her morning in the sun, but there was naught she could do about it now. Betsy reset her hair, and Elaine hurried back to the drawing room in an amazingly short amount of time. Her mother had just finished pouring tea.

Lord Chiverton stood again as she entered. Her efforts to restore herself did not go unnoticed as a small grin softened his face. The smile that had first drawn her to him across the ballroom back in London.

The simple fact that he was here meant something. He could have stayed in London and pretended with the rest of them that she'd ceased to exist. But he hadn't.

He took her hand and gave it a gentle squeeze. "It is good to see you again. I have missed you."

"I've only been gone less than a week, sir."

"Even so." He escorted her to a seat near the fire. "You should sit here. Your hands are cold." Always the gentleman. Perhaps chivalry still survived after all.

"Lord Chiverton," her mother said. "What brings you out to our part of the country?"

"I have a shipment coming into Plymouth." He finally took his eyes off Elaine and turned to her mother. "I don't usually see to these things personally, but this cargo is quite valuable, so I thought I'd come myself."

Lord Chiverton had likely never once taken the slightest interest in what happened with his various ships and cargos. He had a man for that. And a second man for his land. And a third to manage the house. Not to mention that he could have saved himself a day's worth of travel by going straight through Exeter and south.

"We do hope your business is not so urgent that you can't stay a few days." Her mother handed him a plate with a piece of hevva cake on it. "Do you come to Cornwall often?"

He shook his head. "No."

The only people who came here were either miners or fishers. Or smugglers.

"There are some lovely sights to be seen," her mother said. "Isn't that right, Elaine?" She cast Elaine an artful glance. "Elaine is very fond of Arthur's Castle. Perhaps she can take you there."

He looked over at her.

For all his soft brown eyes and face of an angel, she had little desire to take Lord Chiverton to the castle ruins. He might want to see the cave. A place Elaine would be happy never to return to. Especially after today.

"Have you seen the moors at Bodmin?" Elaine asked. "Some of the rock formations are quite astounding. Cheesewring or Rough Tor."

"I have not had the privilege, no. But it sounds fascinating."

Her mother beamed. She'd thought, as Elaine had, that no man would come within twenty miles of poor Elaine.

He set his teacup down and leaned toward her. "Do you often go out walking in a man's coat?"

Just when she thought he'd forgotten. "No, sir. I was down by the water, as you may have suspected, when I . . ." What? Found a woman hurt and alone who later vanished? Sought help from the man who had once offered to marry her? The less he knew about Gareth the better. "Tripped in the incoming tide."

He laughed. "And you were rescued by a handsome gentleman?"

"Something like that." She tried to sound amused. He seemed awfully interested in the owner of the coat. She was certainly not going to let him lure her into a discussion about Gareth Kemp.

"Well, I am glad he was there to rescue you."

Her mother's voice cut across the drawing room. "I do hope you'll be able to stay a while, Lord Chiverton."

"That is very kind of you. But I must first see to my business in Plymouth." He set his empty cake plate to the side. "I wonder, Miss Cardinham, if you would give me a tour of your charming house and grounds."

Havencross was one of the more respectable houses west of the Tamar, but it paled in comparison to the great houses around London. Many of the walls were bare stone. The ceilings were not nearly as lofty as was fashionable in London. And the furnishings had not been updated in some time and gave the house rather a medieval feel.

But she would never refuse a chance to have Lord Chiverton to herself. "If you wish."

Lord Chiverton stood, and Elaine followed him to the drawing room door. Her mother picked up her knitting and scooted closer to the fire, as if having an earl in her house was as common as the daily egg gathering.

"I'm afraid you'll be disappointed," Elaine said as she led Lord Chiverton to the front hall.

He grinned at her with a mischievous gleam in his eye. "I hope not."

She started her tour on the main floor, but Lord Chiverton insisted he wanted to see everything, bottom to top. And so she led him down the rear stairs to the cold and damp basement.

He poked his head into every door, listening intently as she explained how Havencross used to be an abbey and these were the sleeping quarters and food cellars.

"The monks up north were being persecuted by heathens," she explained, "so they came here to escape. It was they who erected the large cross by the elm tree."

"And did they find it?"

"Find what?"

"The refuge they were looking for."

She shrugged. "I suppose so. They stayed, so they must have been pleased."

He looked pensively down the dark and cobwebby hall. "What about you, Miss Elaine Cardinham? Did you not also flee persecution by heathens and come here for refuge?"

He meant the scandal. It was an apt way to describe it. She could not tell his thoughts on the affair, not from the look of curiosity he was giving her now.

"Did you find what you were looking for?" he asked.

"No." All she'd found were bitter memories and heavy burdens. No refuge at all.

He gave one nod. "Perhaps in time."

"Perhaps." She started back toward the stairs. "Let me show you the upper levels of the house. They're much more interesting than these cellars."

Elaine walked him along the main level, skipping over the library door and her sequestered father inside. She stepped lightly to keep the floorboards from creaking, but they creaked anyway, when Lord Chiverton followed. She apologized when he had to duck under the lintel of some of the shorter doors. He didn't seem to mind.

She led him up the stairs to the upper story. From the northward windows, they looked out across the grazing sheep and freshly plowed fields, the black choughs following along. And toward Lowentop, but she did not mention that. To the east, she pointed toward Camelford. The westward windows looked out over the gardens, a short span of heath, and then the sea.

"The Atlantic," she told him, just to be precise. Though surely he already knew. "Sorry," she said.

He took his eyes away from the window and rested them on her. "Why are you sorry?"

She shrugged, not entirely sure herself. "I fear our home is not up to the standards you are used to in London or Warwickshire."

"I think it's perfect." He took a few steps closer. "I'm sorry you left London so quickly."

They'd had little choice, as he well knew. General Forton had bypassed the dual to save his wife's honor and had gone straight to threatening Elaine's father's life. A circumstance also known throughout London.

"I didn't get to say good-bye."

Is that why he was here? To say good-bye?

He placed a hand on her cheek and turned her head until her face was barely a foot from his. "You left so fast, I didn't have a chance to ask you a very important question."

She lifted her eyes to his.

"I have admired you for some time now. More than admired, I fear." He leaned close so his words had nowhere to go except into her heart. "I had hoped—nay, I do hope—that perhaps you might feel the same. It would be my greatest pleasure if you would agree to marry me."

Elaine couldn't believe what she was hearing. This was what she had dreamed about for so long. But his proposal didn't make sense after the disgrace of London.

"What about my father?"

"A scandal one day is forgot the next. I'm not willing to lose you over something that will mean nothing in less than a fortnight."

She looked out the window, carefully keeping her eyes from drifting toward Lowentop.

Lord Chiverton still cared for her. He wanted her for his wife.

This was more than rebuilding a shabby cottage; this was a mansion of marble and gold. And he had come to the ends of the country to tell her so. It was all a bit sudden, but what did that signify? He was under no obligation to offer his hand. He wanted to. He wanted her.

"Can I assume by the smile on your face that you accept?"

She would be a fool not to. He was handsome, wealthy, respected, titled. He would sweep her off her feet and carry her away to his great house in Warwickshire. Her knight of Camelot. "Of course, yes."

He smiled, taking both of her hands in his, kissing first one and then the other. "You have made me the happiest of men."

For the first time since her brother left Havencross and never returned, her future looked bright. A new life with a man she could trust. A man who would not betray her like her father had betrayed her mother. She could not do better than Lord Chiverton.

"Elaine." He gave her hands a squeeze. "May I call you Elaine?"

She nodded.

"I really do have business in Plymouth, and so I must away. I shall return in a fortnight. I will go now to your father, then stop at the vicar's. He can start the banns on Sunday, and we can be married by the end of the month."

So soon?

But why not? This was what she wanted. Waiting would accomplish nothing save prolonging her time in Cornwall. If Lord Chiverton was ready, so was she.

She nodded again.

"Good." He leaned in and kissed her cheek. "I will go to your father."

"Oh." What to say about her father. "He's . . ."

Lord Chiverton stepped away. "I know where he is. I can smell pipe smoke as well as anyone." He winked at her, then left her by the window.

His boots thudded on the stairs as he descended.

Now she must wait. For him to go to Plymouth and come back. And she must tell her mother the good news.

She hurried back to the drawing room. Her mother was still sitting by the fire, her knitting needles dancing a jig. They dropped to her lap when she looked up and saw Elaine.

"By Saint Piran," her mother said. "I never thought we'd see him again."

Elaine sat across from her.

"Where is he now? Did he already leave?"

"He is with father."

Her mother stared at her while a whole host of visages crossed her face. "How is that possible?"

"He is an earl. He can go where he likes."

"Elaine, what has happened?"

"He asked me to marry him."

Her mother leaned back into her chair with a satisfied smile. "I knew he would. The moment I saw his face at our door, I thought to myself, 'He's going to offer.' A man does not travel the breadth of the kingdom to pay a social call."

She supposed her mother was right. Had Elaine been in her right mind when she'd first seen him, she might also have formed such a conclusion. Her morning in the cave with Gareth had left her befuddled.

"I am pleased for you, my dear," her mother said with a smile. "I want nothing more than for you to find true happiness. But I cannot deny I will miss you terribly when you are gone."

Her mother need not say what they were both thinking. She would be left alone at Havencross with only her father for company. If things carried on as they were now, that would be no company at all. Once again, so much of her family's trouble came back to John. If he were alive, he would marry and settle here and her mother would never have to be alone.

Her mother picked up her needles again and started knitting. Without looking up, she asked, "What did he say about your father's slip?"

His slip? As if disgracing the entire family name and breaking his most sacred of vows was an accidental misstep. As if he could right the wrong by merely readjusting his footing.

Perhaps a discreet dalliance was tolerated in the ton, and perhaps Elaine was old-fashioned, but wrong was wrong. And however much some people might be accepting of a little indiscretion, it did not lessen the humiliation for those involved.

"He said it was already forgotten."

"Ah." She tugged more yarn from her spool. "That was generous of him."

It was. Very generous. Elaine could learn a lesson from Lord Chiverton. No good would come from wallowing in circumstances that could not be changed. Better to put it behind her. Her father's *slip*. Gareth. John. All of it.

That was exactly why Lord Chiverton was good for her. He was her crossroads, the place where she buried her shameful past and moved on.

"Mother." Elaine leaned forward and spoke quietly. "What happened? I feel there is more to Father's situation than what the rumors supplied. What did Father tell you?"

"Hush." Her mother's needles sped up. "He didn't tell me anything."

"Cannot you ask him?" She was his wife and had a right to know.

"Of course not." Her mother jerked a length of yarn out of the spool. "I am not speaking with him. Besides, it will do no good to stir the pot until it boils over. We must remove it from the fire as fast as possible. The pot will grow cold soon enough."

Elaine was unsure whether her mother meant the scandal of London would grow cold or her own indignation. By the way her hands were flying, the pot was a long way from going cold. Her mother took everything out on those poor knitting needles. At this rate, they'd have enough woolen goods to clothe all of Cornwall.

Elaine had one or two memories of catching her father and mother stealing a kiss. There must have been love at one time. Somehow it had slipped away, John's death being the final wedge. During their time in London, she'd rarely seen them together—at least not in any affectionate sort of way. They'd spoken when necessary, usually about the weather or their list of engagements or whatever other business had to be dealt with.

For all the blame she'd leveled at her father, her mother had not been quick to offer civility. Surely it must have taken the both of them to get the wedge so deeply imbedded.

The library door creaked open, and Elaine jumped up. She hurried to the hall to catch Lord Chiverton. One last moment alone before he left.

He winked at her again with a contented smile. "He has given consent, and all is settled."

A new start. She thanked heaven Lord Chiverton had come into her life.

"Only three short weeks and we shall be married. How will you like being called the Countess of Chiverton?"

Countess. It was more than she ever imagined. "I shall like it very much, my lord. But . . ." She could feel the heat rising to her cheeks. "That is not the reason I said yes." She couldn't look up.

She'd never said anything so intimate to him before. But he did say that he more than admired her. Hopefully her feeble attempt to return the sentiment would not fall flat.

He took her hand again and kissed it. "I'm pleased to hear it," he whispered. "And now I am off."

Mr. Winkleigh opened the door, and Lord Chiverton strode out. Mr. Dean had his horse ready, and Lord Chiverton mounted up and rode away.

Elaine flopped onto her bed. It had been a whirlwind of a day, and it had sucked her breath away. Everything had changed so quickly. She needed a moment to take it all in.

Gareth's coat lay draped across her changing screen. Elaine stood and walked over to it, lifting it to her nose. His scent brought a flush of memories as powerful as the wind that poured off the sea.

Days of their youth, scouring the beach for shells. The best finds were the mermaid purses—or even better, a sea potato, with its bleached white skeleton and pudgy heart shape. She had a whole collection of them lined up along her windowsill—all of them from Gareth. No matter how low her spirits, Gareth could always cheer her up. How often he had made her laugh until her sides hurt. It was a great talent of his, and she had loved that about him.

She laid the coat down.

Those were memories of the past. Memories she intended to bury. She must bury if she was to have peace in her marriage with Lord Chiverton. She could not bring all the weight of her past into her new life with him; it would only drown them both.

And yet, perhaps she owed it to Gareth to tell him personally that she was now formally engaged to Edmund Crawley, Earl of Chiverton. She had thought to have one of the staff return the coat to Lowentop, but if she set off early tomorrow, she could do it herself. Tell him of Lord Chiverton, and say good-bye.

CHAPTER SIX

Gareth

Gareth rolled up his map of the mine. Things were looking good. Since they'd dropped a new shaft in the southwest tunnel, they'd hit the biggest lode of tin yet. They still had a ways to go before the water level would stop them, but as long as they didn't pull up any dredgy ore, this could be the big hit he'd been hoping for.

He tucked the map into the top drawer of his small desk. It sat in the corner of his room overlooking the lane behind his house. The sky was a brilliant blue this morning, and all was still. Even the wind seemed to have lost its breath, but that could not last long.

Mrs. Penmoor tapped on his door as she stuck her head in. "Mr. Tippet and his daughter have come calling." She grinned at him.

Since the death of his father, more and more of the village wives had come banging on his door, auctioning off their daughters. Miss Tippet had no mother, but Mrs. Swallowford didn't hesitate to play the role. Today it seemed the lot fell to her father. Luckily, Miss Tippet was the most pleasant of the lot.

He gave Mrs. Penmoor a nod.

"They're in the parlor." She gave him a quick dip and ducked out.

Gareth combed his fingers through his hair and straightened his cravat, checking in the mirror that he looked presentable. Why he bothered he wasn't quite sure. He didn't want Miss Tippet to get her hopes up.

What a presumptuous thought.

For all he knew, Miss Tippet didn't care two straws about him. It could be, by some miracle, Mr. Tippet was here with news of the investigation into his father's murder. Gareth snorted. Not very likely since it had been six months and Mr. Tippet had done nothing.

Miss Tippet's artless and open temperament was easy to appreciate, but Gareth had learned his lesson well. He'd not be offering to any woman unless he knew with certainty she wouldn't flee.

But that was just it. He'd been sure about Elaine when he'd asked her. That woman was like a cat living in the sheep shed. Soft and dainty on the outside, but don't get too close, or she'll arch her back and run away.

Gareth found Mr. and Miss Tippet in the parlor, just as Mrs. Penmoor had said. Mr. Tippet stood looking out the window while Miss Tippet perched on the chaise in her best morning frock.

"Tea," he said to Mrs. Penmoor, then gave them a good gentlemanly bow. "Mr. Tippet and Miss Tippet. How nice of you to call."

A pink tinge colored Miss Tippet's cheeks. The flush improved her looks. Gareth was not fond of this fashion for women, to keep their cheeks white as freshly fallen snow. If one was alive, one should look it, not like two days past death.

Tippet came forward. "How are things at the mine, Kemp?"

He always started the conversation by asking about the mines. It was unclear to Gareth whether Tippet asked out of true consideration or because he cared about Gareth's income—for his daughter's sake.

"Very well, thank you. We've just sent a ton of ore over to the smelter." He took a seat across from Mr. Tippet's daughter. "We sank a new shaft, and it appears we'll get quite the keenly gozzan out of it."

They blinked at him.

Foreigners. "We found a lot of tin," he amended.

"Oh! That's grand," Miss Tippet said. "I was just the other day in Wickfern's general store and picked up a tin cup and wondered out loud if that cup was made in your very own Polcart Mine."

Gareth cranked up his smile. "How wonderfully curious of you, Miss Tippet. Pol*kreath* Mine, as I'm sure you know, does not make goods from the tin. We only harvest the ore and process it. Then it is transfered to the smelter, who makes it into ingots, which are then sold to manufacturers."

Miss Tippet nodded. "Oh. Right. I suppose that makes sense."

Gareth turned the conversation to something more along the lines of the lady's interests. "What do you make of this new draper's shop in town?"

"Oh, goodness me," Miss Tippet said. "Why on earth would we need two drapers? And each on a different end of High Street," she added. "It's terribly inconvenient. For once I look at the cloth in Gribble's, I feel I can't make a choice until I compare it to my options in Breward's. So it's all the way up to the other end of High Street. But if Breward's hasn't got anything better, I must turn right around and go all the way back down to Gribble's to make my purchase."

The woman had been spending too much time with Mrs. Swallowford.

"That must be very tiresome," he said. "Perhaps if you started at Breward's instead, you could save yourself one leg of the journey?"

"Hm." Miss Tippet gazed over his shoulder as she considered his suggestion. "Perhaps. I suppose having both stores has its advantages. We do have more to choose from. And one merchant cannot set their prices too high else he'll drive all his customers to the other."

At last, something that showed a glimmer of the intelligence he'd seen lurking inside her. It just took some time to coax it out.

"And how goes the war against the free traders?" Gareth asked Tippet. In the months he'd been here, Gareth had seen not even the smallest dent in the smuggling trade. Nor the murders.

"It's a difficult battle," Tippet said. "But we shall never give up the fight."

A comment that was neither this nor that. Tippet walked the middle line well.

Every time Gareth saw that man, he wanted to rail on him. As far as he could tell, Tippet had done nothing to bring his father's killer to justice, even though Squire Stroud swore he'd been pressing him to do so. In the end, Gareth's pity took over.

Being the Landguard, Tippet took enough railings from the good citizens of Camelford—or should he say the less-than-good citizens. Preventive men did not have it easy in these parts. The local smuggling rings threatened and persecuted them until most either abandoned their posts or converted to smuggling. Gareth had not yet decided where Tippet would fall.

"I've actually come out on a bit of an errand," Tippet said. "I've got a lock in the revenues office that has jammed itself shut."

It didn't help that as head of the Landguard, Tippet also had to collect the import taxes. The poor man was indeed fighting a losing battle.

"I've been told you are the best lock pick around."

Gareth shrugged. The locksmith was the best lock pick in town. But once again, the locksmith had long been suspected of smuggling. Tippet would be hard-pressed to get that man to set foot in the revenues office.

In their youth, trying to break into the gamekeeper's lodgings, John had discovered Gareth's knack for picking locks. John had constantly challenged

Gareth by bringing him all sorts of locks to practice on. Gareth had used tin from Polkreath Mine to fashion himself special tools that could reach in and find the pins with ease.

He'd never tell Tippet this, but he'd already picked the lock to the revenues office many times. And the church. And most every other locked door in town. All with John at his side, goading him on.

"I can come this afternoon."

Tippet nodded. "I'm much obliged."

Mrs. Penmoor entered with a tray of tea and scones ready to be slathered in jam and clotted cream. She bustled out only to return a moment later.

She caught Gareth's attention and widened her eyes at him, tipping her head this way and that, trying to communicate what, he could not fathom.

"Is something amiss, Mrs. Penmoor?"

"You have another *vi-si-tor*," she said with great emphasis, as if drawing out each syllable of the word would allow him to read her mind.

Miss Tippet smiled at him.

Mrs. Penmoor mouthed a word that looked remarkably like *mystery lamb*, but that couldn't be right. Perhaps he was simply hungry for something more than tea, and lamb, however mysteriously prepared, whet his appetite.

"Please show him in," Gareth said.

Mrs. Penmoor's brow puckered as she made one last attempt at transferring her thoughts directly into his mind before shaking her head and backing out the door.

"Would you pour?" Gareth asked Miss Tippet in order to draw the attention away from his housekeeper's strange methods of communication. If one could call them that, since they communicated absolutely nothing.

Miss Tippet seemed pleased with the honor, but before she could set the strainer into the first teacup, the parlor door opened and Elaine walked in, his coat slung across her folded hands.

That was what Mrs. Penmoor had been trying to tell him? A little warning would have been nice—one actually audible to the human ear. He would have instructed the housekeeper to take the coat and send her on her way.

He sincerely hoped Miss Tippet would tuck her intelligence away and think nothing of the appearance of Elaine returning his coat.

He stood to introduce Miss Cardinham, which incidentally sounded nothing like mystery lamb. "I don't believe you know Mr. Tippet, fearless leader of our local Landguard, and his daughter, Miss Tippet."

Elaine appeared about as happy with these circumstances as he did. She offered a quick dip. "It is my pleasure," she said to both Tippets. "And I have met Miss Tippet already," she told Gareth before turning back to Miss Tippet. "It is nice to see you again."

"And this is Miss Elaine Cardinham," he said for the benefit of Mr. Tippet. "Recently returned from London and most happy to be back in her ancestral home of Havencross."

Tippet scowled. Clearly he'd already heard the news of the Cardinham's great fall and wasn't sure they should be associating with such ruined people. To Miss Tippet's credit, she reached out a hand to Elaine. "The pleasure is all mine."

"Thank you," Elaine said.

"Please sit." Gareth motioned to the closest chair.

Elaine perched on the very tip of the seat. She looked to Gareth, then over at Miss Tippet, then pursed her lips. Perhaps she'd wanted to find him here alone. He stole a glance at her, but her eyes were still puzzling something out.

"Do you always wear a man's coat when going out?" Miss Tippet asked.

Elaine looked down at Gareth's coat and seemed surprised to find it in her lap. She handed it to him without a word.

Mr. and Miss Tippet appeared hopeful for an explanation.

"Miss Cardinham fell into the water yesterday. I loaned her my coat."

"I've only come to return it." Elaine stood. "I didn't mean to intrude on your company." She gave the Tippets a brief nod."Thank you again, Mr. Kemp, for your assistance." She left as quickly as she'd come.

She need not have brought the coat back personally. She could have sent any number of servants to do the job. There must have been another reason for her coming to his house. He'd wiped his feet of her. Or at least he'd tried. So when he rose to follow her, he surprised more than just Mr. and Miss Tippet. "Excuse me a moment," he said, then darted out of the parlor and caught up with her just as she was securing her bonnet and stepping over the threshold of the front door. "Miss Cardinham."

She turned.

"What is it that you wanted?"

She tied a neat bow under her chin. "What do you mean?"

"You would not have walked all this way merely to return the coat."

"On the contrary; I enjoy walking very much."

He laughed. "Yes, I know. Unlike our friend Miss Tippet, who finds the length of High Street a bit of a challenge. In any case, that does not explain why you came to see me." He rather believed he was the last person she cared to see. "You haven't had another run-in with Gwenevere, have you?"

"No." She fumbled with the folds of her dress. "I've come to . . . I was hoping for a chance to tell you . . ." She did not finish. She looked at the rosemary growing by the door. At the rock wall leading off to the stable. Even at the slate ellin stones of his roof. It all meant one thing. Her back was arching.

"To tell me what?"

"That Lowentop looks very well."

And now she was on the run. Did she not think he could see through her?

"*Meur ras*," he said because she hated when he spoke Cornish. But he could not help himself. She deserved it after her lie.

"Do not thank me." Her head was down, and Gareth could not see her eyes, but he was already familiar with the fire in them that his words would undoubtedly bring out. "Besides, I do not speak Cornish."

"You are sure about that?" he asked.

"Only the few phrases you taught me. And you were the worst teacher ever. 'Tis a wonder I learnt anything at all." She looked up at him, and for just a moment, the girl he'd loved since childhood was back. "Besides, no one speaks Cornish anymore save you and Broken Betty."

Aye. The broken-witted woman who lived in a hut outside town and bared her teeth at anyone who dared address her in English. She also wore filthy fisherman's garb and wandered the countryside talking to piskeys. For Elaine to compare him to Broken Betty was nothing short of charming.

"Thank you for that."

"Really, Gareth, what can you actually say in Cornish beyond your please and thank-yous and your dreadful cursings?"

"I can recite the entire Lord's prayer. And the ten commandments."

She laughed out loud. This was what he'd been waiting for. A glimpse of the way her nose wrinkled when she smiled, her green eyes bright and alive like the spring leaves bursting from the woodland behind her.

Then she abruptly came to her senses. The girl from his youth was gone, and back in place was Miss Cardinham, recently of London and desperately trying to be from anywhere besides her home.

"I must be going." She turned and hurried off but not before muttering, "*Duw genes*, Mr. Kemp."

He watched her leave, returning her farewell with a soft, "Good-bye, Elowen."

CHAPTER SEVEN

Elaine

So Gareth was courting Miss Tippet. That explained the girl's blush when she had mentioned him the other day.

Elaine had no idea of Miss Tippet's connections and standing. Her father had been a militia man, so he must come from a family with some portion of property. Miss Tippet would be hard-pressed to find a better man than Gareth. He was handsome enough, to be sure. And far from the dandies Elaine had seen in London who had dressed finer than china but had been soft from playing cards and prowling the prospects at Almack's. Not that she'd ever been admitted there.

Gareth had the rugged look of the Cornish—dark hair, lean and sturdy as the rocky cliffs that lined the coast, unbreakable against wave after pummeling wave. He was clever too. Miss Tippet was right to be interested in him.

Elaine climbed over the last stile and entered the lane that led to Havencross just in time to see a carriage stirring up dust out on the main road. Aunt Rose.

She broke into a run, cutting through the house and bursting out the front door just as the coach rounded the drive.

Her mother was there too. "Where have you been all morning?"

"Walking."

"Always walking. It's not seemly to be out wandering the heath."

The Beafords' carriage clattered to a stop. Two footmen rushed forward and began unstrapping Aunt Rose's wheeled bath chair from its resting spot on the back of the coach. The door opened, and Uncle Charles emerged, a large grin on his tall, narrow face.

"Welcome, Uncle," Elaine said, stepping forward and clasping his hands. "I hope your journey was pleasant."

He pulled her in for a hug. "Wonderful. We took a detour through the moors. What fascinating landscape." He held her at arm's length. "Look at you. Quite grown up, I daresay." He extended a hand toward her mother.

She gave him a weary smile. "So good of you to come to us under these difficult circumstances."

The men had the bath chair set up and dusted off. Brixton wheeled it over, and Uncle Charles turned his attention to extracting his wife from the coach. He reached in, and a pale hand appeared, grasping his.

He pulled Aunt Rose forward, lifting her into his arms. "Here you are, my dear." He lowered her gently into the bath chair, smoothing out her muslin dress and tugging it down to ensure it covered her ankles.

Aunt Rose seemed more thin and pale than ever.

Uncle Charles wheeled her over to Elaine's mother, where she reached out her hands. "Oh, my dear sister. What a nightmare you've been through. You must be weary to the bone."

Her mother leaned over to let Aunt Rose wrap her arms around her.

It wasn't until that moment, when her crippled aunt tried to console her mother, that Elaine realized the absurdity of the situation. It should be her mother's job to console her younger sister. Aunt Rose was confined to a chair, her body wasting away, yet she was the one offering sympathy and strength to a woman whose health was excellent, however depressed her spirits might be.

"Come inside," Elaine said. "You must be half starved."

Uncle Charles pushed her aunt's chair, tipping it back to get it up and over the front steps. Brixton helped lift it, and Aunt Rose squealed and laughed when it leaned too far to one side.

The bath chair at last landed smooth and properly on the top step. Uncle Charles nodded a thanks to the footman as he brought Aunt Rose across the threshold. Her aunt veered the chair into the drawing room with the long lever attached to the front wheel.

"Send for the tea, please," Elaine said to Brixton.

"Out walking again, miss?" he asked. He smiled at her and bowed.

That man needed to keep his nose in his own affairs. He was going to get himself in trouble one of these days.

Uncle Charles positioned Aunt Rose in a patch of warm sunlight.

"How did you find the moors?" Elaine asked.

"Exquisite," Aunt Rose said. "You know how I love the moors."

"But it's so bleak," Elaine's mother said. "Nothing but grass and piles of rock as far as the eye can see. All those pagan stone circles make my blood chill. Any moment out there, I just know a puck or hobgoblin or some kind of devil will be after me."

Aunt Rose laughed. "Well, I find the landscape very mysterious, and I can never get enough of it."

"What about you?" Uncle Charles turned to Elaine. "Do you believe there are spirits haunting the moors?"

Bodmin Moor lay on the other side of Camelford, but Elaine's thoughts immediately jumped to the woman she'd found in Merlin's Cave. Gwen. Gwenevere, as Gareth called her, or her ghost or some such nonsense. Perhaps he wasn't so far off. She had seemed to vanish into thin air. But then, where was her shawl, because it too had vanished. And she'd never heard of spirits bleeding.

Uncle Charles chuckled. "I didn't mean to ask you such a troubling question, Elaine. I hope we haven't spooked you with talk of specters and ghosts."

Elaine glanced at her mother. If not for her, Elaine might have shared with Aunt Rose what had happened in the cave. But she'd not add to her mother's anxiety by letting on how far she'd gone on her own. Then there was Gareth's part, which she'd rather no one ever know.

Mr. Winkleigh opened the door and brought in a tray of tea, and the footman—not Brixton this time—followed with another of cold meats, beet salad, and ginger cake. Uncle Charles licked his lips. He was tall and lean and ate everything in sight. One of the great mysteries in life was where he managed to put it all.

Before Elaine or her mother could rise to their feet, Uncle Charles was up with plate in hand. "What can I get you, then, my dear?" he asked his wife.

Aunt Rose smiled at him. "I'm not really hungry."

"Nonsense." He put one of everything on her plate and then balanced it carefully on her tiny lap. "You've got to eat. Husband's orders."

She stared at the plate.

"I insist," he whispered softly, though Elaine was close enough to hear. It was a secret, lovely moment between the two of them, and Elaine turned her head away so as not to intrude.

Only when she and her mother had gotten their food did Uncle Charles help himself. He piled it high, tucked his napkin into his waistcoat, and lifted his fork. "Now then," he said, before taking his first bite, "tell us what happened in London."

As if he were asking about the weather or the condition of the roads.

Elaine's mother began weeping immediately, probably because she had no knitting needles in hand to manage her grief. Uncle Charles turned to Elaine for his answer.

"Well . . ." This was not the easiest subject, especially because Elaine herself was in the dark. "Apparently . . . my father and Lady Forton . . ."

"Oh, hush now," her mother wailed. "Why do you make her speak of such things? She's only a child." This from the woman who'd agreed only a few days ago that Elaine was ruined.

"You are quite right, Harriet." Uncle Charles cast Elaine an apologetic glance. "I do beg your pardon, Elaine."

Of course Elaine had heard the rumors—and plenty of them—but her father's silence and her mother's tears had left her to assume the worst without really knowing for certain if the worst had actually happened. Perhaps there had simply been a breach of etiquette.

If a man and a woman vow fidelity, there should be no straying, not even of the slightest. This casual way society had of overlooking such vows left a bitter taste in her mouth. Such marriages could not possibly bring happiness to either partner. There could be no trust.

Even if her father was guilty of such a breach, it was odd that it had become the rage of the town. They were no one of consequence to rouse the fiery tongues of London society. The whole affair seemed off somehow.

Her mother wiped her nose. "Let us speak of happier tidings. Elaine has some marvelous news."

"What is it?" her aunt asked.

"I am to be married."

A smile broke out upon her aunt's face. "Why did you not say so sooner? This is wonderful news."

"Who is the fortunate man?" Uncle Charles asked as he helped himself to a second plate of food.

"Edmund Crawley, Earl of Chiverton."

Her uncle chewed thoughtfully. "I don't think I'm acquainted with him."

"An earl." Her aunt waggled her eyebrows. "Well done, Elaine."

She couldn't help smiling. What a pleasure to have her aunt and uncle here lightening the mood. This whole house had been nothing but dreary since London.

"That's not why I am marrying him," she said.

Her uncle grinned wickedly. "Then, pray, tell us why you are marrying Edmund Crawley, Earl of Chiverton."

She stirred a spoonful of sugar into her tea. "He is handsome."

Her aunt laughed.

"He is kind," Elaine continued. "He is well-educated. He is attentive. He cares for me. He traveled all the way from London to Havencross to tell me so and to ask for my hand in person." The longer she went on, the bolder she got. "He smells of almond from his shaving soap."

"When did you get close enough to smell his shaving soap?" Uncle Charles asked.

She looked down at her tea. "It is high quality Pears soap, so the fragrance is very strong."

Her aunt and uncle burst out laughing. Even her mother smiled.

Elaine laughed with them. She was going to marry the man; she need not be embarrassed by her affection.

"Well, I am very happy for you," Aunt Rose said. "He sounds quite marvelous. When shall we meet him?"

"He has gone to Plymouth on business but will be back in a fortnight. The wedding is set for the week after that."

Uncle Charles stood. "And that is my cue to leave. When the women start talking wedding plans, I find it best to take myself away." He placed his empty plate to the side. "I think I'll go give my greetings to Francis. Where might I find him?"

"My father keeps himself to the library," Elaine said.

Uncle Charles leaned closer and asked quietly, "By his wishes or your mother's?"

"Both, I believe," Elaine whispered back. As far as she could tell, neither one wanted anything to do with the other.

Before leaving, Uncle Charles removed his wife's plate from her lap. She'd eaten a fair bit of it. "I'll see you later," he said to her.

She nodded, and he strode out of the room, his long legs making the crossing in only a few steps.

When the door closed behind him, Elaine's mother turned to her sister. "It's so good of you to come. You can't imagine the difficulty we've been through. Forced to leave London. Poor Elaine has been beside herself."

"I'm sure it must have been awful." Aunt Rose said in a gentle voice. "But how nice for you to be back in Cornwall. And this news of Elaine's advantageous match must be some consolation." She turned to Elaine. "You must be pleased to be back at Havencross after so many years away."

Elaine glanced around the room. It was comfortable, pleasant. Though the furnishings were a little heavy, they were soft and inviting and warm during the cold winter months. It did feel like home, and yet it didn't.

John should be here playing tug-o-war with the dog on the carpet. And her father sitting by the fire, cursing whatever piece of news he'd read in the paper. Her mother laughing at the latest tale of King Arthur and his knights Elaine had made up for her childhood entertainment. All that was gone now. It would never come back.

Her mother had assumed Aunt Rose was asking her. "My dear sister, you are too kind, but you know this country does not agree with me. Everything is damp and windblown. There is no society. Sometimes it is a very lonely place."

"Then it is a good thing Charles and I have come to give you company. For you know there is no society as good as family." Aunt Rose gave Elaine a wink. "Now. I must hear more about Lord Chiverton. He sounds quite delicious."

"Really, sister. You speak of men as if they were pastries."

Aunt Rose shrugged. "We are stuck with them for a long time. We might as well enjoy it."

"Rose!" her mother scolded.

"Well, at least he adores you," Aunt Rose said to Elaine.

All Elaine really knew about adoration was that Uncle Charles adored his wife and Elaine's father did not adore her mother. Lord Chiverton had said he admired her—more than admired. Not quite the same thing as adore.

He must care for her though—love her, even. At least she hoped he did. She had no way of knowing his true feelings. All she did know was that Lord Chiverton was her knight in shining armor come to carry her away.

"Pish posh," her mother said. "Marriage has nothing to do with adoration."

Aunt Rose merely shrugged her narrow shoulders. She was much younger than Elaine's mother, and though both sisters had had their fair share of troubles, Aunt Rose always seemed to come out better for it.

About half a year before John's death, her uncle's carriage had overturned while they were touring the Lake District. Uncle Charles had walked away with barely a bruise; her aunt never walked again.

"I would love to go out back and take in your view," her aunt said. "Elaine, could I trouble you for a push?"

Elaine leapt to her feet. Nothing would make her happier.

She got behind her aunt's bath chair and gave it a nudge toward the back door that led to the gardens and the cliffs overlooking the sea.

Elaine left the house early, eager to get back down to the cave. She'd not had time this past week with her aunt and uncle here and all the wedding arrangements. She'd been to Camelford three times for cloth and ribbons and trimmings and to be fitted for a wedding gown. The dressmaker was busy sewing away, a few simple sprays of hawthorn blossoms were planned to decorate Saint Piran's church, and her mother had sent to the London house for her strand of pearls. All was well in hand.

Today, Elaine could wait no longer to try to find the mysterious woman she'd encountered in Merlin's cave.

She wouldn't mind getting her shawl back either. She rather liked that one, made of thickly woven indigo silk from the East Indies. Assuming Betsy could get the bloodstain out.

Steps of flat moorstone protruded from the rock wall of the hedge, covered in lichen and winding brambles. Cornwall's version of the stile. Placing each foot with care, she climbed over and onto the path heading north. A glorious day. Sun and warmth and not a cloud to be seen. Even the wind had died down to a gentle whisper instead of its usual scream.

She took off her bonnet and tipped her head toward the sun. An act that in London would have drawn scowls. Sun on the face was for farmers and field laborers. But she was not in London now, and until Lord Chiverton took her back there, she would let the rays warm her skin.

"Careful," said a man's voice. One she recognized immediately as Gareth's.

CHAPTER EIGHT

Elaine

Mr. Kemp sat astride a tall bay he reined to a halt. "It's my understanding that freckles are not in fashion at the moment."

She gave him a dip of her head. "Mr. Kemp." It was long past time for the miners to be at work. Perhaps not today though, for he was dressed quite well for mine work.

"Miss Cardinham." He tipped his hat. "Where are you going?" By the direction of his gaze, he'd already guessed the answer.

"Out for a morning amble."

"Amble?" One of his eyebrows went up. "Alone?"

This was her home. Gareth knew better than anyone that she was well acquainted with the territory.

"Where are *you* going?" she asked.

"Polkreath."

"Alone?"

He laughed. "Not quite the same, though, is it?" He looked very fine and every bit the gentleman perched atop his horse in his stylish suit, his unruly dark hair trying to escape his top hat. His easy laugh brought a smile to her face.

"Never one for being told what to do."

His eyes softened, holding her gaze until she realized she was staring back.

"I do not doubt your skills at navigating the countryside. You were always the best climber of us." He grinned broadly. "Remember when you scaled Gull Top and told John you couldn't get down. Lured him up, I should say. He climbed up to rescue you, but by the time he reached the top, you'd already come down."

Elaine remembered the event very well. "He was stuck up there half the day."

"And you and I ran off and spent the afternoon wandering the hedges, eating the brambles."

"My fingers were blue for days."

"And your lips," he said softly.

Her fingers went straight to her mouth because he was staring at it.

Gareth gazed down the lane for a few moments. "I must congratulate you on your upcoming wedding," he said.

She looked at his boots, polished and shiny, tucked into the stirrup. The whole parish now knew, after Sunday's reading. She'd tried to tell Gareth in person but had failed miserably.

"Elaine," he said.

She dragged her eyes slowly upward.

"I am happy for you." His hazel eyes had a blueish tint this morning from his coat and the clear sky.

Gareth Kemp was a good man. Miss Tippet would be lucky to have him. Elaine had never really found the right time to tell him why she'd refused him. She'd turned on her heel and walked away, leaving him alone in the cave. Foolish girl that she was.

She took a step closer. "I am sorry that . . . " After all this time, she still did not have the words.

"Don't. There is no need." He urged his horse into the lane. "Lord Chiverton is a lucky man. I'm glad you are happy."

"Thank you." She curtseyed again. "Good day, Mr. Kemp."

"Elowen, wait."

She paused.

"There have been smugglers in these parts. Unsavory ones. Truly, you shouldn't be out alone."

"Thank you, Mr. Kemp." He should not be calling her by her old pet name. Especially not in public. "I assure you I'm quite safe."

He opened his mouth to speak but seemed to think better of it. Then he said, "Good day, Miss Cardinham." He clucked to his horse.

Elaine watched him ride away, staring after him and his gentle sway as the horse walked on.

She half hoped he would've offered to accompany her. Though if Lord Chiverton had been here, that would be preferable. Perhaps it was simply wistfulness that yearned for a stroll along the beach with Gareth Kemp. Searching for sea potatoes, exploring the tide pools and coves, both of them with shoes and socks off, wading about in the rocky pools. Her with her skirts hefted up. She blushed to think of it. No wonder he'd gotten the wrong idea.

He turned in the saddle and caught her staring. Again.

She spun around and strode off, determined not to think on him for the rest of the day.

She reached the top of the castle headland and the steep path that led to the beach below. Beyond that, Merlin's cave.

She began the descent. The steepness never ceased to give her a rush of excitement—accompanied by a good dose of fear. Nearly straight down. If she lost her footing, it was quite a ways to the rocky bottom.

Several times her half boots skidded along the dirt, but each time, she managed to regain her footing. When she reached the beach below, she glanced around for any signs of the woman who had called herself Gwen. Though it would be ridiculous for her to still be here. The tide would soon be in, flooding the cave. It was not a likely place for a woman in trouble to take refuge.

Gareth had not believed her about the woman, but Elaine had seen her with her own eyes. Something strange had happened that day, and Elaine meant to get to the bottom of it.

She picked her way across the beach and into the cavern.

"Hello?" she called, not quite sure whether to hope for an answer.

She walked in, stepping out of the warmth and into the cool damp. The cave smelled as it always did: of seaweed, must, and wet rocks. She continued on.

"Hello?" she called again.

The most likely event was that Gwen had been recovered by family or friends and was now convalescing in comfort at her home.

A scuffling sound brought Elaine to a standstill.

"Gwen?"

Nothing.

Gareth's ridiculous musings wouldn't leave her alone. She called again. "Gwenevere?"

Rocks clattered, only for a moment, then the distant din of the waves and gulls returned. Elaine crept deeper into the cavern until she reached the place where she'd found Gwen the first time.

There on the ground lay her shawl, folded and resting carefully on a rock large enough to keep it out of the water should the tide come in.

Elaine glanced around, trying to see who had left it here.

She took the shawl from its resting place and carefully navigated the rocks toward the other end of the cavern where it opened back up to the coast. She couldn't make it all the way because the water filled that part of the cave.

Then she heard the sound of laughter coming from the entrance. She turned and hurried forward.

Silhouetted by the bright sun were two boys tossing a cricket ball back and forth. Barefooted and dressed in rags, they were naught but cages of bones. They must be children of the miners.

The moment they caught sight of Elaine, they froze like rabbits catching the scent of a fox.

"Hello there," she said.

"Hello," one of them said. A fair-haired lad with a shaggy mane the color of sun-bleached flax and a rather prominent black eye. A mishap of youth or the work of another?

Elaine did not recognize these boys, but she had been gone a long time, and if they were local lads, they would have been only four or five when she had left. Not that she'd known all the families, by any means. But there were a few who lived close by that were known to her.

She motioned to the lad's darkened eye. "Are you all right? That looks painful."

"I'm fine, mum." They looked at her as if any moment she might pounce.

"I used to come here to play when I was your age too," she said. This seemed to relax them a little. "Do you come often?"

They glanced at each other, then down at the sand. The other boy, a redheaded, freckled lad, shrugged his shoulders.

"I wonder," Elaine said, "if in the last few days you've seen a woman about."

They both stared at her.

"Other than me." Clearly they thought she was mad. "This woman has long dark hair hanging down her back and bright-green eyes. Probably wearing a green dress and a small gold crown."

The flaxen-haired boy shook his head. "Nay, mum."

They both watched her with large eyes resting above the pink cheeks of boys who were not yet on the voyage to man. Quite charming, even in their rags and with mussed hair.

"That is a lovely ball you have there. Where did you get it?"

No answer—as she'd expected. More than likely lifted from the house of someone living under better conditions.

"May I see it?"

The redhead held it out with a grim look on his face.

Elaine took it, tossing it back and forth from hand to hand, gauging its weight. "Very nice. I'll bet this can really fly."

"It can!" the flaxen-haired lad said. "'Cept we ain't got a proper bat to 'it with." His little chest fell.

Elaine leaned forward to put herself at eye level. "I'll tell you what. My name is Miss Cardinham. I live at Havencross, the big house down the way. Do you know it?"

They nodded in unison.

"I have a bat, proper and strong. You come by anytime, and you can use it. Yes?"

Another set of nods.

"Now tell me your names so I know who to look for."

At this, they gave each other another furtive glance. The flaxen-headed lad elbowed his mate, and the red-topped boy glared at him before looking up at Elaine. "William, mum. And 'e's William too. But everyone calls 'em Willy White-Top." The redheaded William grinned with great satisfaction.

Redheaded William got another elbow in his ribs. "Well, everyone calls 'em Sandy Will on account of it looks like 'es face got covered with sand."

"Shut yer oozle," Sandy Will said, giving him an elbow back.

"You shut it," Willy White-Top said.

"All right, then," Elaine straightened up. Many's the time John had used that same phrase on her. "Willy White-Top and Sandy Will. You come to my place when you need a proper game of cricket, and in return, you promise me you'll keep an eye open for the woman I just described. Yes?"

They nodded again.

"If you see her, you come to Havencross and tell me straightaway." Elaine gave them back the cricket ball.

Willy White-Top grabbed it. He gave Elaine a quick bow, and then Sandy Will did the same. They scurried from the cave on bare feet as light and fast as if they'd been born right here on these very rocks. Little creatures of the sand and stones and cliffs.

Elaine followed them, picking her way around the slippery rocks and the pools of salt water with ease.

She soon reached the top, shawl clutched in her hand. When she rounded the stone walls of the ruined castle, she caught sight of movement coming from across the field, along the clump of tangled and windblown hawthorns.

It was a man on horseback. Beaver firmly atop his head and wearing a coat of dusky blue. She could have sworn it was Gareth Kemp.

He quickly disappeared into the grove. He was watching her though. She felt it by the prickling on her nape. He thought he was so stealthy, but he'd not slipped her notice.

Smugglers about, dangerous ones, he'd warned. She grinned. He was checking up on her. He'd told her not to go to the cave, but he knew her too well. And then he'd followed her to make sure she was safe.

She lifted her hand to shade her eyes from the morning sun and peered after him. It had been Gareth, hadn't it? Who else could it be? In the distance, she caught sight of the two Williams disappearing behind a hedge wall. Odd that the lads were not at work. Boys that age more often than not had to work in the mines or the fishing docks to help support the family. Or attend school, if they were lucky. Even the poor families sent what children they could spare to the parish school.

From their ragged clothes and gaunt faces, Willy White-Top and Sandy Will did not look like boys from families who could spare wage earners for school. More like the lads down the mines, hauling the water bucket or smashing ore above ground with the bal maidens.

Gareth worked at a mine. If that had been him hovering in the hawthorns, perhaps he'd sent the boys down to the cave to check on her, if he was truly that worried for her safety. She turned back and gazed into the woodland, though the horse and rider were gone.

Perhaps he didn't despise her as much as she thought. Or perhaps he was better at forgiving than she thought. Or, more likely, he cared enough not to want her murdered by smugglers.

She could not continue to think on Gareth Kemp. She loved Lord Chiverton, and next week, when he returned from Plymouth, she would not have to wander the heath alone.

The morning was wearing on, and she must get back. The hedges teemed with life on this warm, clear day. A badger scurried across the lane in front of her, darting from one hedge to the other. Butterflies danced over the blooming blackthorn like golden-winged fairies.

She entered the house through the kitchen door. "Good morning, Cook," she said to Mrs. Hale as she slipped a piece of hot bread fresh from the oven off the cutting board. With a slab of butter from the crock and some of last summer's preserves, she grinned at Mrs. Hale.

The butter melted into the warm bread, dripping onto her chin as she took a bite. They should've taken Cook with them to London. No one made bread like Mrs. Hale. Elaine laughed, licking her fingers. She would eat bread and jam every meal for the rest of her life if she could. But her governess had told her time and again that *man cannot live by bread alone—and neither can little girls.* Then she'd been forced to eat her greens before she could go outside and run wild with John and Gareth. To this day, every bite of spinach brought back the face of Miss Bassett.

With her free hand, Elaine turned the knob and pulled open the door to the drawing room. She took another bite of the warm bread, slurping to keep the sticky goodness from dripping.

"Someone's been in the kitchen, I see," came a rather unexpected voice.

Elaine looked up to find an extra face in the room. Lord Chiverton's.

Her feet melted to the floor. She never seemed to be able to make a respectable presentation to him. First wet and muddy, wearing Gareth's coat. And now a thick slice of bread dripping buttery jam onto the floor.

She'd not abandon her breakfast, not even for the earl. She licked a drip from the back side and curtseyed. With a quick gulp she said, "Lord Chiverton. What a wonderful surprise." He was a week early.

Elaine glanced at Aunt Rose, who was pressing a hand to her mouth to keep from laughing. Her mother scowled at her. Clearly she'd raised Elaine to be more of a lady, but how was she to know this would be the exact moment Lord Chiverton would show up after his trip to Plymouth? It was not her fault he'd returned before schedule.

"Good morning, Elaine. Please, do not let me stop you." He motioned to the bread in her hand.

As possibly the most unladylike thing she'd ever done, Elaine stuffed the last of the soggy bread into her mouth, filling it so full she could not speak for some time. The room was silent as she untied her bonnet and removed it from her head, set it on the sideboard, then lowered herself into a chair.

She swallowed with difficulty. "Lord Chiverton. How was your trip?"

He did well to keep a straight face, though not well enough to keep all the mirth from leaking out of his silky brown eyes.

"I was not wholly satisfied with the harbormaster there. Seems I lost a portion of my shipment to smugglers. I believe I might need to find another place to put in. But that is the way of shipping and also very boring. I'm much more interested in hearing about where you've been on this lovely morning." He pointed at her mulberry-colored spencer. "I see you're wearing your own coat. Am I to assume you've not been taking in clandestine meetings with another man?"

Elaine couldn't help a guilty glance in her mother's direction. Of course he was teasing, but he'd landed a little too close to the truth. She would never tell about her meeting with Gareth, nor of the way he'd followed after her.

"I went for a morning walk, that is all."

He watched her, expecting, she supposed, some kind of elaboration on her outing.

"I hope you have not been waiting long." Between Gareth, Gwen, and the two Williams, she was unwilling to provide any details of her excursion.

"Only a few minutes." He winked. "In truth, your timing was quite spot on."

Good to know he hadn't been trapped with her mother and Aunt Rose for too long. Uncle Charles must be with her father.

"No swimming, then, this morning?" he asked.

Her mother gave a horrified look.

"Just walking the lanes, is all." Elaine smiled at him. "Rather uneventful and also very boring."

"You should be careful, Elaine," he warned. "I've heard from more than one local that these paths are dangerous. Smugglers, I've been told. Must be a plague of them. Walking alone may not be advisable."

Everyone in her life assumed she was some delicate flower. Did they not see the stout and windblown trees this part of the country raised?

"You are too kind. But you forget I grew up here. I know this area well. It's quite safe. We do get smugglers, but they are never violent. We leave them alone, and they leave us alone. I know how to watch the wall as well as anyone. I can assure you I'm perfectly safe."

Her mother leaned forward. "My dear, you should heed Lord Chiverton's advice. Have you not heard of the terrible incident only six months ago?"

Elaine shook her head. She'd not heard anything.

"A man was killed by smugglers," her mother announced. "He was walking home from the mines when he came upon them moving their goods, they say. They beat him to death."

Elaine had never heard a word about this. "Here, in Camelford?"

Her mother nodded. "Almost in our own backyard."

"How awful," Aunt Rose said. "Anyone we know?"

Her mother nodded again, this time with a touch of real sadness in her eyes. Elaine's heart thudded. She'd never wish such an awful end to anyone. Not even Broken Betty.

"It was Mr. Kemp. Remember young Gareth, who used to come around? His father."

Elaine stared at her mother. Gareth's father? Why did he not say? The poor man. He'd been very close to his father. To lose him in such a violent way must have been a crushing blow. If only he'd said something, at least Elaine might have been able to offer some small comfort—as an old friend.

No wonder he'd been so concerned about the smugglers. They'd taken his own father. And how easily she'd dismissed him. Good heavens.

It seemed only yesterday she was sitting in the Kemps' kitchen listening to Mr. Kemp play his fiddle while Gareth and John fought their way through a game of chess. Now he and John were both gone.

"Elaine?" Her aunt was watching her. Everyone was watching her.

"This is shocking news," Elaine said. "Such a thing has never happened before." She tried to pull her thoughts off Gareth and back into the drawing room, but the sadness of what had happened to his father, to his family, would not leave her.

"How dreadful." Lord Chiverton set the cup he'd been sipping tea from on the end table. "Was this a person you were close to?"

"He is our neighbor," her mother said.

"He was the foreman of Polkreath Mine," Elaine added.

"Ah," Lord Chiverton said. "Unfortunate indeed."

"So now Gare—Mr. Kemp has taken over as foreman?" Elaine asked.

"My dear," her mother said with some surprise. "You did not know? He recently bought Polkreath and is now the owner."

"Owner?" That explained his fine suit of clothes and his leisurely pace at getting to the mine this morning.

Her mother nodded. "Yes. I'm told the father had set it all in motion before he died."

This was news indeed. Gareth owned Polkreath Mine.

He was very good at keeping secrets. Too good. This was her punishment for not sitting with the tongue-tabbies who came calling on her mother. Had she spent more time in the drawing room and less on the coasts and in caverns, she might have known all this.

Polkreath was one of many lucrative mines marking the West Country. He would be a rich man. He should have told her as much.

Lord Chiverton studied her for a moment before asking, "Do you often get smugglers here?"

Elaine shrugged. "There are always some creeping about, hidden in plain sight. Not like they do down south though. Lizard. Mousehole. They get the worst of it."

"Or the best of it," Lord Chiverton said.

All heads turned to him. How could he say such things? Especially after learning the fate of poor Mr. Kemp.

"Depending on your point of view," he explained. "For many folk, smuggled goods are the only kind they can afford. For others, it means food for their family. A man works all day in the fields doing back-breaking labor and makes what? A few shillings a week. That same man works only one night running cargo and earns nearly double. He can easily bring home two or three times the coin to support his family."

"They are breaking the law," Aunt Rose pointed out. "Not only that, they are supporting the enemy, buying goods from France, taking money out of England's pocket. Those same families could be helped by charitable funds obtained from the crown in a lawful way."

Lord Chiverton shrugged. "Perhaps. But have you ever seen those funds reach the hands of those who truly need it? The fishwives. Children of the miners condemned to a life underground or on the freezing clifftops when they should be going to school."

Lads like Willy White-Top and Sandy Will. Certainly they could benefit from any funds the crown might be willing to allot to caring for the poor. Though it did seem unlikely those funds would reach this forgotten piece of the country.

There were plenty enough scraping together the meanest of lives in the streets and gutters of London. One need not travel all the way to Cornwall to find starving children and mothers suckling their babes with empty breasts.

Lord Chiverton leaned forward. "The smugglers supply goods at a fraction of the cost, and the people reap the benefits."

"I doubt very much the smugglers are in it for the benefit of the people," Aunt Rose said, shaking her head. "Especially since the majority of the funds taken in go to the wealthy man financing the scheme. A man who most certainly is *not* a starving waif nor a child condemned to the mines."

Aunt Rose also made sense. What portion of the operation did help the people? Certainly one could purchase tea or cloth for several shillings less from under the counter, but those few extra coins saved were not worth the life of a man like Gareth's father. With so many people involved in the smuggling rings, it must be a greater boon to the locals than she'd considered.

Lord Chiverton gestured in the general direction of London. "There would be no need for smugglers and privateers in the first place if parliament would only remove the tariffs that make imported goods impossible for the common man to afford." His voice rose with his conviction.

Aunt Rose huffed. "How can you say such things? A man may not agree with every law, but that does not give him the right to go against his king and country. Such disregard for order would make us no better than France."

Lord Chiverton set his jaw. "France—"

"I wonder," Elaine's mother said, "if we ought to have Mrs. Kemp and her son over for dinner. Now that he is a gentleman, so to speak. And she is our nearest neighbor."

The conversation careened into a brick wall—driven there purposely by her mother. And now she wanted to bring Gareth here to Havencross for a dinner party.

Lord Chiverton leaned back in his chair and crossed his legs with a soft chuckle. "Excellent notion. You are very thoughtful, Mrs. Cardinham." He grinned. "I would be very interested to hear his opinions on the smuggling situation."

"I daresay you won't like them." Aunt Rose folded her arms across her chest.

Elaine was inclined to agree with her aunt. After they killed his father, Gareth's opinions would not at all be generous toward the smugglers.

Her mother beamed at them. "'Tis settled, then."

CHAPTER NINE

Gareth

GARETH WAITED IN THE ENTRANCE hall for his mother. She'd been getting ready for dinner at the Cardinham's for more than half the day.

"Mother," he called up the stairs. "If we don't leave now, we will be late."

He couldn't begin to fathom the reason they'd been invited in the first place. It would not have been Elaine's choice, of that he was sure.

His mother's footsteps came pattering lightly down the wooden stairs.

"How do I look?" She stood in front of him and spun, her ample gown billowing out. "Lord Chiverton is there, and I don't want to look like a pauper. You are a gentleman now." She smiled up at Gareth.

She wore a new dress—still black for her husband—with black flowers of some kind embroidered on the diagonal, creating a rather flattering pattern across the frock. Even her hair was done up in an elegant top knot with a few strands curling around her ears. Tasteful and becoming for her age.

"You look quite handsome, Mother. Martha has done well." He opened the front door. "The carriage is ready."

He helped his mother into the curricle, then leapt up beside her and took the reins. With a snap of the leathers, they were off, his mother oohfing as she was thrust backward by the quick start.

They could have walked in almost the same amount of time it took them in the carriage, but his mother insisted that if he was dining at Havencross in the presence of an earl, he should arrive like a gentleman. Just as the horse was finding his pace, they were there.

Gareth hadn't been in this house since John's passing. With the Cardinhams gone nearly that whole time, he doubted much had changed. Yet how different it would be this time, returning as a dinner guest rather than a neighbor boy come to run wild with their son.

They entered the house and were ushered straight to the drawing room. Gareth would have liked to have been here sooner to make a quiet entrance rather than be announced as the last and final remaining guests.

As it turned out, the party was very small. Elaine and her mother. No sign of Mr. Cardinham. He recognized Elaine's aunt and her husband, Charles Beaford. The man he did not know must be Lord Chiverton, of whom his mother had not stopped talking.

So this was Elaine's betrothed. He seemed stuffy and foppish, but apparently that was what she wanted. Chiverton had been staying at The Black Hart Inn this past week, visiting Havencross nearly every day—or so Gareth's informants had told him. Well, good for her. A match with such an eligible man would surely bring her the happiness she'd left Cornwall in search of.

"Mrs. Kemp. Pleasure to meet you." Chiverton gave Gareth's mother a deep bow. He then took Gareth's hand and shook it. "Mr. Kemp. I'm sorry to hear about your father."

"Thank you," Gareth said. "That is very kind."

Over Chiverton's shoulder, he caught sight of Elaine, lovely as ever and desperately trying to tell him something with her eyes wide and one brow cocked askew. Unfortunately, his skills in reading minds had not improved since the day of the mystery lamb.

Chiverton caught him staring and stepped to the side, opening the space between them. "I take it you already know Miss Cardinham?"

Gareth nodded. "We've met a few times. Neighbors since childhood."

"Of course," Chiverton said.

Gareth bowed to Elaine. "Miss Cardinham."

"Mr. Kemp," she said.

Gareth greeted Mrs. Cardinham, who also offered him condolences. And likewise from Mr. and Mrs. Beaford. Perhaps that was what this dinner was about, a condolence for the loss of his father. It was, in point of fact, quite considerate of them.

"I'm sorry Mr. Cardinham can't be with us this evening," Mrs. Cardinham said without offering any other explanation as to her husband's absence. By the hard set of her eyes, he guessed Mr. Cardinham had not been invited by his wife to the dinner party in his own home. Then again, he could be wrong, as taking silent cues was not one of his better skills.

The blush that colored Elaine's cheeks confirmed his suspicion. All was not well at the Cardinham household.

"How is the tin business?" Chiverton asked him.

"Very good," he said, pulling his gaze from Elaine back to Chiverton. "You are from Warwickshire?" Gareth asked, knowing full well he was.

Gareth had heard plenty about this man. Bits and pieces that came to him by way of the innkeeper's wife to the miners' wives to the miners, then to the foreman and then to him, so undoubtedly it was all true. Lord Chiverton was the most handsome man to ever arrive in Camelford. He was the richest. He was the most kind and generous. He shipped goods for the crown. He had the largest fleet. He was the best pheasant hunter. He had the fastest horse. Given enough time, they'd probably make him a knight of the round table.

However interesting this Lord Chiverton, what Gareth really wanted to find out was why Elaine's arcing look.

The butler came in and announced dinner. He'd have to wait till after to get to the bottom of her silent message.

Chiverton took Elaine and led her into the dining room. Gareth was forced to watch from behind as she slipped her hand into the crook of his arm. The strongest arm in the area, according to his chain of informants.

He waited for Charles to push his wife's chair past, then fell in behind with his mother on his arm.

She had a grin from ear to ear. She leaned in and whispered, "Look at us, dining at Havencross. If only your father could be here." She patted his arm.

"Yes, Mother. Dinner at Havencross was the pinnacle of his hopes and dreams."

"Oh, pshaw." She slapped his shoulder.

He was seated between Mr. and Mrs. Beaford. He'd met Elaine's aunt and uncle only a few times before, in his youth when he'd spent time with John. Their conversation was intelligent and interesting, and the dinner passed pleasantly enough. Apart from all the grins and winks between Chiverton and Elaine, that is.

When the last course was finished, the ladies excused themselves, and a footman poured a round of brandy for the men.

"French brandy," Beaford said. "Good thing my wife doesn't know I'm drinking this."

Chiverton laughed. "Indeed." He turned to Gareth. "I hear you're on a quest to rid your coast of smugglers."

Gareth gave him an equivocal nod.

"Can't say I blame you after the unfortunate incident with your father." He swirled his glass and then brought it to his nose. "A shame to go without the French brandy though."

"Too bad there's not a way to rid our coasts of the vermin and keep the brandy," Beaford added.

"True." Gareth pushed his drink away. Anything from France had to pass through the hands of smugglers. "But it does seem rather unpatriotic to give our money to the French when it will only be turned around and used against our own men. And selfish too. What kind of people can't live without goods they know are coming from the enemy? Whose life is worth a glass of brandy or a yard of lace?"

Gareth looked up in time to catch Chiverton's eyes slip over to Beaford with a grin. "Bit dramatic, don't you think?"

Beaford set his full glass down on the table and rose. "I shall leave the solving of Cornwall's import problems in your capable hands. As French goods go, you can have them. I've got all I need waiting for me in the drawing room." He nodded at Gareth and Chiverton, then left.

"He's nothing if not devoted," Chiverton said.

Gareth could not deny it. Beaford had spent a good portion of the meal assuring the needs of his wife were met. Beaford had barely sat with Chiverton and himself for five minutes before needing to be with her again. Though with the present company in mind, Gareth could hardly blame him. He too had little desire to sit and converse with Chiverton.

Gareth rose. "I suppose I'd better check on my mother. She's not had quite the same energy since the passing of my father."

Chiverton nodded. "Of course. We should join the ladies." He scooted back his chair and rose to his feet. "Beaford's not the only one with something valuable in the drawing room." He winked at Gareth and then walked out the door.

Gareth stared after him. A regular cavalier, that one. No wonder Elaine was taken with him. Who could resist such a dashing smile, his grand countenance, and his vast wealth? He hoped she'd be happy with him. Undoubtedly she would be better off, moving in the first circles of society, pin money to buy all the bonnets and shawls her wardrobe could hold. Not things he'd thought really mattered to Elaine, but what did he know?

Gareth entered the drawing room on Chiverton's heels. Chiverton went straight to Elaine, but her eyes flicked to Gareth for the briefest of moments before she smiled up at the gentleman. The evening was getting on, and there was no need for him and his mother to stay longer. He could easily use her as an excuse to retire.

His mother sat on the sofa, deeply engaged in a conversation with Mrs. Cardinham—speaking as though they were both widows, though Mr. Cardinham had to be around here somewhere. Too embarrassed to show his face—or too proud, more likely.

Just as he was about to ask his mother if she was getting tired, Elaine approached him. She'd left Chiverton engaged in conversation with her aunt and uncle and now stood over him, offering a cup of tea. Yet another commodity they'd likely purchased through the *free traders*.

"Thank you," he said, taking the porcelain cup and saucer edged with gold.

"We paid full price," she said, reading his thoughts. This was a skill he had better start practicing.

She sat across from him on a small chair, stirring her tea. "I was sorry to hear about your father, Mr. Kemp."

"You're very kind," Gareth said.

Elaine took a sip of her tea, keeping her eyes on the creamy brown liquid as she spoke. "I wished . . ." At last, she looked up and said quietly, "Why did you not tell me he was the one killed by the smugglers?"

Gareth shrugged. It was big news at the time. He assumed everyone already knew. She really had cut herself off from Cornwall completely to have missed that bit of information. "I did not know you didn't know."

"Your father was a good man," Elaine said. "One of the best."

Gareth drained his tea cup and set it aside. This was why he'd not said a word to her about it. Rather than healing, her sympathy cut deeply, opening raw the wounds he'd been working so hard to close. It was easier when he'd believed she cared nothing about him, but the sorrow in her eyes was real. He had knack enough in thought reading to recognize that.

"And why did you not tell me you are now the owner of Polkreath Mine?" This she said so quietly it took him a moment to understand.

"Would it have mattered?" he asked.

She quickly looked away.

He should not have said that. Not after her sincere sorrow for his father. It wasn't like him to be petty. Really, he had put her and her silky copper hair and her crinkly-nosed smile far behind him. When she'd left for London, he'd thought he'd never see her again—and he'd gotten along very well these last five years. It made no sense that now, when all was past, he should feel the need to goad her.

She would be here for only another week or so until the wedding. Ten days to be precise. Not that he was counting. Then, as before, he'd likely never see her again. She would move to Chiverton's estate in Warwickshire and perhaps he might see her at church next Christmas.

Gareth looked up to see Chiverton standing behind Elaine. He hadn't seen him come over.

Chiverton cleared his throat and lifted what was left in his glass. "I propose . . ." He stood poised with his drink raised until all eyes were on him. "An outing."

"Oh," Mrs. Cardinham said, taking up a pile of knitting. "Wonderful idea."

"What do you have in mind?" Beaford asked, resting a hand on his wife's chair.

"The ruins of Tintagel. Mrs. Cardinham mentioned it to me some time ago, and I've been yearning to go ever since." Lord Chiverton tossed the rest of his drink down his throat.

Some outing. Chiverton might as well take that glass of brandy and exchange it for milk. Those ruins weren't much farther than Gareth's own backyard. He and John and Elaine had been there countless times. He'd expected something a bit more exiting—Newquay, perhaps, or even as far as St. Ives.

Mrs. Kemp clasped a hand to her chest. "The ruins are treacherous. Are you sure you'll be safe?"

"Nonsense, Mother," Gareth said. "They are perfectly safe."

"What do you say, Kemp?" Chiverton asked. "Are you up for an excursion?"

It sounded more like a challenge than an invitation. Elaine ducked her head, studying her tea like she could predict the future from its dregs.

No tea reading was necessary. He could clearly see how this outing would turn out. They would all go to Tintagel together. The air would be damp. Lord Chiverton would be gentlemanly. And the awkwardness of the whole situation would leave them all exhausted.

Gareth took one more glance at Elaine. She flashed him a single dark look, but it was enough for him to understand her clearly. His skills were improving—at least where Elaine was concerned. She would prefer he skip the entire affair.

He gave Chiverton a nod. "It would be my pleasure."

Chiverton let out a *ha* of triumph. "Then it's a plan." He paused his celebration, his eyes falling on the Beafords. "I do hope you'll be able to join us, Charles." Chiverton seemed uncertain about the man's situation regarding his wife—confined as she was to her chair.

Beaford opened his mouth to speak, but his wife beat him to it. "We should be delighted to be part of the company." She smiled up at Chiverton. "It's been ages since I've been out there, and I do so love it."

Chiverton's glance slid back to Beaford.

He nodded. "My wife has spoken. And as everyone knows, I never go anywhere without my wife."

"You don't need to tell me that." Mrs. Beaford rolled her eyes for the benefit of the group. "I can't ever get away from him."

"Do you know what would make this outing perfect?" Gareth's mother asked.

Chiverton gave her a little bow. "The pleasure of *your* company?"

Mrs. Kemp waved a hand at him. "Oh, goodness me. I could never. That is a journey for the young." The spark in her eyes gave Gareth a sinking feeling. "You must ask Miss Tippet to join your party. I'm sure she would make a great addition."

Gareth immediately regretted his decision to go.

His mother turned to Elaine and Mrs. Cardinham. "Miss Tippet is new in the neighborhood," she explained, "and she has quite caught the eye of every eligible man in the district." She directed her gaze straight at Gareth.

Thank you, Mother. He shifted in his seat, looking everywhere except at Elaine.

Chiverton pounced, grinning broadly at Gareth. "Indeed. Miss Tippet must certainly be included. Mrs. Kemp, I shall leave it to you to offer the invitation."

Gareth's mother nodded. This was the kind of responsibility she thrived on.

What Gareth couldn't understand was Chiverton's interest in him. He was certainly of no consequence to the Earl of Chiverton. He could have easily planned this outing without Gareth, but instead, Gareth was the first Chiverton had sought consent from.

"It is settled," Chiverton announced. "Let us set the date for two days from today. What say you?"

Elaine nodded.

"I say very well." Gareth rose to his feet and crossed to his mother. "We'd better get you home. I'll send for the carriage." He left the drawing room and went himself to the stables. The sky had clouded since he'd been inside the Cardinhams' home, and the air tickled with the promise of rain. Good. A nice cold rainfall was just what he needed.

CHAPTER TEN

Elaine

ELAINE PACED BACK AND FORTH in the entry hall, twisting the ties to her bonnet in her hand. Lord Chiverton was to be here over an hour ago, and still there was no sign of him or his carriage on the approach to Havencross. What could be keeping him?

They'd been planning this outing to see the ruins of Tintagel Castle for the past five days, but time after time, a note had arrived stating that *matters of business* had detained him. Always with his deepest regrets.

At least the notes had arrived on time. She understood gentlemen had business that needed attending, but to be shunted aside time and again worried her that something had gone wrong. An accident. Or perhaps smugglers had gotten to his goods again.

In the meantime, Aunt Rose and Uncle Charles had their coach readied and loaded this whole time, awaiting Lord Chiverton. Aunt Rose's bath chair was secured to the back, and she waited on a chair Brixton had brought out for her.

Uncle Charles had spent the last hour pacing back and forth, muttering under his breath. He walked over to his wife and asked if she needed anything.

"Calm down, Charles," Aunt Rose said. "I'm sure he'll be here any minute. One cannot always perfectly predict such things. He is dependent on the ostlers at the inn to ready his rig. The state of the roads. For all we know, there was a herdsman with a flock of sheep blocking the Camelford Bridge. That alone could hold him up for some time."

Her uncle nodded and kissed her hand. "I'm sure you're right, dear." But that didn't keep him from taking up his pacing again. And his muttering.

The neigh of a horse and the rickotting of wheels on the packed dirt lane reached her shortly before a high-slung phaeton rounded the bend. Hardly the best choice for driving along the rocky lanes.

"Excuse me, miss." Mr. Winkleigh appeared beside her. "But there be two boys at the servant's door asking for you. They claim to know you."

It took her a moment to figure out who it could possibly be. Then she grinned. "A red-haired freckled lad and a lighter one?"

He nodded.

The two Williams. Perhaps they'd learned something of the lady Gwen. "I do know them. Thank you, Mr. Winkleigh." She set off to the rear of the house.

Sure enough, there stood Willy White-Top and Sandy Will. One of the kitchen girls stood guard, ready to shoo them away should they be trouble. "Fetch some ginger fairings from Cook, please," Elaine said to the girl.

The boys' eyes lit up as the maid nodded and left.

The two lads glanced at each other. It was fitting they shared the same name since they seemed like one body with two heads rather than two individual boys. Here they were again, wandering the backcountry when most young ones their age would be busy in the mines or at lessons—if they could afford it. She wished she'd told the kitchen girl to bring something more hearty than biscuits. Beef pasties or stargazy pie, to put some meat on their bones.

"Do you have news of the woman?" she asked the Williams.

"No, mum," Willy White-Top said. "We ain't seen nothun like that."

"And we been lookun 'ard," Sandy Will added. "Ain't that true?"

Willy White-Top nodded so vigorously she worried his head would topple off. From behind his back, he brought forth the cricket ball.

She laughed. "You've come to use the bat."

This time it was Sandy Will who bobbed his head up and down.

"What's this about cricket?"

Elaine spun around to find Lord Chiverton right behind her. "Sir. You startled me."

He grinned. "Forgive me, my dear. The footman told me you had business with two boys, and I had to see it for myself." His smile broadened. "I thought maybe I had competition, but I can see I overestimated their attachment."

Elaine turned to find the stoop completely absent of Williams. She looked out over the lawn to see their skinny forms disappearing into a row of trimmed hedges.

"Williams," she called.

They did not reappear. The girl returned with a stack of fairing biscuits wrapped in a napkin.

"Never mind. They've gone." Elaine looked up at Lord Chiverton. Those boys had been very leery of Elaine that first day they'd met. The sight of another stranger, especially one so fine as Lord Chiverton, must have spooked them.

"I'm terribly sorry," he said. "I didn't mean to frighten them. In fact, a few swings with a bat would be a fine diversion. Alas, today we are off to Tintagel."

Elaine kept her eyes on the hedge in case they decided to come back once the fright wore off, but there was no sign of them.

"Just some local boys I met the other day." She turned away and closed the door.

"Skin and bones. Poor little waifs." Lord Chiverton took a step closer. He touched her hand, just the tips of her fingers, but it was enough to send a fluttering up her arm. "Lucky they have such a lovely benefactress to watch over them." He gave her fingers a soft squeeze.

She tightened her hand on his in an intimate gesture she'd never used on any man before.

His smiled broadened. "Come now." He winked and handed over her bonnet. "I believe there is an ancient castle waiting for us. And I, for one, cannot wait to see the birthplace of our nation's greatest king."

Elaine laughed, setting her bonnet on her head and tying the strings close to her chin so it wouldn't blow off in the open-topped phaeton. "I wonder," she said, "what our monarch would think of you claiming a man of myth and legend is a better ruler than our own dear King George."

They reached the front drive, and Lord Chiverton helped her up into the carriage. "Before we go, I'll have you know I fully believe in Arthur, his knights, and the beautiful city of Camelot."

No wonder she was fond of him. "You and Mr. Kemp, both. I thought men were supposed to be the practical ones and the women those with romantic notions."

Lord Chiverton walked around the horses. He put his foot on the step and hoisted himself up into the phaeton. "So, Mr. Kemp is a romantic. You seem to know him well."

"No, not very well." She smoothed the front of her frock. "We are neighbors. And I knew him as a child, but that was many years ago. He was a friend of my brother, John."

The stable boy handed Chiverton the reins. He snapped the leather, and the animals set off. Elaine looked back over her shoulder. Her aunt and uncle's carriage fell in motion right behind them, driven by Coachman Dean. She'd tried to convince her mother to come with them, but she was having a day of poor nerves and insisted they go without her.

Her mother had never been keen on the old castle ruins nor walking the rocky coast by the sea. She doubted her mother had ever been down to Merlin's cave in her entire life. It had always been John and Gareth who'd taken her to the water's edge or over to see the mine or to explore Bodmin Moor.

Lord Chiverton took his team out onto the lane and turned them north toward Lowentop. He looked well the part of a gentleman sitting tall on the seat of his high flyer, his beaver perched upon his head at a jaunty angle while locks of his light hair curled out along the brim. He was far too fine a man to be here in the West Country whilst the rest of his colleagues enjoyed the London Season.

He looked over at her, catching her gazing. "How very lucky I am to have the prettiest tour guide in the country."

Elaine turned away. She hated the flush his compliments brought to her cheeks and how they left her with no idea what to say in return. He was still watching her; she could feel his gaze through the straw brim. She lifted her eyes to him. "It is my pleasure."

He held out his elbow. Aunt Rose and Uncle Charles were in the coach behind them and were no doubt watching their every move. What did that signify? They were to be married in only five days. She had no reason to hide her affections.

Elaine slid her hand around his arm, and he snugged it tight. "I'm glad you are well," she said. "You postponed our outing so many times I thought you must have had a terrible accident."

He shook his head. "No such thing. It's all this business of shipping. Again we lost a good deal of merchandise to the smugglers. I'm now thinking of relocating my whole operation." He looked down at her. "But that is neither here nor there and should not be talked about on an outing of pleasure."

He turned the carriage down the lane that cut across a little wooded area of planted trees, shaving almost a mile off the main road. It was used mostly by farmers as they crossed from one field to another.

"Why are we going this way?" she asked.

"'Tis shorter, is it not?"

True, but few people went this way unless they were locals. Nor was it the smoothest path for his high phaeton. Lord Chiverton maneuvered his carriage well along the untamed track, and in only a few more minutes, they turned into Lowentop.

Gareth was striding across the lawn with a rifle slung over his shoulders and two hounds bounding at his heels. His eyebrows rose slightly when he saw her seated so neatly beside Lord Chiverton.

Lord Chiverton brought the phaeton to a halt. "Ho, there, Mr. Kemp."

Gareth nodded, a smile building on his face. "'Morning. Or should I say good afternoon?"

"My apologies," Lord Chiverton said. "I had some trouble getting out of the inn."

Elaine retied her bonnet in order to extricate her hand from Lord Chiverton's arm.

"As a matter of fact, it gave me time to do some shooting," Gareth said.

"Bit early in the season for a hunt, isn't it?" Lord Chiverton asked.

"Quite so," Gareth agreed. "I've been out taking care of a troublesome badger that keeps getting into the chickens."

"Ah. I hadn't thought of that. Something we don't see much of in London."

"Would that be badgers or chickens?" Gareth asked.

Lord Chiverton laughed. "Badgers, I suppose."

Gareth switched his gun to the other shoulder. "Miss Tippet is inside with Mother. I'll go fetch her."

Gareth disappeared into his house and returned moments later with Miss Tippet. She wore a colorful pink dress and carried a parasol in a matching shade. All of it trimmed in light blue ribbons.

Uncle Charles opened the door to the coach and handed Miss Tippet in. Aunt Rose said something to Gareth that made him smile, but Elaine could not hear it from her distance. The coach door closed, and they were off again.

The path took them down toward the edge of the cliffs that overlooked the ocean. She never tired of the view nor of the waves as they rippled and curved along the water. It always reminded her of John. She'd spent more time with him than anyone, excepting Gareth.

It didn't take long for them to reach Trevanna. They drove through the little village, and Lord Chiverton stopped at the top of the path leading to the ruins. Brixton, who'd been riding on the bench with her uncle's coachman, came forward and took the reins.

Lord Chiverton jumped out and then took Elaine's hand and fair near lifted her to the ground. He had more strength lurking under his fine clothes than she'd imagined. Not that she'd spent much time contemplating the physique of Lord Chiverton. At least not that she wanted to admit.

Gareth was the first out of the Beaford's carriage. He handed Miss Tippet down, then went immediately to the rear of the carriage and helped remove the bath chair. Uncle Charles joined him, and soon it was ready for Aunt Rose.

Uncle Charles lifted her from the carriage, cradling her in his arms like a fragile treasure. She smiled up at him, and Elaine looked away. It was a look meant only for the man dearest to her heart. Her eyes instead went to Gareth, who was already watching Elaine.

Lord Chiverton offered his arm again. She turned and wrapped her hand around it. Gareth and Miss Tippet fell in step beside Aunt Rose, while Uncle Charles pushed the chair along the packed dirt of the path leading to Tintagel.

"A perfect day for our adventure, do you not agree?" Lord Chiverton said.

The sky shone a brilliant blue, scattered with soft puffs of clouds whiter than fresh bleached linen. That did not guarantee that in the space of an hour they wouldn't have wind and rain.

"I agree—for the moment," Elaine said. "You should know that the weather changes faster than a man changes his mind."

A bark of a laugh came from behind them. A sound she attributed to Gareth, so often she had heard it. It was quickly followed by a loud cascade of laughter. Miss Tippet.

"What on earth does that mean?" Lord Chiverton asked.

"Only that the weather is rather fickle," Elaine said. "Friendly one moment and raging the next."

Gareth let out another guffaw. "Sounds more like the women I know."

"Hear, hear," Lord Chiverton agreed.

"Well, I agree with Miss Cardinham," Miss Tippet said. "In the months we've been here, the weather can't seem to make up its mind."

Lord Chiverton and Gareth exchanged a look. "You've perfectly described the gentler sex, Miss Tippet," Lord Chiverton said.

Miss Tippet glanced over at Elaine, appearing somewhat uncertain as to why the men were laughing so heartily at her comment.

"Watch your step here, Miss Tippet," Gareth said as they approached the scattered and crumbling walls of the castle.

The ruins of Tintagel were divided, a few larger structures up against the cliffside of the mainland and a scattering of other ruins out across the island-like headland. John had told her that the great castle stretched across them both, but then the narrow land connecting them collapsed, taking a large portion of the castle with it.

They had reached the first set of ruins on the mainland, where several tall walls still remained, indicating the inland part of the castle.

It would be quite difficult for Aunt Rose to make it to the island and nearly impossible for her to go down to the cave. Elaine was happy to accommodate. The day would likely go much better if they didn't go to the cave at all.

"Now, then," Lord Chiverton said. "Tell us about the significance of this place and our mighty King Arthur."

All eyes turned to her. She hadn't planned on giving a history lesson today, but she would do her best. "It is said that this is the place where Uther Pendragon—King Arthur's father—first fell in love with Igraine, Arthur's mother. Unfortunately, at that time, Igraine already had a husband."

She stopped. Until this moment, she'd not realized how like her own father's indiscretion this story was.

How cruel these makers of myths and tales to take the worst of humanity and use it to tell a story about the greatest king to ever rule England. Now more than ever she wanted nothing to do with it.

"It sounds quite scandalous," Miss Tippet said.

Gareth stepped in, taking over for Elaine as she stumbled on the words. "Shortly thereafter, Igraine's husband was killed in battle. She was free to marry Uther." He motioned to the ruins out on the island. "It is here that the young king was born."

Lord Chiverton's head turned, taking in the prospect before him.

Elaine inched closer to Gareth. "*Meur ras.*" She whispered her thanks in Cornish.

He nodded, turning toward her with eyebrows raised at her language choice.

"What about Gwenevere?" Aunt Rose asked. "When did Arthur fall in love with her? That's my favorite part of the story."

Here too was a problem. For this subject took her far too close to Gareth's proposal five years ago.

"This is only the birthplace of King Arthur," Elaine said. "Gwenevere came later. After Arthur removed the sword from the stone and became king."

"But you can still tell the story." Aunt Rose leaned forward in her chair with little notion of the discomfort she was causing.

Elaine was still standing right next to Gareth. Her mouth went dry at the thought of repeating these words in front of him. But she could not deny her aunt and the eager way she waited for Elaine to continue. So she forged on.

"It is told that when it was time for Arthur to take a wife, he went to Merlin." Elaine carefully kept her eyes away from Gareth. "Arthur told Merlin he would marry whomever Merlin advised. But Merlin turned the choice back to Arthur, asking him if there be any maiden Arthur loved more than any other."

"What did he say?" Miss Tippet asked.

Before Elaine could answer, Gareth took up the telling. "Arthur said he loved Gwenevere, daughter of King Leodegrance. Arthur declared to Merlin, 'She is the most valiant and the fairest lady that I know living or, yet, that ever I could find.'" Gareth's eyes flicked to Elaine's.

Those were the exact words he'd used on her when he'd taken her hand in the cave below. She wanted to dive headfirst off the headland to escape the snakes gnawing at her insides.

Aunt Rose sighed with her hand over her heart. "True love."

This time Gareth's eyes fell hard on Elaine. "Yes, I believe it was."

He may as well have driven a stake through her heart. She'd never meant to hurt him. She wished once more that Merlin would magically appear and turn back the hands of time, that she might undo her mistakes of the past. But he did not appear. All she had was Lord Chiverton to take her far away from all this.

"What a beautiful story." Miss Tippet twirled her parasol.

"Well, Gwenevere was very beautiful," Gareth said pointedly. He cleared his throat and then smiled at Aunt Rose. "After some time, King Leodegrance consented to the union. The great round table of Camelot was actually a wedding gift from Gwenevere's father."

"Is this place Camelot?" Miss Tippet asked.

"That is the great mystery," Gareth said with flair. "No one knows for certain where the mighty castle of Camelot was. Perhaps here. Perhaps at Glastonbury in Somerset. Perhaps Caerleon in Wales."

"Perhaps France," Elaine said in an effort to show Gareth his words had not affected her. "As it seems to be a French word."

"Don't be daft," Miss Tippet said. "He was the King of England. He would never cavort with the enemy, much less have his castle over there." She tipped her head, indicating a direction Elaine supposed was meant to be across the channel but instead led directly to Scotland.

"Indeed, Miss Cardinham." Gareth chuckled. "Don't be daft."

Aunt Rose laughed but quickly stifled it, covering her mouth with a handkerchief.

"The folks in Camelford claim it was there." Uncle Charles pushed his wife closer. "Camelford. Camelot. Not sure they have much else for their claim beyond linguistics though."

This excited Miss Tippet, as if having a lost kingdom in her own neighborhood was all one could hope for in life. "That does make sense."

Gareth gestured toward the east. "Let us not forget that the great round table of King Arthur currently resides in Winchester. They also lay claim to Camelot."

Lord Chiverton smiled grandly and swept his hand across the view in front of them. "This is Camelot. I'm sure of it. How can there be any doubt?"

"Well," Uncle Charles said. "First, there is—"

"Nonsense," Lord Chiverton interrupted. "Look at this place. It is perfect. Ready transport by either land or sea. Impregnable to siege. And the whole coast is riddled with caves in case one needs a place to lie low. As you see. Perfect."

"That must be why it is abandoned," Gareth pointed out.

"Disagree all you like, Mr. Kemp, but Camelot was here. I can feel it in my bones." Lord Chiverton gazed out over the ruins and past the cliffs and water, his eyes focused on something far more distant than the horizon. "And my bones are never wrong."

Something about his deep voice and the intensity with which he'd spoken sent a chill across Elaine's skin. His conviction was almost enough to turn her back into a believer.

It was quite a romantic notion—one that had fueled the childhood imaginations of John, Gareth, and herself. That the great seat of Camelot was so near her own house. King Arthur and his knights would have ridden across the same land she so often walked. Their feet treading on the same stones. Same beach. People coming from all over the realm to see the greatness of their king.

Miss Tippet rushed forward and stood beside him. "I believe you are right, Lord Chiverton." She looked up at him, beaming.

But Lord Chiverton's eyes, when they finally left the deep places of the horizon, went straight to Elaine.

He nodded to her as if he'd somehow, through the windblown hair at the back of his head, seen her lean toward his words. He smiled at her, reminding her of why she'd taken a liking to him in the first place.

Through the ballrooms teeming with eligible ladies, through the concert halls of eager eyes, even past the fine carriages where handkerchiefs fell like snow, Lord Chiverton had found Elaine. A nobody of significance from Cornwall. He'd smiled at her like that at the Wilmslow's ball, then had crossed the floor and asked for an introduction.

She still could not understand how, after the fall of her family from what little station they'd had, he was here, gracing her with his brown, velvet eyes and carefree grin.

Lord Chiverton strode toward her, tucking her hand in the bend of his arm. "Come, Miss Cardinham," he said softly. "I very much want you to show me the rest of this place."

Though the wind blew a cool breeze off the water, warmth spread to her fingertips. What would Gareth think of his boldness? Why did it even matter? They were to be married. Lord Chiverton had every right to request the company of his future wife. She was happy to oblige.

Still, as Lord Chiverton ran his hands along a weathered wall, she stole one quick glance at Gareth. His back was to her, and he was speaking to Miss Tippet. The woman had been left on the precipice of the cliffs when Lord Chiverton had so abruptly abandoned them.

She was all smiles and laughter, not even seeming to notice she'd been completely overlooked. It was a testament of her agreeableness. Gareth was so contrary that she would do him good.

CHAPTER ELEVEN

Elaine

THEY MOVED ALONG THE RUINS, Uncle Charles pushing Aunt Rose in her chair, keeping mostly to the packed pathways and areas of low grass.

Piles of crumbling stones in hues of slate and gray crisscrossed the site. A wall here. A forgotten archway there. Most of it unidentifiable mounds of rock. In Elaine's youth, Gareth had held her hand, steadying her as she walked along the tops of the walls. She would tiptoe along the stones, clutching him for balance. His hands were always large and rough from work.

It hadn't taken long for the ruins to lure Lord Chiverton away from her side. He now stood in the open space between two partial walls, speculating to Gareth what he thought the room was used for.

"This must be where the king slept. Or perhaps this is the very room where Arthur was born."

Miss Tippet nodded, agreeing with every speculation, no matter who said it or how much it contradicted the previous supposition.

"Possibly," Gareth said. "Though I believe most scholars consider this the upper courtyard and guard rooms." He pointed across the narrow rocky path that connected the mainland to the small headland. "Across there is the heart of the castle."

Miss Tippet nodded again. "Makes sense, doesn't it? To have the king's quarters within the safety of the island fortress." That was quite sound reasoning coming from Miss Tippet.

Lord Chiverton followed Gareth's pointing finger. "I see." He loped off, picking his footing far too quickly for any semblance of safety.

"Careful!" Elaine called out.

Lord Chiverton's head turned back, glancing over his shoulder with a wide grin. He looked just like John used to before setting off on an adventure.

She'd come to take for granted the allure of Tintagel. The rocky point of land it was built upon and the uniqueness of the castle's situation—all of it was quite extraordinary.

Uncle Charles came up beside her. "He seems eager."

Elaine nodded. "Very eager." She directed his gaze toward Miss Tippet, who stood at the cliff edge with her hand clasped over her heart, gazing with trepidation at the path that dropped steeply away. "And some are not so eager."

"Goodness sakes." Miss Tippet cast a nervous glance at Gareth. "Is it safe?"

Gareth offered her his arm. "Only one way to find out."

A few drops of color drained from her face, but she rallied herself and gave him a determined nod. Gareth and Miss Tippet set off arm in arm.

Aunt Rose leaned forward in her chair, taking in the view. "I haven't been here in ages. I'd forgotten how beautiful it is."

"Indeed," Uncle Charles agreed.

"I'll stay here with my aunt," Elaine said to Uncle Charles, "if you want to cross over and walk around with the others." A break from all of them would suit her well. Save Uncle Charles and Aunt Rose, of course. She never tired of them.

Uncle Charles looked down at his wife tucked safely into the wheeled chair. He wagged his eyebrows at her, and Aunt Rose's face lit up. "Don't be ridiculous," he said. "I never go anywhere without my wife."

He took his place behind her chair and leaned into it, pushing the wobbly wheels across the rough track. Elaine moved along beside him, doing what she could to help the chair over the clumps of tussock grass and rocks.

Uncle Charles tipped the bath chair forward and started down the path. More than once, she and Uncle Charles had to dig their feet in to keep Aunt Rose's chair from rolling out of control. Her aunt spent the whole time laughing, like it was nothing more than a carriage ride through the park.

Getting her back up on the other side proved even more difficult.

Gareth noticed their efforts, and once Miss Tippet was safe and sound on the headland, he skidded his way back down to help. In the end, the terrain proved too steep and the chair refused to cooperate. Uncle Charles lifted Aunt Rose into his arms, and Gareth took up the bath chair, hauling it up the cliffside path.

Elaine followed behind him, useless in this grand endeavor. The whole excursion was Lord Chiverton's idea. He should be the one maneuvering that chair up the hill.

"Careful, Mr. Kemp," she called when the track narrowed.

He turned back with his lips in a pinched line. "Thank you, Miss Cardinham, for your helpful warning. I've never climbed this path before."

He was too brassy by half. She'd only meant to help. He may have climbed this route a hundred times, but she'd bet her best boots he'd never done it carrying a bath chair. She should keep her mouth shut next time and let him trip. Just a small stumble, of course. She didn't want him dead.

They soon had Aunt Rose up on the headland and settled back into her chair. Both men had a sheen of sweat across their brows. Had there not been ladies present, she imagined Gareth might have stripped off his coat completely. But that would never do—not in front of Miss Tippet.

Lord Chiverton was nowhere to be seen. His explorations must have taken him too far down the sloping headland or off to the side where the oldest ruins were.

"Where has Lord Chiverton gone off to?" Miss Tippet asked as Uncle Charles settled the small knit blanket around his wife's legs. One of the many creations of Elaine's mother.

"Who knows," Gareth answered. "Could be anywhere. Down the other side to the iron gate, the well, the old ruins." He pointed to the rubble farther up the hill. "You see, Miss Tippet, where we are standing now was built by Richard, Earl of Cornwall, in the fourteenth century. Up beyond is the structure that would have been standing during Arthur's time. That is where he was born."

"Oh," breathed Miss Tippet, looking eagerly at Gareth. "I'd love to see it."

"And so you shall," Gareth said. He did not offer her his arm as he'd done crossing to the headland. He simply motioned for her to walk with him in the direction of the ancient ruins. Miss Tippet followed with one hand on her bonnet to keep it on in the growing wind. Already she'd had to close her parasol because of it.

Elaine stayed with Uncle Charles and Aunt Rose, helping to guide her aunt's chair in the opposite direction toward the more level ground. The wind blew in off the water, crashing onto the cliffs and rolling up and across the island top. There would be rain before the day was out.

These old stones and half-buried foundations revealed little of what life had been like here on this barren crop of land all those centuries ago. What stories they could tell. What secrets they could reveal. She let her fingers graze the lichen walls and skim atop the grass sprouting between the cracks, as if she could draw their secrets out of them.

Was King Arthur the chivalrous knight he was made out to be in Malory and Monmouth? As a child, she'd clung to the legends, sure that somewhere a place like Camelot still existed. Life had shown her differently.

It would be lovely, though, if it were true. A place of courtly valor and gallantry, where integrity and courage were prized above all. A shame no such place endured in today's world. Such fanciful ideals were merely the stuff of myths and legends. She was no longer a child.

"My dear," Aunt Rose said to her husband, pulling Elaine out of her reverie. "Perhaps you'd better find Lord Chiverton to be sure he hasn't gotten himself into any trouble. We haven't seen him for some time."

He situated the bath chair securely and stepped aside. "Will you be comfortable here with Elaine while I'm gone?"

"Yes, yes. I'm sure I'll be fine." Rose smiled up at him.

Uncle Charles bowed to his wife and then set off at a quick pace across the rocky terrain. Aunt Rose lifted her face to Elaine, and her smile faded to something she'd seen mothers give other mothers when their children are being silly. "I love that man more than words can say," her aunt whispered, "but sometimes a woman needs the company of another woman."

Elaine laughed. "Come. We don't need a man to enjoy these crumbling dwellings." Elaine leaned into the bath chair and pushed Aunt Rose up along the worn paths and onto a level piece of ground where the remaining walls formed a cross. The old chapel. Even though Arthur was a king among kings, he wasn't too proud to worship the Almighty. Another trait to admire in him.

"What do you think about the Arthurian legend?" Elaine asked her aunt.

Aunt Rose turned in her chair, looking back at Elaine. "What do you mean?"

Elaine shrugged. "Do you believe in King Arthur and his Camelot?"

Aunt Rose smiled. She gazed out across the lines of stones crisscrossing each other as they laid out the foundation of something that could have been wonderful or could have been nothing. Just another ruined castle in this country pock-marked with them.

"I do believe," her aunt finally answered. "But not in the way you're asking, I think."

"How so?"

"Was there an exact place on some map labeled Camelot? I do not know. Nor do I know if King Arthur united all the Britons and helped to find the Holy Grail. It all sounds a bit much."

"But?"

Aunt Rose laughed. "Yes. There is a but. I do believe in the idea of Camelot. I believe that we each must find our own Camelot. Somewhere in this world, there exists a place where we might find the idyllic life we seek. A place of joy and peace, love and respect, where we are whole."

Elaine paused in her pushing. *An idyllic life where we are whole.* Interesting words coming from her aunt, considering her life was anything but idyllic and whole. She would never walk again. Never bear children.

Elaine released the chair and walked around the front so she could see her aunt's face. The woman's soft smile convinced her that perhaps for some, such a place was not so far off. "And where is your Camelot, Aunt?"

"At the moment, I believe it is wandering the cliffs of this tiny peninsula looking for Lord Chiverton."

"Do you mean Uncle Charles?"

"Of course. Look at me." She motioned to her legs, useless and limp. To the chair she was dependent upon to go anywhere. To her frail frame, pale from whatever else the accident had done to her body. "Most men would have given up on me. Abandoned me. Left me home in my sickbed while they occupied themselves with loose flirtations or the races or the thrill of the foxhunt. I am loved far more than I deserve. With Charles, I have found my Camelot."

The bond she'd witnessed between Aunt Rose and Uncle Charles truly was something special. Nothing like her own parents' relationship. Nor any other she'd ever seen.

The great homes in London, with their balls and concerts and feasts, were grand places, but she'd rarely glimpsed any sort of ardent affection between husband and wife. Not that she thought them all unhappy. Indeed, many seemed pleased with the lives they'd created. But it had never been the union Aunt Rose had just described.

It seemed impossible to know if one had found their Camelot or not until it was too late. Would her mother have married her father knowing then what she knew now? Perhaps her mother had not had a choice.

More often than not, marriage was predicated on reasons other than love. Money. Alliance. Scheming parents. Havencross had been on the verge of becoming another set of ruins in this harsh country until her father had married her mother and her ten thousand pounds. She'd never asked why her mother had consented to the match—or if it had been thrust upon her.

But Lord Chiverton had not asked for money nor an alliance. His parents were already dead and beyond the ability to scheme. This proved the depth of his affection for her. He must be her Camelot.

Aunt Rose reached out and took her hand. "Remember, even the mighty King Arthur did not build his kingdom in a day. It takes time and work to create such a life."

Time. Of course. Once she was married to Lord Chiverton, they could begin building their own Camelot together. Marriage was the starting point, not the ending. The door she must enter first before finding her idyllic life beyond.

Lord Chiverton would take her away from Havencross. She could put Gareth and John and her father behind her and turn her attentions to her new husband and a new life beyond Cornwall. That would be her best chance at finding the life she wanted. The life Aunt Rose described.

Her aunt reached up and took Elaine's hand. "The one thing I have learned, dear niece, is that it is usually much closer than we think."

CHAPTER TWELVE

Gareth

GARETH LEANED AGAINST THE WALL of the ancient chapel, completely concealed by it as he listened to the conversation between Elaine and her aunt.

Such a romantic notion, this idea that Camelot was a state of mind. And utter nonsense. He'd already learned that life was simply one disappointment after another. Rejection. Death. And more death.

If Camelot was real, he'd not found it yet. He'd found the opposite. Elaine's prompt dismissal of his affection. The death of his closest friend. Then his father's murder. Hardly idyllic.

Miss Tippet appeared again beside him. She'd wandered in and out of the ruins with great stamina—much more than Gareth had expected from the woman recently complaining about the length of High Street.

"What do you think this room was? The nursery, perhaps? Or guest chambers? Maybe the kitchen." She glanced around, then added, "Where did they get the wood?"

An astute observation, considering the headland was barren of all but rocks and tussock grass waving in the breeze—a breeze that had already stiffened in the time they'd been there. "I don't know," he said. "Perhaps they had it brought in from the Forest of Halwill."

"Of course," Miss Tippet answered. "That makes sense. He was the king; he could have brought it from wherever he wanted." She moved right on to her next question. "Did he worship the Green Man? I've heard that people from the West Country worshiped the Green Man."

"Hello?" Elaine's head peeked around the corner through a gap in the wall.

Miss Tippet had given him away.

"Miss Cardinham," Gareth said. "Miss Tippet was just asking me about the Green Man." Gareth crossed into the remains of the chapel, where Elaine and her aunt had been talking. Miss Tippet followed close behind.

"I've heard that many people here in the West Country worshiped the Green Man. I was wondering if that was true," Miss Tippet clarified.

"Interesting question, Miss Tippet," he said. "Many of the churches in this area have carvings of the Green Man—a face of a bearded man surrounded by leaves and vines."

Miss Tippet was a curious creature. She had jumped from question to question faster than a rabbit zigzagging its way across an open field.

"I think there was some confusion in those days as to whom they should worship," he explained. "As the old ways died out, making way for Christianity, there was some overlap in what to believe."

"What does that mean?" Miss Tippet asked.

"It means that even though we are standing in what's left of a Christian chapel, they also believed in wizards and dragons and probably the Green Man."

"So they weren't Christians?"

"They were," he said. "Just confused."

"Oh, look!" Miss Tippet pointed out into the sea off the headland.

Gareth followed her white-gloved hand. Out on the water, a small skiff was rowing away around the edge of the cliffs and quickly moving out of sight.

"Who was that?" Elaine asked.

"Smugglers." Gareth had no doubt about it. There was a good chance they were the same ones who had killed his father. Blackguards. These vermin clung to their territory like ravens guarding their nests. Curse them all.

He turned and looked up the long path to the carriages in the distance. If he left now, he could make it to Camelford in less than an hour and rally some men to go after them. Old Jonesy over to Tremerton had a little dinghy he could borrow—if the ancient thing still floated. He could go to Mr. Tippet if that poor excuse for a Landguard could be moved to act. But by St. Just, he'd see those men hanged.

He felt a hand on his arm. Elaine's.

She shook her head. "You will never catch them. They will be long gone."

She was right, of course. He'd never find them. But it was the way her fingers wrapped around his arm that took his mind off the smugglers. So at odds with her civil and distant demeanor toward him of late. She'd read his mind precisely, without a single word. Perhaps he needed lessons from her.

"Catch who?" Miss Tippet asked. "The smugglers? My father says it is a wasted effort. By the time one smuggler is caught, five more step up to take his place."

Elaine's hand tightened on his arm, restraining him. "Like the Hydra," she said. "An apt description, Miss Tippet."

Miss Tippet had just confirmed what he'd feared all along; he would be getting no help from the Landguard to bring his father's killers to justice. Tippet had probably already been bought by them, cheerfully volunteering as one of the new five.

"Look what I found," Beaford called as he came striding across the grass, the great and honorable Lord Chiverton at his side.

Elaine jumped. She took a few steps back from Gareth, folding her arms across her front, then letting them fall to her sides.

"What?" Miss Tippet asked, striding forward to see whatever it was she thought Beaford might have found.

Beaford stared at her for a moment, then looked pointedly at Chiverton.

Miss Tippet kept her eyes on Beaford. "What did you find?"

"Lord Chiverton," Beaford said.

Miss Tippet seemed rather disappointed, despite the fact that Chiverton was considered the handsomest man to grace Camelford in the last decade. What more could she have been hoping for?

The man cut a fine figure as he crossed the green, going immediately to Elaine's side. She seemed eager to please him, though Gareth found little to recommend other than looks and land. Perhaps that was enough for her.

As to fortune, there was no guarantee he wasn't in need of funds to keep his estate intact. But if that were the case, Gareth doubted he'd be interested in Elaine. She had a small dowry but not enough to attract the really desperate men.

He should ask around and see what he could dig up about Chiverton. After her father's humiliation at being driven from London by an irate general, it was more than a little bewildering that such a man would still associate with a woman whose family had been scandalized in such an indelicate way.

Or perhaps Gareth was letting his cynicism rule the day. He could not fault a man for wanting to be with Elaine. He'd tried himself to gain her hand—and he'd been promptly and firmly put in his place.

Chiverton was the kind of man she had set her sights on from the very beginning. He also hoped the man would fall off the cliffs onto some very jagged rocks below. Far below.

Chiverton took Elaine by the hand. "Forgive me. Charles here has reminded me that I've been gone far too long. I'm afraid the allurement of this place took hold of me." He glanced around the group, his eyes landing on Miss Tippet. "Do you not agree with me, Miss Tippet? There is a kind of magic here that draws one in and doesn't seem to let go?"

"Yes. Oh, yes. I've never seen anything like it."

Chiverton turned to Elaine. "And what about you, my dear?

She cast Gareth a somber glance, one he did not think he was meant to see.

After his unwanted proposal, Gareth highly doubted she would use the word *magic* to describe Tintagel. He had inadvertently but most effectively ruined it for her.

She gave Chiverton a smile. "Yes, it's very enchanting." Her time in London had honed her skills at evading.

Chiverton took her hand in a gallant gesture. "The ruins of Tintagel are not the only thing that is enchanting."

Gareth nearly choked. *Smooth-tongued as a snake, Chiverton.* If he'd paid any attention to her at all, he should know by now that she disliked such attention in front of a crowd, even if that crowd consisted of friends and family.

Elaine tugged her hand away, her face now redder than a ripe tomato. But she did seem pleased by his compliment. Too pleased. He hoped again that Chiverton would take another walk along the clifftops. Then with any luck, a strong wind would come up, and whoosh. Problem solved.

Not that Chiverton was his problem. He was Elaine's husband-to-be. And Gareth had washed his hands of her. He'd promised himself not to think on her anymore. Unfortunately, the more he was around her, the more difficult his task.

"Now," Chiverton said. "Who wants to go down to the cave?"

Beaford glanced down, grim-faced, at the steep slope leading to the beach and cave below.

"I'm afraid I've got my heart set on seeing the well and the northern ruins. You'll have to count me out," Mrs. Beaford said.

She fooled no one, except perhaps Miss Tippet. She meant to keep her loyal husband from having to carry her all the way down—then all the way back up—the winding, uneven, and rather treacherous slope.

"That's my cue," Beaford said, leaning into his wife's chair and pushing her off. "See you after," he called over his shoulder.

Chiverton started back toward the narrow bridge of land with Elaine's hand tucked neatly into his perfect arm. It was from here the trail wound down to the beach and Merlin's Cave.

Gareth escorted Miss Tippet down the steep slope to the beach. She clung to him, taking care with each step until Gareth thought it would be nightfall before they reached the bottom. The tide was well on its way in. Hopefully Miss Tippet didn't mind getting her boots wet.

He guided her across the sand, catching up with Chiverton and Elaine at the cavern's entrance. From the piece of conversation he overheard as they approached, Elaine was trying to get Chiverton to go in without her.

CHAPTER THIRTEEN

Elaine

Now Gareth was upon them. Why couldn't they have gone to St. Ives? Even Port Isaac would have been better. Every place on this forgotten island only brought to light the parts of her past she wanted kept in the dark.

Being here with this group, walking the grounds, listening to Gareth explain to Miss Tippet the same things he and John had explained to her—it pressed upon her. The memories hurt like someone had opened her heart and proceeded to pull and tear on every regret she'd buried there. John. Gareth. So many mistakes.

She wasn't ready to enter Merlin's Cave with Lord Chiverton. He was her hope for the future, and the cave was part of her past—the past she meant to leave.

A flash of dark green cloth caught her eye. It came not from within the cavern but from off to the north, along the coast of the mainland. A dress just like the one Gwenevere had worn.

"You go in," she told Lord Chiverton. "I'll wait here."

"Nonsense. I couldn't possibly."

"You are very considerate," Elaine said, but just now was not the time for the chivalry she'd been pining for. "You forget, I grew up here. I've seen the cave many a time, and I'm perfectly fine on my own." As she'd already proven since he'd been doing his own wanderings for a great portion of the outing.

He gave her a sheepish smile. "I do hope you'll forgive me. It was not my intent to be so long absent. In my efforts to discover the wonders of this place, I lost myself." He took a step closer. "I fear I am remiss. You are far more splendid than this site, no matter its wonders."

Gareth coughed loudly from behind her. "Excuse me." He pounded a fist on his chest. "I got a taste of something unsavory."

His quip did not escape Elaine. Insufferable man.

"Are you well?" Miss Tippet asked with a little pucker to her brow.

"I am now. Thank you." He started across the sand. "Come now, Miss Tippet. We must get in and out before the tide comes in." He did not wait for her as he stomped across the beach.

Miss Tippet lifted her skirts and tiptoed after him.

Elaine took a few steps toward the cliffs to the north. Why wouldn't he just go in without her? Gwen was getting away. "Go on." She motioned for Lord Chiverton to follow. "The cave is not to be missed, and I'll be fine out here."

Lord Chiverton winked at her, then turned. In a few strides, he reached Miss Tippet, who was having somewhat of a difficult time navigating the terrain. He offered her an arm, and she took it, shifting her skirt to one hand.

Elaine didn't wait to see if Miss Tippet survived the crossing. The moment their backs were turned, she set off to follow the green gown.

There it was again. A flash of green disappearing behind a bend in the cliffside wall. Elaine leaned with one hand on the rock face while she held up her skirts with the other, picking her way one stone at a time along the steep water's edge.

She used to scale these treacherous shores with barely a care for the salty spray upon her face or the water lapping at her boots. The wind blew harder now, whipping her dress around her ankles and into the cliff.

She rounded the corner in time to see a figure with long, dark hair and a circlet of gold on her brow. Her gown of holly green hung long and fitted to well below her waist, and a thin girdle of gold rested low on her hips with one long strand down the front. Rather ostentatious for a woman who seemed to be living in the rocks.

Gareth had been teasing Elaine when he'd called the woman Gwenevere, but this thought settled deeper and deeper into Elaine's mind. If she painted a picture of what Arthur's Gwenevere looked like to her, it would be this woman's exact likeness. She had appeared out of nowhere in Merlin's Cave, then vanished in the same place. Elaine did not believe in ghosts, but there was something about this Gwen that had Elaine questioning.

The woman looked directly at her before disappearing into a cave. It was most certainly the same woman she'd found wounded the other day.

"Gwen?" she called, but the woman did not reappear.

Elaine struggled for footing as she clambered along the rocks after her. The wind tugged her bonnet loose, and she had no free hand to catch it before it sailed away onto the waves. She'd never gone this far before, and solid footholds were quickly becoming harder and harder to find.

She reached the opening of one of the many small caverns that perforated the coast. She climbed up on her knees, ruining her blue-trimmed muslin with mud stains that would never come out. She struggled to her feet and peered into the darkness. A short distance ahead, the narrow tunnel curved out of sight.

Gwen had gone on around the bend—or disappeared again. This woman couldn't possibly be living in such a place, yet this was the second time she'd seen her near the Tintagel ruins.

She could be a vagrant. Or a smuggler—as Gareth would undoubtedly assume. She looked like neither. Her clothing reminded Elaine more of the dresses in the stained glass of Saint Piran's chapel. Her circlet of gold gave the impression of wealth and standing.

Perhaps Gareth was right and the woman was a figment of Elaine's imagination. An invention born of her fascination with Gwenevere and Arthur.

Elaine inched her way forward. All she wanted was a peek around the corner just to see what lay beyond in the recesses of the narrow walls. Every step deeper into the cliffside blurred the light coming in through the mouth of the cave. Visions of smugglers lying in wait just around the bend grew more vivid in her mind.

Why had she followed Gwen here? What was it about this mysterious woman that prompted her to scale the watery cliffs? It was a fool's errand, and she was done.

Elaine hurried back to the entrance. She stood on the lip of the cave, staring down into the rising tide pounding into the rocky walls. Without question, this was a fool's errand. If she didn't leave now, she'd be trapped by the water. Or she'd have to take a swim. To top it all off, the wind had brought rain, and dark splashes of water dotted her dress.

But what if Gwenevere was there, waiting just around the bend? This might be Elaine's last chance to see her again face-to-face. To ask her once and for all who she was and why she'd been lying injured—near death—one moment and then gone the next.

She'd come this far, not to mention a perfectly good frock gone to waste. And if she did not go around that bend and at least see, she would always wonder.

She stepped carefully along the rocky floor of the tunnel, retracing her steps. She brushed off her muddy dress and smoothed her windblown hair.

If Gwenevere was waiting for her, she would meet her with as much dignity as she could muster.

She peered around the bend. It took her eyes a few moments to adjust to the dark, but the moment they did, she let out a scream.

On the ground not two steps away lay the crumpled remains of a corpse.

Elaine slapped both hands over her mouth, but it did little to keep another cry from escaping. She backed up until she was pressed against the cold dampness of the cavern wall.

She could make out a rotted pair of tall boots on the corpse's feet. In that first moment, she'd thought it was Gwenevere, but this was a man's body. Though the term *body* could hardly apply. All bones and rotted clothes, it was.

She'd seen enough. Elaine turned back toward the mouth of the cave, putting the awful thing behind her and out of sight.

Who could it be? Who could have died here and not a single soul had cared enough to give him a proper place of rest? A smuggler, perhaps. No honor among thieves, as the saying went. A pirate, maybe. A victim of a shipwreck. It was no secret that if the sea didn't take them, the wreckers would. The law stated that if a crewmember was found alive, the cargo belonged to him. The wreckers who came plundering made sure none were found alive.

From what she'd made out of the clothing and boots, it was not a fisherman nor a sailor but a man of some means. Despite her need a moment ago to stay as far from the bones as possible, she suddenly found she wanted another look. It was hideous but also intriguing. A puzzle that needed solving. Like a story that, despite its disturbing events, had to be finished—to see how it ended.

She took three great breaths, then, lifting ever so slightly the hem of her gown, tiptoed back into the depths of the cave, quietly so as not to disturb the soul of the dead.

She crouched over it. The boots were tall and somewhat fine. The coat, once brown, was now mostly shreds of moss and lichen. And around his neck draped a gold chain. A locket or something hung on the end, but it had sunk into the ribs and under what was left of the lapel.

With one eye closed against the disgustingness of it, she gave the chain a little tug. Out came a tarnished quizzing glass. A good-sized one with a letter carved into the hilt.

C.

For Cardinham.

This could not be.

She recognized that quizzing glass. Her father had given it to her brother shortly before he had disappeared. He had loved that thing and never took it off. And the coat and boots. She saw them clearly now.

Elaine tried to scream again. She opened her mouth, but now it would not come. She staggered her way toward the cave entrance. She had to get away. The uneven ground tripped her, but she did not fall. Someone caught her.

"Elaine."

She recognized Gareth's voice, though she could not see clearly.

"We've been looking all over for you. I was afraid you'd fallen into the waves." He looked down at her. "*Re Just*. What has happened?"

"John," was all she could say. "It's John."

CHAPTER FOURTEEN

Gareth

ELAINE LOOKED LIKE SHE'D SEEN the devil himself. Not to mention the state of her gown, torn and filthy. Her boots soaking wet. Her hair windblown and tangled.

"John," she whispered repeatedly, wildly. Then her strength seemed to give out, and her knees buckled.

Gareth held her up. She clung to him so tightly he could feel her heart hammering against his chest.

"Come now. What has got you so upset? Are you hurt?" He'd heard her cry from outside the cave.

She shook her head. "Gareth," she whispered. "I found John."

She had lost her senses. "John is gone. You know this."

"No, no, no. I found his body." She pointed into the depths of the cave where the tunnel bent out of sight. "Not his body. His bones."

"What?" He peered into the darkness, seeing nothing but rock.

She nodded as if unwilling to repeat her words.

"Are you sure?"

"Yes." She waved her hand down the tunnel. "Go and see for yourself."

He left her there with her arms wrapped around herself and shivering in the cold. Around the turning, he found the remains. One could hardly miss them as they lay half slumped against the wall. Garish white bones covered with all damp growing things. A few slick strands of hair clinging to the skull.

He bent for a closer look and felt a hand on his back. It was Elaine leaning over his crouched form, her palm resting on his back as she peered over his shoulder.

"See there." She pointed. "The quizzing glass. Remember how he used it to examine every rock and insect until we were sick and tired of waiting for him?"

Gareth lifted it from the corpse and turned it in his hands. "Yes. I believe you're right." He carefully lifted the chain over the skeletal head and stood.

"The moment I saw that, I knew." She looked up at him the way she used to, before she'd left for London. "I know it is him, Gareth. It *is* John."

"Elowen." He put a hand on her shoulder, and she leaned into it. "What a fright you have had. What a horror. And then to discover it is your own brother."

Most women would be in hysterics by now, trapped in a cave by a rising tide with the body of a dead man. And not just any man but the bones of her brother. He drew her close again. She did not protest, so perhaps she was more hysterical than he'd supposed.

This coast was riddled with caves. Hundreds of them exactly like this. Many of them much easier to get to. "How on earth did you find him here? What possessed you to climb the cliffs to this exact spot?"

"You won't believe me if I tell you."

"What?"

She stepped away. "It was the woman I met before. Gwen. Remember? She led me here."

"Gwenevere." He remembered well that day a few weeks ago when she'd come banging on his door for help. He'd doubted the soundness of her mental capacities, but today had changed his mind.

Elaine shrugged. "I don't know who she is. But she knew John was here and led me to him."

Gareth slipped the quizzing glass into his waistcoat pocket. "We will take this to your father. And notify the magistrate, Squire Stroud. But first we must get you out of here before we are trapped for the next twelve hours waiting for the tide to go out. Lord Chiverton is looking for you."

Elaine took one giant step away, bumping her head on a low part of the cave. With that one mention of Chiverton, she transformed into a different person. Back into the new Elaine who lived in London and was engaged to marry one of the finest bachelors in the country. Elowen to Miss Cardinham in the blink of an eye.

"How is your head?" he asked as she rubbed it.

"It's fine." Her hand came down. "We must hurry." She turned and led the way back to the entrance of the cavern.

Rain poured down. Hopefully Beaford had made it back to the carriage with his wife by now. Mrs. Beaford was all too frail to be out in weather like this.

The sea lapped at the rocks below. If Elaine's attire hadn't already been ruined, it would be now. And Gareth's boots. Again. Perhaps he'd send a bill to her father, for this was the second pair he'd waded through saltwater in for Elaine's sake.

"I'll go down first, then you climb down to me. Can you do that?"

She nodded, pulling her hair out of her face as the wind flurried it about.

Gareth maneuvered his way down the rocky cliff face. When he secured his footing, he called to her.

She made her way slowly. As soon as he could reach her, he put a hand around her waist, easing her onto the small landing where he stood.

"Well done. You always were the best climber."

She smiled at him. "And you were always the worst. Too impatient to be cautious."

Her words were too true. He wholeheartedly believed his impatience had been his downfall when it had come to Elaine Cardinham. He'd jumped the fence far too early, she'd rejected him, and he'd come down hard on the wooden spikes.

Gareth took her hand, steadying her as they teetered from rock to rock, making their way toward the small beach underneath the castle. They were almost knee-deep in water by the time they rounded the cliff edge.

"Ho, there!" Chiverton waved at her. "We found her," he shouted over his shoulder to Beaford, who was searching along the old dock carved out of the rock centuries ago.

Chiverton waited on the edge of the lapping water, keeping his Hessians out of the sea.

When Elaine was close enough, Chiverton reached out to her. She immediately let go of Gareth's hand, and he released her. Handing her over to a man not willing to dampen his boots for his betrothed.

Elaine was safely returned, and that was that.

He tried not to see the way she leaned into him for comfort. He certainly looked away when Chiverton's hand slid around her waist. And he definitely did not see when Chiverton placed a gentle kiss on her wet and worried forehead.

Gareth hurried ahead of the love-struck couple to meet up with Beaford. "Where is Miss Tippet?" Gareth asked when he caught up.

"They are waiting in the coach." Beaford indicated up the hill near the town of Trevanna. "How is she?"

For a moment, he thought Beaford meant Miss Tippet, but no. His inquiry was for Elaine. "Cold. She had quite a fright." Gareth started up the lane toward the carriages, and Beaford fell in step beside him. "She somehow found her way to a cave in the cliffside."

Beaford glanced over at Gareth.

"Inside the cave, she came across human remains. Bones and rotted clothing. And this." He took the quizzing glass from his pocket and held it out to Beaford.

The man took it from Gareth's hand, turning it this way and that.

How well-acquainted Beaford was with John, Gareth could not say. As Mrs. Cardinham's brother-in-law, he must know most, if not all, the details of John's disappearance, though he seemed uncertain about the origins of the glass.

"That there is John's quizzer," Gareth said.

Beaford's eyebrows shot up. "John Cardinham? My nephew?"

"Aye. Miss Cardinham found it on the skeleton."

Beaford came to a stop. He gazed at the glass, then up at Gareth. "Are you telling me Elaine discovered the corpse of her brother?"

"Yes."

"But . . . anyone could have taken this. Stolen it or . . . The body could be anyone."

Gareth set off walking again. "It could be, but I believe it to be John. The clothes—what was left of them. The situation that led to his discovery. All of it inclines me to believe it is John."

They climbed higher up the steep hill that led away from the castle ruins. "What do you mean, 'the situation'?"

Gareth wasn't sure what held him back, but he hesitated to mention the mysterious woman. He skirted the details while still giving way to the essence of the matter. "Think about it. Look around you. Elaine could have gone anywhere, but something drew her to that particular cave. She was very close to her brother, as you know."

Beaford nodded. "Yes, she was. As I recall, John wasn't the only boy she was close to." Beaford's gaze turned away, up the dirt lane to the village and its ancient houses. But Gareth didn't need to see his face to catch his meaning. He had no idea what Elaine may or may not have shared with the rest of her family.

If she'd confided anything to Mrs. Beaford, her husband undoubtedly knew of it. But if Beaford was merely fishing, Gareth would not so easily supply.

Gareth nodded. "Yes, I believe you're right. There was a dog, I think. A hound she was quite attached to."

Beaford snorted. He handed the quizzer back. "Here. You should be the one to take this to Francis. He respects you, I think. For whatever reason, I can't understand. Good thing he doesn't know about the hound."

Beaford was too close to the truth for comfort, though Gareth still got the impression the man was only feeling the waters. It was all five years in the past, and he'd not open that door again, not with Elaine's uncle.

Gareth tucked the quizzing glass back into his pocket. "I'll come directly. After I take a moment to make myself presentable."

By the time they reached the waiting carriages, the rain had slowed. Beaford opened the door to the coach his wife and Miss Tippet were waiting in and peered inside. He exchanged some words with his wife but Gareth could not hear them in the wind.

Down the lane, Elaine and Chiverton followed, leaning close. Chiverton had draped his coat around her shoulders. Gareth wanted to spit into the gorse bush. She had no business connecting herself to a man like that. A London man. He didn't blame her for wanting more than he had to offer; he was, after all, a lowly foreman's son—or he had been back then. But he couldn't help this nagging feeling that she deserved better than the Earl of Chiverton.

For all her protestations about the West Country's disadvantages compared to the glories and wonders of London, she was not a city girl. She was a girl of the heath and hedgerows. That she'd lasted five years utterly amazed him. Perhaps she really did love that peacock of a man, even if he was a few knots off from center.

Chiverton must have made some sort of joke, for she turned her face up toward him and smiled, the curve of her mouth tipping up the corners of her eyes just enough to produce a few lines of laughter across the bridge of her nose. Not that Gareth could see these details from his position; he simply knew them by heart.

He turned and spat into the gorse for real this time, aiming carefully at the yellow flowers wedged in among the needle-sharp spines. A ridiculous shrub good for nothing but inflicting pain.

"Everything all right, Kemp?" Beaford asked, his eyes darting to the forms of Elaine and Lord Chiverton.

"Yes, sir." He wiped his mouth with a handkerchief. "Just a bit of saltwater still caught in my throat."

"Perhaps you should come home with us to Havencross. Even in your current state." Beaford nodded toward Elaine.

She turned her head, and the distress on her face became clear. Though she'd been grinning only moments ago, the shadow of her discovery lingered behind her eyes. It would be better to deal with the incident sooner rather than later.

Beaford leaned close and whispered, "I assume you are aware of the circumstance which took them from London?"

"I am."

"Good. I don't believe she has spoken to her father since her arrival at Havencross."

That was hard to imagine.

"For what it's worth," Beaford whispered even more softly, "I don't believe the accusations are entirely true."

Gareth looked up sharply. "How do you mean?"

But by this time, Elaine and Chiverton had joined them, and Beaford said no more.

"Elaine." Beaford stepped forward and reached for his niece's hand. "Why don't you ride home in my carriage with Rose? It's warmer and out of the rain. Mr. Kemp can take the phaeton with Lord Chiverton." He gave Gareth a devious grin as he loaded Elaine into his coach.

That man saw far too much. Or maybe it was his wife who did the seeing and passed it all on to him. Mrs. Beaford, with her kind and trusting face, seemed to prompt people to talk. Add to that her confinement to the chair and she came across as the gentlest creature on earth. Who wouldn't confide? Yet keen intelligence lurked beneath her delicate facade.

"Where is the footman?" Beaford asked.

"He went up to the village," the coachman said.

Gareth peered up the steep lane. The man was not in sight. Mr. Cardinham should have him fired for this.

"We cannot wait," Beaford said.

The coachman nodded.

When the coach door closed on the Beaford carriage, Gareth climbed onto the high seat beside Chiverton.

"Ever been in a high flyer before?" Chiverton asked.

Gareth shook his head. Of course he hadn't. The only folk in these parts who rode in them were those who valued their lives at naught. The seat box was perched well above the carriage wheels, making the center of balance too high. Chiverton had the folding top pulled closed to keep out some of the rain, but this was really a fair-weather carriage.

"Wait till you see the beauty of these steppers. No two horses pull faster or more smoothly."

"I'm sure it will be the high point of my year."

Chiverton gave him an exhilarated grin. "Hold tight, old man."

He cracked the whip, and the horses lunged forward, bravely taking on the hill out of Trevanna village. Beaford's carriage dissolved out of sight. At this rate, he'd be to Havencross in only moments. Or tossed over the hedge into the newly sown fields.

Chiverton's horses were top-notch, but his driving left much to be desired. He took every bend and bump in the road at top speed. Tossed over the hedge was becoming more and more the probable outcome. Gareth leaned and rolled, sometimes coming to his feet to counterbalance the rig as they careened around the corners.

Chiverton's warning to hold tight was superfluous as blisters formed on Gareth's hands from clinging to the side rail. If this was how Chiverton always drove, it was a miracle he was still alive. Gareth would not have wasted all that time wishing ill upon him from the cliff's edge had he known Chiverton's driving was already suicidal.

The horses barely slowed as they approached the final bend leading up to the Havencross lane. Chiverton clucked them on, barreling into the turn.

Fool and double fool. Only a blockhead would drive like this on unfamiliar roads. On the other side of the turn, hidden by the hedge, a puddle always formed when it rained, leaving a large hole in the ground. Every driver west of the Tamar knew better than to round a blind corner at breakneck speed. There was a reason it was called *breakneck* speed.

Gareth readied to make a dive for it. Whatever happened to Chiverton's phaeton was not going to happen with him inside it.

As Chiverton leaned into the bend, Gareth leapt from the seat, taking advantage of the low-hanging branch of a stunted oak tree. The rig whizzed past under his dangling feet and rounded the bend.

He heard Chiverton let out a curse just before steel ground on rock with a splintering crash. The horses whinnied, and a large phaeton wheel careened into sight, smashing into the hedge. A handful of crows squawked and fluttered into the sky. Then all was quiet.

Gareth dropped to the ground, his hands bleeding from the rough tree branch.

He ran around the bend to find Chiverton sitting in a puddle of mud beside the pieces of his high flyer. The surprise on his face was worthy of a kingdom. Sadly, however, he seemed unhurt.

"Tough luck, old man," Gareth said, striding over to calm the horses. Chiverton had never looked better. Gareth spoke to the animals, rubbing their necks until they stopped pawing at the earth.

Chiverton stood, trying to brush the mud from his buckskin breeches but mostly just smearing it. "There go my new boots."

Yes. Too bad he'd wasted his opportunity to ruin them by helping his future wife instead. Now he'd just ruined them in an act of lunacy.

Gareth swatted some twigs off Chiverton's back. "I should have warned you about the roads here in Cornwall."

Chiverton shook his head. "It wouldn't have helped."

At least the man was honest. "You all right?"

"Nothing injured but my pride, as they say." Chiverton surveyed the ruins strewn across the rocky ground. "And my high flyer." He picked up a wheel, with its red spokes, then he tossed it aside and picked up the padded driver's bench. It was as if he didn't know which piece to mourn most.

"We've got a man over in Camelford who's a wizard with carriages. I'm sure he can fix it in no time." Gareth bent over and unhitched the horses from the rig. "Havencross is only a quarter mile on. Best get these boys safely stabled."

Chiverton took the lead of one of the animals and set off, walking with a noticeable limp in his left leg. It seemed there was a just God after all.

CHAPTER FIFTEEN

Elaine

ELAINE AND THE BEAFORDS HAD taken the longer way home, where the roads were better, so she'd not seen anything of the wreck Gareth was describing.

"You're limping. Are you hurt?" Elaine asked Lord Chiverton.

"Perfectly fine; just landed a bit off. Nothing to worry about."

She wasn't, not really. Thoughts of confronting her father to tell him about the body of her brother left very little room in her mind for Lord Chiverton's overturned phaeton.

She took off her filthy pelisse and handed it to Betsy. Her hem was in shreds and her bonnet drifting out into the Atlantic, but that hardly mattered.

Aunt Rose appeared, Uncle Charles pushing her through the front door into the entry where they all stood divesting themselves of the worst of it. Uncle Charles's carriage had ridden off to take Miss Tippet back to her home.

Lord Chiverton yanked off his soiled coat. "Blasted thing cost me a king's ransom."

"I'm sorry about your phaeton." Elaine assumed he was talking about his carriage, but perhaps she was mistaken. "And I'm sorry about your coat."

Mr. Winkleigh and Gareth stood at the foot of the steps, speaking in hushed tones. Gareth would be asking the whereabouts of her father, explaining that there was news that could not wait.

"I don't have time for this," Lord Chiverton said, pacing furiously across the entryway floor. "I don't have time to go to Camelford and back. I've got other business this evening."

It was unclear to whom Lord Chiverton was speaking. Uncle Charles was busy lifting his wife out of her chair, proclaiming again how she'd overdone herself today. Gareth was following Mr. Winkleigh down the hall toward her father's library. Elaine supposed he must be talking to her, though she knew nothing about Camelford's carriage maker nor the piecing together of high flyers.

"You can take our coach if you need transportation," she said. "Or a horse, as the rain has let up and it is the fastest way into Camelford. You can ford the River Camel up north and save yourself the trip down to the bridge. I'm sure the coach maker will do all he can to have your carriage up and working as soon as possible."

Lord Chiverton ran over to her and kissed her hand. "Brilliant idea! Thank you, my love." Then he darted out the front door.

Gareth must have taken it upon himself to inform her father. That was brave of him. Just before the library, he paused, catching her eye, his eyebrows raised, asking if she wanted to join him.

She could let him deal with her father all on his own. He would do it well. Her father had always gotten on with the elder Mr. Kemp, and Gareth too, when he'd come to run with John. After the long silence between her and her father, perhaps now was not the best time to attempt conciliation. But if she waited for the best time, she might be waiting forever.

Those first few days, she'd hated her father for ruining her chances with Lord Chiverton. But Lord Chiverton was here and their marriage quickly approaching. If Lord Chiverton had been willing to reach out to her even after her family had been disgraced, should she not also be willing to at least face her father with the matter of his own son's death? After all, it was her fault he'd died in the first place.

She gave Gareth a quick nod and hurried down the hall to where he waited for her.

Mr. Winkleigh opened the door to the library and announced them as if her father might not remember her. Perhaps he didn't, so long he'd kept away. Though the finger could easily point in the other direction.

Her father rose when they entered, his shock as plain as plain across his face. "Elaine?"

He'd been seated in a tall-backed chair upholstered with dark, oiled leather and woven tapestry. It was his favorite seat, there by the fire. Elaine used to crawl onto his lap, and he would read to her the stories of King Arthur and his knights. Of chivalry and honor. Battles with men and monsters.

All that had been before John had died. Since that time, her father had withdrawn more and more, removing himself from his family life by bits and pieces until London happened.

"Sit down, please, sir," Gareth said.

Her father scowled at Gareth's order, but Elaine had to agree. He should be sitting for the news they brought from Tintagel.

"I want to tell you something, Father," she said.

He sat.

He'd taken John's loss so hard. This news might push him farther away. Or to have it all settled might bring him back. She had no way of knowing how he might take it—nor the best way to deliver it.

Her father had always been a practical man. She went straight for the truth. "I found John."

Her father leapt up. "He's alive?"

The burst of light in his eyes was too much. In the momentary flash of hope, Elaine couldn't bear her part in the loss of John that night.

Gareth quickly came forward, holding out the quizzing glass in the palm of his hand. "I'm terribly sorry, sir."

Her father took it, rubbing his finger across the engraved *C*. He sank back into his chair. "Where did you find this?"

Elaine opened her mouth to speak but found she did not have the words. Each mention of her brother brought back the horrible vision of his desiccated body crumbling in the damp and forgotten cave.

Again Gareth spoke for her, doing a much better job than she could have.

"At the coast, near the old castle, Miss Cardinham discovered a hidden cave," he explained. "Inside it was the body of a young man long dead. His clothes were those of John, and we found this around his neck."

Her father took a long, slow blink. Perhaps he had been hopeful all these years that his son would come home. She had known better. John would never disappear without a word to her or Gareth. And he wouldn't have left his errand unfinished. Her father looked up at her. "This is what it takes for you to finally come talk to me?"

Elaine glanced over at Gareth. His eyes were fixed on his boots, all stained and warped from their foray into the sea.

She did not answer her father. They lived in this house together; he could have come and spoken to her at any time.

Her father lowered his head. "Perhaps if I had not lost my son, things in London would have been different."

Elaine found no correlation between John's death and her father's blunder in London. How dare he try to pin his own mistakes on the loss of his son.

"How can you say so? The loss of John was devastating to all of us, but Mother and I did not turn our backs on our family. You cannot pile up wrongs and blame them on a single misfortune that occurred years ago. Each choice we make is its own. Many men have had greater losses than yours and not brought their family to ruin."

Her father sank deeper into his chair, drawing his shawl around him, barricading himself from her words.

She should feel pity for the man, but she did not. Look at her Aunt Rose. She could not have children. She could not walk. Elaine didn't even want to think of all the other things she could not do. Things Uncle Charles or the nurse must do for her. Yet she did not wallow in her hardships nor did she throw her husband to the wolves.

Her father mumbled something.

"What?" If he had the nerve to defend himself, he should speak up.

"I didn't ruin anyone," he said.

"Just because Lord Chiverton has it in the goodness of his heart not to care about the downfall you brought upon us, it is not justification for you to say we are not ruined. You cannot hide in your library forever, Father."

"I'm not hiding." He spoke louder, as if adding volume could give strength to his lie. For it was clear to everyone in the house he was doing exactly that.

"I will not speak with you if you are untruthful." They had strayed far from John's bones now. Elaine considered turning on her heels and marching out the door. "Perhaps it is John's fault you will not come out of this room."

That struck the wind from his sails. His shawl settled back into place, and he took a moment to adjust the fire screen. "You are wise for your years, Elaine. Perhaps too wise. What I meant was that in London, I did not do that of which I am accused."

She could not speak of such details with her father. It was untoward. Gareth should be the one to press him. She nodded at him, tipping her head in her father's direction. Gareth did not take her meaning. He shrugged apologetically.

Ask him, she mouthed while her father stared into the fireplace.

Gareth looked appalled. He shook his head.

Elaine prompted him again, gesturing frantically and pointing at her father.

Gareth waved a hand for her to stop. "Fine," he whispered. "Sir," Gareth began. "Elaine does not understand your meaning. Could you be more clear? For her sake."

He was supposed to leave her out of it. This didn't help at all, yet Gareth looked triumphant.

"I don't know where the rumor began," her father said without taking his eyes off the fire, "but it exploded like gunpowder. By the time it reached the gossip chains, nothing more could be done. Everyone knows such news cannot be countered, whether it be truth or not."

If this was true, he should have said so long before now. He could have defended himself if he was innocent instead of letting his reputation go to ruin. At least for her mother's sake, he should have spoken up.

"How can I believe you?" she asked.

"Perhaps you can't," he said. "But that is neither here nor there. Perhaps your mind is set and I cannot convince you, just as any attempts to change the minds of all of London would have been futile. So I let it lie. Why fan the flame when 'tis better to let it burn out."

Almost the same thing her mother had said. *The pot will cool down soon enough.* Perhaps he had tried to talk to her mother and she'd turned him away with the same response. That was not how Elaine wanted her marriage to be. She wanted a union with no secrets. No lies. Able to talk with each other about even the most difficult subjects.

Even Gareth looked skeptical. "They said you were at her house."

"And so I was. In the drawing room. Talking."

"Who else attended?" At last, Gareth was asking the right questions.

Her father sighed. "No one. We were alone."

"What were you talking about?" Elaine asked.

Gareth seemed surprised by that question. "Why does that matter?"

"It matters," she said.

"Nothing of importance." Her father rose to his feet. "And that's the last I'll say about it. Now, we've gone far off the topic you came in here for. One that I'm greatly concerned about." He suddenly sounded like her father again, calling down his authority as head of the household instead of shrinking from it.

"Sir," Gareth said, his voice clearing the room of the unease that had settled in. "We should retrieve John's remains as soon as possible. With the tide in, it will be easier to reach the location with a boat. If you'll leave it to me, I'll arrange for a skiff and have the body brought here."

"That is fine. Thank you, Mr. Kemp."

Gareth bowed to her father, then retreated quickly out of the room, avoiding being dragged back into another conversation about her family's troubles.

The door closed behind Gareth. Her father looked older, tired. Worn out. Or perhaps worn down. If he had been wrongly accused for whatever malicious reasons, he must be suffering greatly. Either way, his regret seemed real.

"I'm sorry about John," she said. It was the best she could offer.

"Yes." Her father settled back into his chair. "But are you sure it's him?"

The quizzing glass was still clutched in his hand. He studied it again. "Someone could have stolen it from him and then died later."

"It is him, Father. I know it. I feel it as sure as I feel the rain on my face or the warmth of the sun." Gwenevere would not have led her to any body—only to the body of her brother. Of that Elaine was also sure. The way she'd lured her along the cliff face and how she'd looked at Elaine before entering the cave—it was all very deliberate.

"Does your mother know?"

Elaine shook her head. "Not unless Uncle Charles or Aunt Rose said something." Aunt Rose had seemed especially tired by the time they'd gotten home. Uncle Charles had mentioned several times on the way back from Tintagel that she was going directly to her bed. Lord Chiverton's mind had been consumed by the wreck of his carriage and sudden lack of transport. He must be long gone by now to try to put the thing back together again.

"I should be the one to tell her," he said. "Will you have her sent in?"

Elaine did not expect this. She wasn't sure her mother would even want him to be the one to tell her. The news of John would fall hard on her, and she'd find little consolation from the man she couldn't bear the sight of.

"If you wish." She'd not step one foot between her mother and father where his indiscretion was concerned. She hurried out, closing the library door behind her.

Gareth stood in the hallway, waiting.

"I thought you went to get a boat," she said.

He pulled her away from the door, where her father might overhear. "I wanted to make sure you were all right."

She shrugged. That was not a simple question. "Do you believe him? About his innocence?" she asked.

Gareth thought for a moment before answering. "I'm not sure what to believe. Your Uncle Charles believes him, I think. He mentioned so earlier today."

If Uncle Charles believed him, that was something. He was not the kind to be easily swayed in the wrong direction.

"But, then, why start the rumor in the first place?" Elaine spoke softly, careful to keep her voice from carrying to any servants or back to her father.

Gareth leaned closer to hear, their heads almost touching. "You think he started the rumor himself?"

"No. He would never. I only meant the rumor had to begin somewhere, with someone. Who was it, and why would they choose my father? We are no family of consequence. We have a little money but nothing to envy. So why would anyone in London choose to slander us?"

"Who can say? Perhaps your father was an easy target. Perhaps more happened than your father claims. Perhaps the target was not your father at all but was the other woman, and the Cardinhams were swept up in the storm."

She hadn't thought of that. It could be that the woman in question was meant to bear the brunt of it. She'd not considered that Lady Forton might also be suffering. But even if what her father said was true, it did not mean he'd done nothing wrong.

"Regardless," she said. "He can hardly call himself innocent."

"Unless he *is* innocent," Gareth pointed out.

"But there are different levels of innocence. He may not have committed an unforgivable sin, but even a small wrong is still a wrong."

"I'm not sure I take your meaning," Gareth said.

"Father says he was at the woman's house, alone with her in the drawing room. So what were they discussing?"

"The price of tin?" He grinned.

"If they were discussing investments in a tin mine, that is one thing. There would have been another person present, right? For propriety's sake."

Gareth leaned even closer. "You think they were having an intimate conversation. Discussing things of a personal nature."

Elaine nodded. "That is my fear, yes. If Father was baring his soul to a woman alone in the drawing room, is that not also being unfaithful? Upon marriage, he vowed to love, honor, and comfort his wife, forsaking all others. If he went to another woman for comfort, even though it be only words, he has broken the covenant he made to love and to cherish his wife and none other."

Gareth was staring at her as if she was missing something important.

"What?"

"You are right," he finally said. "No marriage can be a happy one where there is not also unity of mind and spirit." Still he looked at her as if there was more he wanted to say.

"Then we agree."

Gareth nodded. "Elowen," he said. "Where is Lord Chiverton, your husband-to-be?"

"He went to Camelford to get help for his carriage. I thought you knew that."

"I did," he said with a sigh. "I must go and retrieve your brother's remains. Please excuse me." He turned and walked away.

Yes. John. Her mother needed to be informed about him. Elaine followed Gareth's footsteps back toward the main staircase. A footman stood sentry at the door.

"Brixton, tell my mother that my father wants to see her in his library."

The footman nodded and strode off, eyeing her tattered dress.

She went straight to her room and rang the bell for Betsy. When she looked in the mirror, she let out a moan. Not a single strand of hair was left in her knot. She'd ruined many dresses before, but none as badly as this. It wouldn't even be good for an apron. And her boots. She sat on the edge of her bed and worked on the laces.

Betsy appeared, took one look at her, and shook her head. "I'm surprised Lord Chiverton will still have you in such a state. I'll call for a bath."

An hour and a half later, her hair was clean and reset. Her dress new, and a dry pair of shoes on her feet. No word had come yet from the rescue party, but it was probably too soon to expect them to have returned.

Aunt Rose had gone to bed. Uncle Charles had left with Gareth to oversee the recovery of John. Her father was still in his library, probably pacing by the window, awaiting the return of his only son. She could hear her mother sobbing through her bedroom door.

Hers was a house of individual suffering. Where her family should be drawn together, comforting each other, they were instead pulled apart.

Lord Chiverton had ridden off on her father's mare and not returned.

She went out the back door and crossed the lawn, following the path that would take her to the edge of the cliffs. She peered up to the north, looking for any light coming from Tintagel. It was too far away, of course. And they would bring him in a wagon, for there was no place to moor at Havencross.

Water from the sea beat against the rocks, always trying to break through but never able.

Poor John. Trapped all these years in a bed of cold and stones. It would be nice to lay him to rest in the churchyard, where she could go and talk with him sometimes.

Never once had she believed him to be alive. She'd known, just as Gareth had known, that he was gone. When he didn't return that night, she'd known. He hadn't wanted to go out in the first place. A storm had come in, and the wind howled. But Elaine had begged and pleaded, and John had surrendered.

It was hard to believe her father had clung to hope. John loved Havencross. He was West Country through and through. If Father had let him, he would have gone down into the mines with Gareth or out netting the pilchards with the fishermen. When Father wasn't looking, John helped the Kemps plow their fields.

Father had been so different then. Laughing. Fun, though the word seemed so wrong for him now. He had let that one moment—the loss of his son—define the rest of his life.

And she was no better. John's death had stunted them all, like the trees along the coast, too battered by the elements to reach their full height. Bent and beaten by the weight of it all.

Gareth had blamed the smugglers. He always blamed the smugglers. Finding his body like that, left to rot in a forgotten cave . . . Perhaps Gareth was right, though it surprised her that smugglers had not cleaned him of his boots or the quizzing glass, anything of value.

She shuddered as the image of his corpse filled her mind. Indeed, it was no accident that Gwenevere had led her to her brother. Perhaps this was Merlin's way of reminding her again that she had made her choice, her mistakes, and there was no going back. Not now, not ever.

CHAPTER SIXTEEN

Gareth

GARETH LUMBERED ALONG, SNAPPING THE reins occasionally as he and Beaford made their way to Havencross. John's remains lay in the bed of the wagon wrapped in a shroud of sailcloth, Beaford beside him on the bench in silence.

What a job it had been to get his friend's bones out of the cave and down to the boat. Now Gareth was a filthy wreck, and Beaford hadn't fared much better. The morning at Tintagel ruins seemed ages ago. Much had happened since they'd wandered off on the ill-conceived outing. Poor Miss Tippet had been dropped off at her house by the coachman. She took it well though, wishing Elaine a quick recovery from her shock and all the best for her family.

Gareth's mother was pushing him to make her an offer. Now that he owned the mine, he had the financial means to marry. By the time his children grew up, he would be wealthy enough to be on equal footing with families such as the Kemps and Squire Stroud. Quite above the Tippets. But that mattered little to him. His idea of a wife . . . well, his idea of a wife had already refused him.

Gareth had taken the shortcut back to Havencross. When he rounded the final bend in the road, he had to rein the horse to a stop. Chiverton's broken high flyer still blocked the road.

The man had worked up a big enough bother about it that Gareth had expected a team of men would have come out by now and carted the whole thing away.

Beaford jumped down to help push the main bulk out of the path. Then they were on their way again.

Gareth wanted to swing his fist at Chiverton for deserting Elaine. He should have been the one to go after her when she'd gone missing at the castle ruins. He should have been the one to wade into the water and carry her out. And he should have been the one at her side when she had confronted her father.

Worst of all, she could not see that the man cared more for his perfectly matched trotters than the woman he intended to marry. This whole marriage business was off. To Gareth, it mattered not at all what the London gossips said about the Cardinham family. Ruined. Not ruined. What was that to him? But Edmund Crawley, Earl of Chiverton, would care. A man of his station could not marry, would not marry a girl so below him—especially not one that came with disgrace. Unless, of course, he truly loved her.

Chiverton did not paint a picture of love. Why Elaine was so taken with him, Gareth could not say. He must assume that the man's wealth and position as earl appealed to her. Or his good looks.

That was fine. He'd had nothing to offer a gentleman's daughter back then save his heart, which was entirely hers. Or it had been, back then. He'd been a fool to even ask, but he could not help himself.

The wagon rolled up the lane and into the Havencross courtyard. The front door opened, and Mr. Cardinham came out, his face glowing white in the twilight. Elaine followed with her mother clinging to her arm.

Cardinham turned and held a hand out, stopping his wife. "Harriet, stay. I do not think you will want to see this."

"It's my son. Or it is supposed to be. I cannot rest until it is confirmed by my own eyes." She let go of Elaine, coming forward to stand beside her husband.

The wind died down, leaving a calm and eerie silence in the night. The hush that fell over the courtyard was thick as iron yet delicate as lace.

They leaned against the side of the wagon, all three of them—Elaine and both her parents. Gareth would have thought Elaine had seen enough, but perhaps not.

At a nod from Cardinham, Beaford pulled aside the sailcloth.

Mrs. Cardinham let out a gasp and pressed a handkerchief over her mouth.

They'd done their best, he and Beaford, to arrange the skeleton in a dignified way. It had been rough seas, and getting it out of the cave and into the boat while pieces of bone and leathered sinew were falling off was not an easy task. They'd laid him on a plank to try to keep him intact as they'd lowered him into the skiff; it had helped some.

Mrs. Cardinham let out a wail. "It's nothing but bones. Our beautiful John. Now look at him."

Mr. Cardinham had gone even whiter. He reached out in an attempt to comfort his wife, but she turned away, burying her face in her handkerchief.

"At least now he can have a proper burial. A place in the churchyard with all the rest of the Cardinhams," Mr. Cardinham said.

Mrs. Cardinham sobbed on while her husband's efforts to console her were met with an icy glare.

Quite the opposite of Elaine's reaction when Gareth had done the same earlier that day. The sadness in her eyes clearly showed as she looked on. It could have been for John or for her parents' broken marriage.

She'd put her hair up in a simple knot at the back of her head. He liked it that way. She used to wear it like that when they roamed the moors, then she'd snag it on a gorse branch. With one quick tug, she'd pull out the hair pin and a cascade of copper and gold would tumble down her back.

Elaine looked over at him. He quickly reached into the cart and lifted the sailcloth back over the bones.

"Bring them around to the kitchen," Cardinham said. "We'll put him on the table in the store room."

Beaford nodded, and he and Gareth lifted the plank out of the bed of the wagon and carried it around to the back of the house. It weighed almost nothing, with so much life gone out of it.

They left him wrapped in the canvas and placed the plank on the table.

"Who could have done this?" Mrs. Cardinham moaned.

"Perhaps it was the same man responsible for Mr. Kemp," Cardinham said.

All eyes turned to Gareth as if he might be able to pull out of thin air his father's murderer.

"I do not doubt for a moment that this was the act of smugglers," he said. "It is likely that John stumbled upon a stash of hidden goods and was silenced. But this was five years ago; I highly doubt the culprit will ever be found."

After all, he'd been looking for his father's killer for months now, and he had nothing to show for it.

"If I discover anything, I'll let you know." Gareth gave them all a little bow and slipped away. His part was over now that the body was recovered. He and John had been the best of friends, but that didn't mean they were equals.

He climbed onto the bench of the cart and urged the horse onward, toward Lowentop.

In the last few years, there had been four deaths in the Camelford area that could not be accounted for. Old David Lidgey, the fisherman. Widow Reede, who'd left her three small children home alone and had gone to dig clams. She lived a ways out near Treknow, and by the time her body had been discovered, her children had nearly starved.

Then there was the Gribbin lad. A great bully of a youth whom Gareth already believed to be mixed up in the smuggling game and very possibly deserved what had come to him.

And his father. Add to that John Cardinham, a gentleman's son, and that made five.

Five people who'd lost their lives so the public might have a cup of tea at a better price.

Something had to be done. But what? He could go again to the squire and complain, but that would do little good. They needed more wardens, more customs officials and revenuers to patrol the waters and keep them clear of the free traders.

More and more Gareth believed Tippet to be among the gang leaders, if not the operator himself. He would be only one more in a long string of men the crown sent to stop the smugglers who then embraced the crime instead.

The wagon rattled along the rough track until he came to Chiverton's wreckage again.

Gareth wanted nothing more than to get home, get out of his filthy clothes, and take a bath. Salt from the sea coated his hair. He had been wetted and dried and wetted and dried more times than he could count. But Chiverton's phaeton was not safe.

"Whoa." He tugged on the reins, and the cart rattled to a stop.

He may as well gather what parts he could rather than leave them here overnight—or until Chiverton got around to cleaning up his mess, whenever that might be.

Lord Chiverton may have been from gentler parts, but he was a fool to think he could leave his damaged phaeton in the lane all night and not have it looted. Whether lost at sea or on the land, a wrecked vessel was fair pickings in the eyes of many.

Gareth picked up the wheel that had come off and loaded it into the back of the cart. He rounded up the bench, which had snapped in two—one piece thrown off to the side and the other still partially attached to the seat box.

He reached up and gave it a tug to see if it would come off, for the upholstery, with a little mending, could be reused. His hand hit something under the seat.

In the darkness, he could not see it clearly, but by its cold and rigid feel, he thought it a metal box. He retrieved the lantern from his wagon and came back, shining it under the driver's seat.

It wasn't so odd to have a place to store something under the bench. There was little room in a carriage such as this—one meant only for show, with no thought of practicality—to keep anything safely tucked away. But this particular box had a lock on it. Perhaps that should not be so odd either, but it was ever so tempting.

Gareth glanced over his shoulder. There was no one in sight.

What did a man like Chiverton keep hidden away? He passed the lantern across the ruins until he found a splinter of steel, long and slender. This would do. He slipped it into the lock, feeling for the pins, working them until it clicked open.

Lifting the lamp, he opened the lid. Inside, he found two items: a pig-sticking knife and a folded paper.

Gareth stepped away. A pig sticker was common enough. Every farmer had one for the butchering of pigs. Gareth doubted Chiverton had ever butchered a pig in his life. A few pheasants, perhaps. Some quail. Though more likely he shot them and brought them home to his butler, never giving them another thought.

It was a good idea for any man traveling the roads to carry a weapon in case he was set upon by thieves. It was only that a pig sticker was the weapon of choice of smugglers.

If a smuggler was caught carrying a firearm or a sword, the penalties were steep—death or transportation. These farm tools could be just as deadly without incurring any penalty of law. Gareth wouldn't have thought twice had he opened the box and found a pistol. He would have congratulated Chiverton on his foresight, though he'd still have been a fool for leaving it here unattended.

Gareth took the letter out and held it to the light. It was sealed with a wafer bearing no mark and was addressed with no more direction than *T. S.* Two letters that had no part in Lord Chiverton's name. It must be an outgoing correspondence.

The clatter of horse hooves drew Gareth's attention. Someone was coming. He tucked the letter into his pocket, then tossed the pig knife on the floor of the carriage to make it look like the strongbox had flung open on its own and its contents had spilled out. He stuffed the broken spoke deep into the hedge, then fixed the lantern back on his cart.

By the time the horse and rider rounded the corner, Gareth was innocently gathering parts of the rear iron and spring.

"Ho, there, Mr. Kemp," Lord Chiverton called.

CHAPTER SEVENTEEN

Gareth

GARETH LOOKED UP AND SMILED. "Lord Chiverton. Glad to see you, sir. I hope you had some luck in Camelford finding a man to fix your phaeton?"

Chiverton swung a leg over and slid off the horse, landing gingerly. He must still be favoring his injured leg.

"I admit I haven't had time to get to Camelford yet. I had some urgent business earlier and have just now gotten away." He glanced at the spring iron in Gareth's hand. "Are you planning on fixing it for me?" he said with a grin.

"Me? No. I'm not handy with mechanical things. I was just on my way home from Havencross and thought I'd gather up the pieces before they disappeared into the hands of wreckers."

"Ah. That is good of you." He stood silent for a moment, then said, "It's very late. Did you stay for supper?"

"No. We just now finished delivering the remains of Mr. Cardinham's son."

"Oh yes. I'd forgotten about it. Piece of nasty business, that."

How could he have forgotten the discovery of John Cardinham's bones? "Yes. It was quite distressing to the ladies of the house."

"Certainly. And rightly so. It is not in their constitution to see such things."

Gareth wanted to swing the spring iron into the man's gut. How could he be so irritatingly stupid?

"And how is Miss Cardinham holding up?"

Should that not be a question for Gareth to ask him—the man about to marry her? "It is not my place to know," Gareth said. He tossed the iron into his wagon before he did something he might regret. Though he doubted there would actually be any regret.

Chiverton gave him a quick nod. "I'm off to Camelford in a bit of a hurry. I just came by to check on things." He fished a folded pocketbook from his coat and held out a five-pound note. "For your trouble. I do appreciate it."

Gareth would dance naked on the hedge tops before taking money from Lord Chiverton. "It's no trouble," he said.

Chiverton shrugged and replaced the note. He strode to the front of the rig and reached under the seat, then paused.

"Hm. That's strange." Chiverton had the pig sticker and was turning it in his hand.

"What?" Gareth asked with perhaps a little too much surprise.

"Nothing," Chiverton said.

Gareth retrieved the folding head cover that had torn off and carried it to the wagon, wedging it under the wheel to keep it in place. "Well, I think that's all I can salvage without tools. But if I were you, I wouldn't leave the carriage body here unattended for long. There's questionable men about."

"Good advice," Chiverton said, though he seemed a little preoccupied. "Uh, did you . . . I see my strongbox has come open, but I could have sworn it was still locked before I left."

Gareth leaned in and studied the metal box with a good amount of concern. He shook his head in puzzlement. "There was no one about when I got here, and that was only a few moments before you showed up. As I said, questionable men in these parts. I hope nothing valuable is missing?"

Chiverton tossed the pig knife into the wrecked phaeton. "No. Nothing at all. Wasn't anything of value in there to begin with."

"Well, that's lucky." Gareth smiled. He pointed to his wagon. "I'll have these part in my stables when you need them. Unless, of course, you want to take them with you now. Lowentop is not more than a few minutes' walk from here."

Chiverton was pawing at the base of the hedge with his foot, searching. In the dark, it was hard to see much of anything. Perhaps he might give up quickly and come back in the morning, but by then, who knew what the wind might have blown away.

"No, no. I appreciate your taking them," Chiverton said. In the night, his face stood out in contrast to his dark clothing and the blackness of the hedge. He was looking at Gareth, watching him as he climbed onto the bench.

"Good night, then, sir." Gareth snapped the reins, and the wagon rolled away.

When he lumbered into the Lowentop drive, he whistled for Tomas, instructing him to stow the broken phaeton parts in the stable.

Gareth clambered out of the driver's seat. At last, he was home. What had started as a simple outing to the castle ruins had turned into . . . what? He couldn't find words to describe the events of this day. May he never have a day like it again.

His mother came running out, her dainty feet skimming along the walkway. "Gareth, where have you been? I've been sick with worry. Utterly sick. I thought for sure you'd fallen into the cove and been washed out to sea. Or worse." She choked back a sob.

His mother knew he'd gone out to Tintagel, but he'd not had a chance to explain to her why the long delay in getting home. He should have sent word, considering she always imagined the worst.

"Sorry. We had a bit of an emergency, and it took the whole day to work it out." He put his arm around her and turned her back toward the house. "We found the body of John Cardinham."

She gasped and stumbled on the threshold.

Gareth led them back to the kitchen because he was too dirty for the parlor. "It was Elai—Miss Cardinham. She discovered him. Naught but bones and tattered cloth. I think it quite unnerved her."

"The poor girl." She poured some water into a kettle. "Where?"

He shed his filthy coat, tossing it on the table. "In one of the sea caves not far from the castle ruins."

His mother spun around. "Smugglers! I knew it." She sloshed some water as she swung the kettle over the fire. "Probably the same filthy scoundrels who took your poor father. It's not safe here anymore, Gareth. Not safe at all. I can't even walk into Camelford without fearing for my life. Mrs. Dawlish agrees, especially after her own son was mysteriously killed not more than a fortnight ago."

He shook his head. "Mother. That was a mining accident, and everyone knows it."

She shrugged. "That's what they want you to believe, but Mrs. Dawlish is not so sure. She says—"

"I'm very sorry for Mrs. Dawlish. Really, I am. But there is no question about her son's death. He fell in the mine. He was trying to save money and work off the light of other men's candles and fell fifteen feet down a new shaft. No mystery. Only foolishness."

"That's not what Mrs. Dawlish says." She had her hands on her hips now, staring him down.

He didn't want to argue with her. He could easily understand why Mrs. Dawlish would have difficulty accepting that her son had died at the hands of his own poor judgment. She was likely the one urging him to cut costs. It would ease her mind to blame the smugglers, but Gareth wished she would not fill his mother's head with more cause to worry.

He dropped into a chair near the fire and tugged off his boots. As he bent over, the letter from Chiverton's strongbox fell out of his waistcoat pocket.

"What is that? Have you received a letter?" She picked it up off the floor with a soft grunt.

Blast. This inane conversation with his mother had stripped it from his mind.

"It's nothing. Just some details about the mine I need to attend to." He took it from her hands. "Call me when the bath is ready." He left and traipsed up the stairs to his room.

Gareth closed his door and slipped the letter out of his pocket. He read the direction again. *T. S.* It could be anyone and was obviously prepared for hand delivery, as there was no town or otherwise to direct a postman.

It was probably nothing. People corresponded daily with all sorts of matters. Chiverton had ships in Plymouth, so a business letter would be apropos. In fact, he had mentioned a run-in with smugglers who'd helped themselves to some of his cargo, so perhaps a pig sticker was not so far from expected.

To be perfectly honest with himself—something Gareth ardently tried to avoid—his feelings for Elaine might be clouding his judgment. His own brother could be marrying her and he would be under equal suspicion—if he had a brother. He should have left the letter where he'd found it.

There was nothing for it now. It was too late to return it. He'd already dug his pit by lying to Chiverton about it. He couldn't very well go tromping back saying, *Surprise, I actually did have your letter.*

He might as well read it. It was not his business, and he had a strong feeling he should keep himself out of it. And he would have if it weren't for Elaine.

He tipped his head back and stared at the black timbers of his ceiling. Why could he not let her go?

For five laborious years, he'd thought about her. Dreamed about her. Watched and waited for the stinging news he knew would come. And come it had. He'd nearly ripped his prayer book in half when the banns were first announced. Elaine Cardinham, daughter of Mr. Francis Cardinham, to marry Edmund Crawley, Earl of Chiverton.

Over the last week or so, he'd dug into the books to find out as much as he could about Chiverton. Real facts, not the hearsay babble he'd been getting. He'd found next to nothing. Good name. Ancient family. Apparently they'd had a little trouble, steadfastly sticking to their Catholicism during the reign of Henry VIII, but since then had seen the light and were now converted. Other than that, he'd found very little.

So why couldn't he let it alone? He would shed this need to watch over her, to keep her close, if he could. But the passing of five years had taught him he could not. And when he saw her that day, standing on the edge of the world with the wind stroking her hair . . .

Enough. She was engaged to another man. An engagement that seemed by all appearances mutually agreeable to both parties. He had no right to interfere. He should turn and walk away. And by St. Just, he would. As soon as he got his way into this letter.

He pried open the wafer and unfolded it. One glance told him he'd not be reading it. It was written in French.

Was Chiverton a spy for Napoleon's army? Well, this just kept getting better and better. Gareth would put a stop to this whole thing if he thought Elaine was getting herself entangled with a turncoat. He'd not see her swing from the gallows. Not for that fop.

He searched the contents for any word he might recognize—a name or a place—but he found none.

He could ask Elaine to read it. There was nothing on the page to implicate Chiverton, leastways not as far as he could tell. But if the contents *did* contain something that incriminated him, it might be enough to make Elaine change her mind about marrying him.

Listen to himself.

He was being absurd.

The engagement between Chiverton and Elaine was official. Three weeks of banns had been read. No going back. And what in the name of black pilchards made him so sure Chiverton was involved in anything? So he had a strongbox. So he had a pig sticker. So he had a letter in French. Odd, to be sure. But not so very out of the ordinary that it proved any kind of wrongdoing.

Elaine was not stupid. She would not get herself involved with a man she didn't trust or who was mixed up in something he shouldn't be. Yes, there was that scandal clouding the name of Cardinham. Many would lose interest because of that. Gareth hadn't, so why must he assume the worst of Chiverton? If Chiverton saw half as much in Elaine as he did, of course he would still want her.

Martha knocked on his door. "Your bath is ready, sir."

Good. This was just what he needed—to wash the dust and filth and past away and start over.

He folded the letter and tucked it on his desk under the chunk of raw tin he used as a paperweight. He was done assuming the worst. Elaine had chosen someone else, and the least he could do was respect that choice and be civil.

He stripped off his shirt. Miss Tippet was a good soul, kind and generous. What she lacked in education he could supply with some books, perhaps a tutor, and a good helping of common sense.

If Miss Tippet's father had taken up with the smugglers, that would be a problem. Gareth wanted no association with the free traders. As yet, he could prove nothing.

There was a knock on the front door. Gareth glanced at the small clock on his mantel. Past ten o'clock. Who would be calling so late?

He opened his door and listened. It was a man's voice. Chiverton. He must have come by to see why his ears were burning.

Bath or earl first?

He took under advisement his own counsel from only moments ago and decided to be civil. Better to not keep the earl waiting. He found a clean pair of breeches and stepped into them, then tossed on a shirt. That was as far as his civility went. Bare footed and in nothing more than breeches and shirtsleeves, he descended the stairs.

"Oh, sir. I was just coming to get you," Martha said as she was coming up. "Lord Chiverton is here in the parlor to see you."

"Thank you."

She paused, and her eyes widened as he went past her, heading to the parlor in such a state of undress. He didn't care. Enough had happened today that he gave very little thought to his attire—especially at this hour.

Perhaps in London they kept late nights, but here, when one must be up at dawn to see to the stock and the mines, one went to bed with the sun.

His mother perched on the sofa, and across from her, near the hearth, sat Chiverton. She had stoked the fire to near smelting levels, and Chiverton's face was bright red.

Again, Gareth had to admit that he'd unfairly judged the man. Rather than offend his mother, he endured the fires of Hades.

"Oh, there you are," she said, her eyes gleaming for having an earl in the house. Or perhaps it was simply the heat. "Lord Chiverton has called." She would have a mouthful to brag about tomorrow.

"Thank you, Mother," Gareth said, motioning her to the door.

"Really, Gareth." She shook her head as she passed. "You're barely dressed."

The door closed behind her, and Gareth opened a window. "Sorry about that; she gets a little overzealous with her hospitality sometimes."

Chiverton crossed the room to stand by the open window. "Forgive my lateness; this was my first chance to get away."

"It's all right."

Chiverton stared for a few moments into the inferno. "Polkreath must keep you very busy."

"Yes. It takes a good deal of my time."

"Your mother tells me even at this late hour you were occupied reading a letter."

Blast his mother. She little knew what information she was giving over. Gareth smiled. "Yes. Did she tell you we are sinking another shaft? I've got more miners clamoring to buy a work space off it than I have room to fit them in. It's a good lode, and every miner in the district wants a piece of it."

"They pay you to mine?"

"The men buy their piece to mine, yes. And they make their money based on how much they pull up. A family working together can do quite well." Gareth leaned forward. "I have a feeling, Lord Chiverton, you are not here to discuss the business of tin mining."

"You are correct. I know it's late, but I was hoping I might sift through the pieces of my high flyer. I seem to be missing something."

Gareth lifted his eyebrows in a show of surprise. "Absolutely. What is it you are missing?" He rose to his feet, and Chiverton followed.

"Well, it's a little embarrassing," Chiverton said, and he did turn a fair shade of pink, though that could also be from the fire. "A letter. Like a besotted fool, Mr. Kemp, I penned a love letter to Miss Cardinham. I don't want it floating the countryside. It's personal. And ridiculous. But so it is."

"I hope you didn't go so far as to include poetry," Gareth said.

Chiverton laughed. "I fear there may be." He followed Gareth to the back of the house. "I thought, why not give the pieces you retrieved one last look. It would be worth it to keep the letter from falling into the wrong hands."

Gareth fitted a candle into a lantern and closed the glass. "Wrong hands?"

Chiverton cringed a little. "I suppose any hands besides the intended are the wrong hands."

Gareth stuffed his bare feet into a pair of boots. He was a good actor, this earl from Chiverton. Either that or he really had written a love letter to Elaine in French. In no way did the letters *T. S.* make sense when applied to Elaine. Gareth couldn't even think of a loving epithet. Tender Sweetling? Treasured Sundew? Still, he supposed there was the possibility that the letter was meant for Elaine. *T. S.* could mean something entirely different in French.

He nearly asked Chiverton what language he'd written in but didn't. Too close to the truth.

Gareth opened the back door and led them out into the night. "I've had the broken parts moved to the stable. This way."

CHAPTER EIGHTEEN

Elaine

THEY WERE A QUIET BUNCH at breakfast the following morning. Elaine's father had joined them for the first time since arriving home from London. Aunt Rose had not. Too tired, Uncle Charles had informed them.

Yesterday's trip to Tintagel had been too much. Aunt Rose worked very hard at pretending she was as strong as anyone. In truth, her frail body could not tolerate so much exertion.

Elaine could not help but feel partially responsible for her aunt's condition; she'd wandered off and prolonged the outing. But if she hadn't, she wouldn't have found her brother's remains. And if she hadn't found his remains, perhaps her father wouldn't be sitting here with them to break his fast—his first real step at reconciliation.

Uncle Charles filled a plate with more food than her aunt would eat in a week.

"We have servants for that," her mother said. "There's no need for you to carry trays of food about the house."

"I'm happy to do it. How else will she know I still love her?" He turned his head and gave her father a nod. Uncle Charles poured a cup of tea and set it on the tray. "I shall be upstairs if I am needed."

"Do give my sister our best," her mother said.

He tipped his head and departed, carefully balancing the tray in his arms.

Elaine went back to her breakfast. Poor Aunt Rose. Her constitution was so weak. Every infection, no matter how insignificant to one of stout health, caused a great deal of suffering in her aunt.

"Harriet." Her father's voice cut into the stillness of the breakfast room like shattering glass. "I will be going to the vicar this morning to make arrangements for the interment of John. Perhaps you would care to join me?"

Elaine's buttered bread hung halfway to her mouth. The recovery of John's body must have affected him more than he let on to be speaking so suddenly to her mother like this, after so many weeks of silence.

Her mother stared at her father for a few moments, then seemed to come to herself, scooping a spoonful of preserves and scraping it with great force across her bread. The bread tore from the pressure, but that did not stop her mother from spreading.

Elaine was one person too many in this room. She put down her food and wiped her mouth. "Excuse me." She scooted away from the table and made a dash for the door. Once through, she closed it softly but couldn't bring herself to leave.

She leaned in, pressing her ear to the frame.

Her mother spoke first. "I don't think—"

"I insist." Her father's words were soft but firm.

No one said more. Leastways not in the minute she stood waiting.

This was progress. An olive branch, contrived though it may be.

To her knowledge, no other attempt had been made by either parent to bridge the gap of silence. They were stuck with each other *so long as they both shall live*. Wouldn't the years to come be more bearable if they could find at least enough ground for civility?

She pushed off the wall without making a sound and started toward the back door, carefully avoiding the kitchen and store room, where the bones of her brother still lay. A handful of daffodils would be just the thing to brighten her aunt's room.

Elaine gathered up her cutting shears and a basket and stepped out into the garden. She took a deep breath. The fresh air always cleared her mind. She made her way through the rows of hedges and shrubs, taking her time filling her basket until the sound of scuffling came from the other side of the hawthorns. A badger, most likely.

She set her basket down and climbed a few steps up on the stile. Crouched behind a large bracken sat two lads, one with white hair and the other with red.

"Willy White-Top and Sandy Will."

They looked up at her, rabbit-eyed.

"What are you doing in my hedges?"

The two lads scurried to their feet. They each elbowed the other, trying to push their friend forward. At last, Willy White-Top spoke up. "We want ta see the bones."

For a moment, Elaine could not speak. As if her brother's remains were some sort of warped entertainment. Her fright must have shown on her face, for the boys backed away.

As appalling as the idea was, it would give her a chance to get them in the house and fed a proper meal. She could have Cook pack up some extras to take home to their families. Surely whatever parents or siblings they had would be as starved as them.

"Did you bring your ball?" she asked.

Willy White-Top wedged it out of his pocket.

"Good. Maybe you'll have a go with the bat after. Yes?"

Their eyes lit up. For all their troubles, they were still just children wanting to play. She wished these boys were the only waifs with nothing to live on, but she was not that naive. The workhouses were full of families—mothers with no husband to provide any kind of sustenance to her children. She would do what she could for these little ones.

"Very well," she said. "I'll show you the bones."

They seemed more relieved than anything. Perhaps they were also hoping for some food since the last time they were here, Lord Chiverton scared them off before they'd had a chance to play with the bat or take a bite to eat.

They climbed over the stile, which was really just a few stones protruding out of the hedge wall. She started off toward the house, the two boys following dutifully behind her.

After about twenty paces, she stopped. "La, I forgot my flowers."

She turned back, but Sandy Will was already running for them. "I'll get 'em." He returned moments later. "'Ere ye go, mum."

"Thank you." She took the basket from him. "I'm such a ninny sometimes. You should have seen me in London. My mother was constantly reminding me of what I had forgot."

"You been ta London, mum?" Willy White-Top asked.

"I have."

"What's it like?"

"London?"

The boys nodded.

"It is busy, busy, busy. Morning visits. Parties and concerts at night. Balls. Barely a moment to one's self. No peace and quiet at all."

The Williams looked at her, heads askew. Concerts and balls were likely not what young boys were interested in.

She could do better. "The streets are crowded with people and horses. You can't cross the road without a carriage wheel threatening your foot or a horse puffing its wet breath down your neck." This had them staring wide-eyed, so she went on. "Vendors selling every sort of thing. Spices from the East Indies. Swords of the Saracen. Piemen who'll toss a penny for a pie. Regiments in uniform marching here and there, ready to fight the French. And the theater. Stories of adventure, mystery, and murder all played out on a grand stage."

The lads walked with her as she spoke, their eyes turned faraway as her descriptions played out in their minds. She may have overdone it a bit, but what did it matter? If they ever happened to London, they would learn well enough for themselves.

Elaine opened the door to the kitchen, and the boys followed her through into the heat of the baking bread and capon roasting over the fire. In a small alcove set off from the kitchen was the store room with its large oak table covered with a shawl. How small the remains of her brother appeared underneath the embroidered silk. It was hard to believe all that was left in this world of John lay underneath it.

Cook looked up, surprised at Elaine's sudden appearance—accompanied by two waifish lads.

"Something hearty for the boys, please, Cook. And perhaps something sweet."

The cook gave Elaine a quick nod, eyeing the Williams. She went to the pantry and started sorting through the foods.

Elaine guided the boys to the shrouded table. Before lifting the cloth, she gave them a stern look. "This is my brother, mind. Do you know what that means?"

Willy White-Top nodded, but Sandy Will shook his head.

"It means that this is more than just bones. It was the son of Mr. Cardinham, master of the house, lord of the manor. My brother and best friend."

"Be respectful," Willie White-Top said.

"That's right." Elaine lifted the cloth, exposing the stark whiteness of all that was left of John. He had been the brightest part of her life throughout her childhood. It seemed fitting now that his bones shone brighter than anything else in the dim kitchen.

Sandy Will let out a breath of awe. He leaned up against the table, his eyes roving over the remains. Elaine had expected Willy White-Top would be the one to oo and ah over the bones, but he held back, looking on from afar.

Sandy Will lifted his hand, ready to stroke the long white limbs of John's arm. He stopped and looked up at Elaine. She nodded. Why not. John would not have minded. In fact, he would have been the first to gather up the cricket gear and take the boys out for a game.

Sandy Will let his fingers gently run along the bones. Hard to believe these sticks and knobs were the framework of life. The remains of John's clothes—his boots, the tatters of his coat, the buttons from his breeches—lay organized in a neat pile beside the bones. Her mother must have done that, or perhaps Mr. Winkleigh.

Willy White-Top moved closer, following his friend's lead. He too raised a finger and very gently touched the skull.

Elaine turned away. This was not how she wanted to remember her brother—a relic of bone. A sideshow curiosity.

Cook had returned from the pantry and was bundling pasties, cold ham, and currant cakes. Elaine went over to help, adding a few extra cakes to each packet. Cook expertly folded them up, working the napkin into a simple knot to keep it together. With two sons in the mines, she well knew how to tie a supper up for transport.

Elaine returned to the table and covered the bones. "That's enough of that. Cook's got something for you."

Sandy Will had gone white as whey and stared at Elaine as if she was a ghost. Willie White-Top looked down at his bare feet.

"What is it?" Elaine asked.

Sandy Will shook his head. He took a bundle from Cook and gave them both a bow.

Willy White-Top followed suit, then they both disappeared out the kitchen door. Perhaps they weren't as ready to see the bones as they'd thought. They were only children, after all.

"Don't you want to use the bat?" she called after them, but they did not look back. It could have been the excitement of food that had overtaken the lure of cricket.

Elaine leaned against the door frame, watching the Williams dash across the lawn and disappear behind the holly tree. At least they would be well fed in their beds tonight. If they had beds. Perhaps tomorrow she'd walk into Camelford to find out whom they belonged to.

She snipped the stems of the daffodils and arranged them into a willow-patterned vase. Not quite as perfect as the flower arrangements she'd seen in

London, with all their roses and tulips from the hot houses, but it was bright and cheerful and filled the room with sweet aromas of the living.

The stairs creaked like always as she climbed to Aunt Rose's room. After Elaine's quick knock on the door, Uncle Charles's head appeared.

"Elaine, come in." He opened the door wider.

Her aunt was lying in bed, her face drained of color, and there were dark circles under her eyes. She looked paler than ever. Uncle Charles had claimed she was only a little bit under the weather; clearly, he'd underplayed the severity of his wife's illness.

"I brought you some flowers. Thought it might brighten your room."

"They're lovely. Thank you." Aunt Rose tried to sit up, but Uncle Charles laid a hand on her shoulder to keep her down. Uncle Charles was ever her willing servant—until it came to her health. Then he would not budge.

Elaine sat on the edge of the bed. "How are you feeling?"

"I am well enough." Her voice rasped and squeaked as if it fluttered by. "Just my usual bout. I'm sure it will pass in a few days."

Elaine's eyes went to Uncle Charles's for the real story. He smiled and nodded. "It will pass. It always does."

She did not believe him for a moment. Something more was going on here.

"I have no choice but to recover quickly," Aunt Rose said. "I am determined not to miss your wedding."

That gave her aunt only four days to recuperate. Perhaps she should speak to Lord Chiverton about postponing.

"What are they going to do with John's remains?" Aunt Rose asked.

"Father and Mother have gone down to the vicar to see about getting him buried in the family tomb."

"They went together?" Uncle Charles seemed quite pleased by this. "That is something."

Aunt Rose nodded, but a fit of coughing kept her from speaking. Uncle Charles held a teacup to her mouth, and she took a few sips. It seemed to calm her lungs.

Betsy knocked on the open door. "Excuse me, Miss Cardinham, Mrs. Kemp is here and wishes to speak with you." Betsy dipped her head. "She's in the drawing room."

Elaine leaned over Aunt Rose and gave her a kiss on her forehead. "Get well," she said.

CHAPTER NINETEEN

Elaine

Mrs. Kemp paced to and fro in the drawing room.

Elaine cleared her throat to catch her attention. "Mrs. Kemp."

The woman spun around gracefully. Her bonnet was askew, and a sheen of sweat glistened on her brow. She must have hurried to get here.

"Miss Cardinham." She gave Elaine a little curtsey. "Thank you so much for seeing me."

"My pleasure." She would never refuse to see Gareth's mother.

"I'm looking for my son. Have you seen him?" There was an edge to Mrs. Kemp's voice, a frantic undertone. She'd always been a worrier.

How many times had Elaine, John, and Gareth come home from their adventures only to be forced to listen to Gareth's mother enumerate in great length all the ways they could have died or been injured or gotten lost or been drowned or gotten run over by the harvest wagon.

"Is he not at the mine?"

Mrs. Kemp shook her head. "No. I had Tomas check there first."

"I've not seen him since yesterday." Not since he brought home her brother.

Mrs. Kemp nodded. She gave a smile, but it was a fleeting and fretful thing. "He got home late yesterday evening but disappeared again. Didn't sleep in his bed and didn't come for breakfast. I thought maybe with him being so fond of you, he might be here. Or perhaps you might know of his whereabouts."

Good heavens. Was she implying that her son was here with her all night? No, of course not. But did she know about what had passed between them? Hopefully not.

"I'm sure he's out working somewhere. Or perhaps he went to town. Lord Chiverton had a carriage accident yesterday. I think it very likely he's off helping him find the carriage maker to get started on the repairs."

That seemed to bring her some relief. She smiled and sat down. "Yes, of course. I had not thought of that. Lord Chiverton did call late last night. That must be where he is. Though he's going to feel the back side of my spoon when he gets home."

Gareth Kemp was a grown man capable of handling himself perfectly well in the world. Wherever he was, surely he was fine.

"Thank you, Miss Cardinham." She stood and made her way to the door, already preoccupied with this new notion.

"Good day, Mrs. Kemp," Elaine called after her.

The front door opened, and Elaine heard some chattering—her parents greeting Mrs. Kemp as they returned from the vicarage. She also recognized a third voice, Squire Stroud.

She waited for them in the drawing room. Her mother entered first, eyes red-rimmed and face wilted. It must have been a hard morning at the vicar's. She handed her bonnet to Mr. Winkleigh and dropped into a chair by the fire.

Her father came next.

"Why is the squire here?" she whispered at her mother.

Her mother shrugged her thin shoulders. "He wants to find out what happened to John, I suppose."

Her father gestured for the magistrate to enter the drawing room, then he ordered tea from Mr. Winkleigh.

The man's large round belly entered the room first, followed by his large mustache, bald head, and ruddy cheeks. He had bright, clear, youthful eyes in great contrast with the rest of his body. When she was younger, his vast size frightened her. But since then, he'd proved to be a kind but serious man who took his responsibilities as magistrate earnestly.

Elaine dipped her head at him. "Squire Stroud."

Before they'd left for London, the squire had frequently dined with them. He was a widower with no children of his own. Sometimes, during the Sunday service, he would bring John and Elaine a strawberry pastille, sneaking it to them when their parents were not looking.

He lowered himself into a chair that groaned with his weight, or perhaps Elaine had groaned in sympathy.

"The squire is here to inquire about the discovery of John's remains," her father said.

As magistrate, it would be up to the squire to determine if there needed to be an inquest regarding John's death. And if there was an inquest, well, that was only one more reason to postpone the wedding.

Squire Stroud nodded. "I understand you are the one who found the . . . him." His blue eyes watched Elaine with a mix of sympathy and curiosity.

"Yes. I found him in one of the caves near the ruined castle of Tintagel."

The squire considered this for a few moments. "How did you find him?"

"I found him long dead."

Her father snorted, then quickly cleared his throat.

Squire Stroud's lips did not even twitch. "I mean, how were you able to locate the remains, considering that area is one frequently explored by excursionists and locals both? How had he not been found before? After all this time, how were you alone able to find him?"

She feared this would be his question. She would never mention the woman in green. If the squire found out there was a mysterious woman haunting the coast, no doubt there would be a search. Gwenevere would be a suspected accomplice in John's death, the death of Mr. Kemp, and the other deaths Elaine had since heard about: the fisherman, the widow, and the Gribbin lad. Or perhaps Gwenevere would vanish again, never to return. "I can't explain it," Elaine finally answered. "Something drew me there."

"And what did you find?"

"A long and narrow cave. As I went deeper, I stumbled upon the bones of a man." She continued her story, describing her shock, then her realization that it was her brother, based on what was left of the clothing and the quizzing glass.

"And you were with Mr. Gareth Kemp?"

That was another area she did not care to elaborate on. "The tide was coming in, and I was trapped by the water. Mr. Kemp, Lord Chiverton, and my Uncle Charles set out searching for me. It was Mr. Kemp who finally found me."

"How was it that Mr. Kemp knew where to look if the cave itself was so hidden and remote?" Squire Stroud was leaning forward now.

It was clear he'd already formed an opinion of what had happened to her brother and that he was simply waiting for her to speak the words to confirm it. A fox lying motionless in the bracken, waiting for the rabbit to fall into his trap.

But there was no trap. It had been five years. Nothing could be done. The squire did raise an interesting question though. How had Gareth been the one to find her—and so quickly?

"He knows that area better than anyone." Certainly better than Lord Chiverton and her uncle.

Squire Stroud leaned back into his chair as if his trap had sprung.

"What is it you suspect?" her father asked.

The squire pursed his lips. Though he was the magistrate and it was his duty to deal with matters such as these, he was not the highest-ranking man in the parish. Her father was. But her father had been happy to waive his right to magistrate. The position had been offered to the squire.

Squire Stroud had no part in the tin mines, and Elaine thought he'd always resented what he called *easy money*. He believed a man's wealth should come from the ownership of land, not the funding of mines. For this reason, Elaine did not entirely trust his objectivity regarding Gareth.

"We know young Master John has been gone these past five years," the squire said. "Most likely his death, like the others, came at the hands of the smugglers." He paused as if waiting for the rest of the room to catch up.

Apparently none of them did, as she, her mother, and her father all stared at him, wondering what he could possibly mean.

He gave them all an exasperated look. "The young Mr. Kemp has come into a great deal of money over the last several years."

Elaine was already shaking her head. It was clear as day where he was headed now.

"Owner of Polkreath Mine. A carriage. That kind of money does not come from honest work. Not so quickly."

"You're saying Gareth Kemp is a smuggler and killed our John?" Elaine's mother spoke for the first time. Squire Stroud's story had stilled her knitting needles, and she was on the edge of her seat. If her mother believed for one moment that Gareth was capable of this, Elaine didn't know her at all.

"It makes sense, does it not?" The squire settled back into his chair. "Young Master John discovers his friend's doings. Gareth stops him any way he can. Gareth knows the alcoves and hidden places along the coast and leaves the body where it will never be found."

"No." Elaine was on her feet. "That is simply not possible."

Squire Stroud watched her carefully, as if every move of her body could be the final piece of evidence he needed to arrest Gareth.

Gareth and John had been the best of friends. The very idea that Gareth might have been at all involved in John's death was utter madness. That he was a smuggler, preposterous.

"Are you also accusing Mr. Kemp of killing his own father?" Elaine asked, her voice rising. "Did the elder Mr. Kemp also discover his son's underhanded activities and have to be *dealt* with? Absurd." Elaine glared at her father. He should know better.

"It does seem rather far-fetched," her father said. He'd come to her aid, but he did not seem wholly convinced of Gareth's innocence.

The sound of shouting came from the back garden. Elaine peered out through the glass but could not see what the commotion was.

A few moments later, Mr. Winkleigh entered. He set out a tray of tea and scones with cream and preserves.

"Thank you, Mr. Winkleigh," her mother said.

"What's going on outside?" her father asked.

The old butler's eyes went to Squire Stroud, then to Elaine. "Two local lads in a bit of a mix-up," he said.

The Williams? She thought they were long gone.

Mr. Winkleigh did not leave the room. Though he addressed her father, his eyes kept going back to her. "Got into a scrap of trouble is all, sir." There was something he wasn't saying.

"I'll see to it, Father." At the very least, this would give her the opportunity to get out and away from the squire's half-witted theories.

She followed Mr. Winkleigh into the corridor. "What is the trouble?"

When the door to the drawing room closed, Mr. Winkleigh said in a quiet voice, "The lads were caught stealing."

"Stealing?" Good heavens. After all she'd done for them. There must be some mistake. "I gave them the food; they did not steal it."

"It's not the food, miss." He motioned for her to proceed him down the hall toward the kitchen.

She strode along, and he followed on her heels, still offering nothing of what the boys were accused of. "What is it they have stolen?"

He cleared his throat, then quietly answered. "A piece of Master John."

Elaine stopped. She stared at Mr. Winkleigh. "Do you mean . . . a piece of his . . . a bone?"

The old butler simply nodded.

Why on earth would either of the Williams do such a thing? She'd only ever shown them kindness. After all her warnings about respect for the dead, that he was her cherished brother, not just a pile of sticks and stones, they dared to pilfer a piece of him. It was unthinkable. And also a little bit disturbing.

Elaine hurried on, entering the kitchen with her lips pursed tightly.

The two boys stood in the center, heads hanging low. Sandy Will's knees quaked, and Willie White-Top's hands twisted and turned as he held them in front of him. They'd better be scared; she was not going to let them off lightly.

She planted her hands on her hips. "What have you got to say for yourselves?"

The lads did not look up.

Mr. Winkleigh intervened. "I think you should see this." He held out a long curved bone. A rib, it looked like. "This is the piece they took."

She looked back at the boys now trembling harder than ever. "Why?" she asked, though she wasn't sure if she was asking the lads or Mr. Winkleigh or the world in general. None of this made sense.

"Look closer," Mr. Winkleigh said. "Here." He pointed to some dark markings on the bone.

Elaine leaned in. A figure had been carved into its surface. She did not touch the bone, but she pulled Mr. Winkleigh's hand holding it closer. It seemed to be some kind of symbol. A bird, like a crow or a chough, with what appeared to be a lantern hanging from its beak.

She looked up at Mr. Winkleigh. "This looks like a smugglers brand."

Mr. Winkleigh nodded.

"Are you saying John was somehow involved in smuggling?" She could not believe it.

The squire's theory about Gareth rang in her ears, but it could not be true. It was hard to tell who was involved in smuggling rings and who wasn't, so secretive was the whole scheme.

But this was all nonsense. Neither of them was a smuggler of any kind. They could never have hidden that from her.

Mr. Winkleigh shook his head. "I'm not saying any such thing." He placed the rib back on the table in the spot it would have been during John's life. The smuggler's brand came to rest over what would have been John's heart. "Just thought you should see it."

In any case, this mark had been made long after his death. If John had been involved in the smuggling and not simply a victim, why bother to carve this symbol above his heart after his flesh had rotted away.

"We should show this to my father, but after the squire leaves." No sense adding fuel to the fire that stoked Squire Stroud's far-fetched ideas, but her father should definitely know.

Which brought her back to her first question. She stood in front of the boys again. "Why? Why did you take this bone?"

Willy White-Top shook his head. "We didn't know it 'ad that on it."

Of the whole pile of bones laid out on that table, they'd happened to select the one with the marking on it? Never.

Unless there were more that had been branded. "Mr. Winkleigh, could you please check the bones that none others are marked."

"Already done so. Couldn't find nothing else."

Elaine turned back to the boys. "Do not lie to me. Why are you after this bone?"

A long moment of silence followed, then a faint whisper from Sandy Will.

Willy White-Top's elbow landed hard in Sandy Will's side.

"What was that?" Elaine bent forward to listen.

"He'll kill us." His little voice barely made a sound.

That was probably the most truth she'd ever gotten out of them about the whole affair. This explained much about the two wandering children. They *did* work—not down in the mines, not at the fisheries, not with the bal maidens, but with the smugglers. Along with their parents, no doubt. A part of her didn't want to know who they belonged to anymore. It was so much easier when the smuggling went on beyond her sight. Now the lads were caught up in something that could very well lead to their demise.

"Who?" she asked again, but both sets of lips remained shut tight. "You must tell me. It could lead us to the man who killed my brother. The man who killed Mr. Kemp."

"What are you talking about?" Her father stood in the doorway to the kitchen.

At last. "Is the squire gone?" she asked.

He gave a nod.

"Come and see this." Elaine motioned him over to the table, and Mr. Winkleigh lifted the shroud. She pointed at the mark, and her father bent close to study it.

He lifted the rib, and all three of them peered at it.

"A smuggler's brand?" he asked.

"I believe so," Elaine said.

"Have you ever seen this before?" he asked the butler.

"No, sir. Not this one."

"Why is it on the rib?" He ran a finger over the mark at the same time a click came from behind them.

Elaine spun around in time to see the door swing shut and nothing of the two Williams. She ran to the door and flung it open just as the lads reached the edge of the lawn. "They're getting away!" she cried.

CHAPTER TWENTY

Elaine

Elaine pulled her cloak tighter around her shoulders against the cold and drizzle of the day. Her feet sank and sloshed with every step into the damp field. Last night's rain had left the fields a marshland. The shortcut to Gareth's had not been the best idea. Better to have kept to the lane.

The Williams had not been recovered. She doubted she'd ever see them again. Her father had sent men after them but with no luck. They'd be in hiding now. Likely whipped raw by whomever it was who had sent them to retrieve the marked bone in the first place.

At the pleas of her mother, her father had not called Squire Stroud back to investigate. Her mother was ready to move on. As she'd said for the millionth time, finding out who had done it would not bring her son back. She was right, of course. Especially since Elaine was the one ultimately responsible for John's death, and if she had a way to bring him back, she would have done so long before now.

Elaine had talked to her father about the mark, but he'd not let go of the squire's theory that Gareth was somehow involved. After tossing and turning in her bed all night, she'd decided to ask Gareth herself. He knew more about the people and their goings-on than anyone at Havencross. He might recognize the brand.

The wind was silent this morning, and the clouds hung low, stroking the fields with foggy fingers. She stopped and looked out across the heath. A few trees here and there, though they kept themselves sparse. Patches of yellow gorse. The rest blanketed from sight behind a vale of gray mist. This was the weather she'd convinced herself she was happy to leave behind.

Now here, standing in the crisp air with the gulls calling from beyond the fog, this was why she loved it. A mysterious, almost magical landscape.

No wonder the legends of Arthur and his knights wandered these forgotten parts.

And no wonder it was so perfect for smugglers. She glanced over her shoulder. The mist crowded in and thoughts of Gareth's poor father found along the nearby ditch hurried her on. She'd walked these fields for years with never a thought for danger. Now too much had happened.

One by one, the vitals of her life had been stripped away, leaving her carved out and hollow, like the reed whistles Gareth had made her when they were children. She thanked heaven again for Lord Chiverton, counting her blessings that he still cared for her.

She turned into Lowentop through a gap in the stone wall. Gareth's dogs bounded at her, barking as if to wake the dead.

"Hush, there," she said, reaching out so they would recognize her scent.

Gareth did not appear. Hopefully he was not down at Polkreath already. She'd tried to get here early enough to beat him out, but that was not easy to do.

She knocked on the rear door, just as she used to do. Perhaps she should have gone around to the front, but this didn't feel like a formal visit, not this early in the morning.

Mrs. Penmoor answered the door. She gave Elaine a little bow. "Miss Cardinham."

"Hello, Mrs. Penmoor." Elaine stepped across the threshold into the warmth of the kitchen. "I was hoping to see Mr. Kemp before he set off today."

The housekeeper shook her head.

Elaine had been too late after all. He'd already gone.

"Wait here, please, miss." Mrs. Penmoor set down her lump of bread dough and left the kitchen. She heard the woman's feet plodding up the stairs.

Elaine scooted a chair closer to the fire and sat, lifting her feet toward the heat to dry off the morning dew.

Mrs. Kemp entered. "Oh, you poor dear, you'll catch your death for sure. Get her a blanket, Mrs. Penmoor, and a nice cup of warm tea. Better make it comfrey."

It was a sign of Elaine's former place at this house that Mrs. Kemp thought nothing of meeting her in the kitchen.

Mrs. Penmoor handed her a thick wool blanket, but Elaine declined. The fire was plenty warm.

Mrs. Kemp pulled a chair beside her. "Mrs. Penmoor tells me you have news of Gareth."

"News?" She hadn't heard anything about Gareth—at least not anything more than what his mother must know. Perhaps there was an announcement to be made about him and Miss Tippet. That was the only newsworthy bit of information she imagined Mrs. Kemp might mean.

Elaine's heart stumbled like a horse that leapt over a low wall only to find the ground falling away on the other side. Would Gareth really marry Miss Tippet? She was all wrong for him.

"Miss Cardinham?"

Elaine had not heard a word of what Mrs. Kemp had just said.

"We haven't seen him yet since two nights past. I thought you might have heard something of him."

"He is still missing?" That explained Mrs. Kemp's furrowed brow. "I'm sure he's busy either at the mine or somewhere else. He might still be with Lord Chiverton trying to fix the phaeton." That would also explain why she hadn't seen Lord Chiverton for the last two days either. They were to be married in only three days' time, and she thought Lord Chiverton would have come by yesterday. He must still be busy with his carriage situation.

Mrs. Kemp was shaking her head. "The phaeton is still in our stable."

Squire Stroud's blue eyes appeared in her mind. If Gareth had anything to do with the smugglers and John's death, he would have known they'd find the mark. He might have fled. The truth was she knew very little of what he'd been up to these past five years. And his wealth had significantly improved.

If only she'd never heard the squire's half-witted theories. They were playing tricks on her mind. There was absolutely no chance, not one in a million, Gareth could be involved in smuggling.

"I'm sure he's with Lord Chiverton. Even though they have not yet come to recover the broken carriage, it does not mean they are not together working on it. Perhaps they had to go as far as Launceston."

Mrs. Kemp did not look at all mollified. "Wait here." She left the room soundlessly.

Elaine waited, her feet still resting on the hearth. A faint wisp of steam rose as they dried.

Mrs. Kemp returned. "You're an educated woman, are you not, Miss Cardinham?"

"Uh, well. I suppose I've had my share of schooling." She and John had had a governess until John was sent off to school. Then it was just Elaine and Miss Bassett.

Mrs. Kemp glanced around the kitchen, but it was empty of anyone else. Mrs. Penmoor had left them alone to talk. "I found this in his room, and it's got me worried sick about him." She held out a small folded note. "Only problem is I can't read it. It's written in some sort of code."

Elaine took it. The direction on the front contained nothing more than *T. S.* The wafer was broken and left no clues as to the sender. She glanced up at Mrs. Kemp, the woman's hair pulled back in a frantic knot and her eyes brimming with belted panic.

Mrs. Kemp had no one left in her family beyond Gareth. There was a child who had died in infancy, and then her husband had been taken from her. It was no wonder she was quick to raise the alarm. Still, it was hard not to let the contagion spread.

She unfolded the letter. It was not written in code. It was a few short lines of French.

Elaine's French was rusty at best. As hard as they'd tried to push it on her, she'd found it of little use. Her eyes went straight to the end to identify the sender, but there was no signature. Wait, there was something there. She held the letter closer to the fire. With the bright light glowing behind it, she saw a symbol that turned her insides to stone.

A chough holding a lantern in its thin, curved beak.

What had John gotten himself mixed up in?

"What is it?" Mrs. Kemp leaned over her shoulder. "What does it say?"

"I don't know. I haven't . . . Let me try to decipher. It is in French."

Mrs. Kemp returned to her chair and perched on the edge of the seat.

The lettering was rushed and difficult to make out, but she was able to read it without too much trouble.

Schedule unchanged.

Dragon's head prepared.

Three spouts mark the spot.

Twelve smocks ready.

"What is it?" Mrs. Kemp asked again.

"It's hard to say." She wasn't sure how much to tell Mrs. Kemp. She didn't understand it herself, but it smacked heavily of smuggling. "Did Gareth write this?"

"I found it on his desk. I don't know where it came from, but it's not in his hand. And Gareth didn't know French." She was already speaking of Gareth as if he were gone.

Elaine studied the letter again. *Schedule unchanged.* That seemed straightforward enough. *Dragon's head prepared* meant nothing to her. *Three spouts* . . . Water spouts? That made no sense. Maybe she'd translated it wrong. A smock was a long, heavy shirt worn mostly by the local farmers.

Under no circumstances would she tell Mrs. Kemp that her son might be a smuggler. No. That was not what she meant. She didn't believe he was a smuggler; he'd just gotten mixed up with them somehow. Just like his father had, and they all knew what had happened to him.

Elaine took a deep breath. Steady on. Don't make Mrs. Kemp fret more than she already was. "I'm not sure what it means. The words seem to be nonsense. Perhaps if you let me take it to my father, he will know."

Mrs. Kemp nodded. "Yes. Yes. Mr. Cardinham will know what to do. Oh, if only my husband were still here; he'd have everything worked out."

Elaine tucked the note into her reticule, donned her bonnet, and pulled her cloak snugly around her shoulders. "I'll send word as soon as I know anything."

Mrs. Kemp nodded.

As soon as she cleared the gap in the stone wall, Elaine had the letter out again. The day had not cleared during her time inside Lowentop. Rather, the fog had closed in even more, and she could scarce make out more than a few yards around her. She'd better keep to the lanes and avoid losing her bearings in the heavy mist.

The words of the letter tumbled through her mind. *Dragon's head. Dragon's head. Dragon. The head of a dragon.* She smacked her palm on her forehead. Gareth would have chided her for her lack of knowledge of the Cornish language. *Pen* was the Cornish word for a hill or headland. Half the names in Cornwall started with *pen. Dragon's head* would become *Pendragon.* Uther Pendragon.

Whatever it was that was happening—and she felt safe assuming it was a lugger ship making a drop of contraband—would be happening at or near the seat of Uther Pendragon. Tintagel castle.

The clatter of horse hooves came thundering down the lane. She leapt to the side, quickly tucking the letter away in her reticule.

A horse appeared like a ghost from the mist.

"Elaine?" Lord Chiverton reined his beast to a halt and slipped off. He rounded the head of his horse and stood in front of her. "I was just coming to see you." He took her hands in his. "Your fingers are like ice. Where have you been?" He rubbed his gloved hands over her red fingers.

"I've been over at Lowentop. Mr. Kemp has been gone a few days, and his mother is quite the worrier." She didn't mention that this time her worries might be justified. "We thought he might be with you, helping get the repairs started for your carriage. Have you seen him?"

Lord Chiverton shook his head. "He was helping me, and he very kindly took my high flyer and stored it in his stable. I haven't seen him since late two nights past though."

He offered his arm, and she took it. Here was a man she could depend on. She leaned closer, and he rested his arm around her shoulders, warm and heavy, grounding her.

"I can see you're worried too," he said.

"No," she said. "Not really. I'm sure he's fine. It is his mother I'm concerned for. It is not like Gareth to keep her in distress."

"Well, let's get you home and warmed, and we can figure out how to find him. I am at your service."

He pulled the reins over his horse's head, holding them with one hand and her with the other, leading them both down the lane toward Havencross.

She turned over the words of the letter in her mind as they walked. Smocks and spouts. What could it all mean? If she could figure it out, perhaps she could warn the squire and put a stop to their plans.

Lord Chiverton was speaking to her. She nodded and agreed without really hearing. Perhaps it would be better to take the letter to Mr. Tippet. It would be something if the Landguard could intervene in time to capture the smugglers.

"Elaine?"

"Hmm?"

He grinned. "I get the feeling there is more on your mind. I had to say your name three times to get your attention."

She did have much on her mind. The letter most of all. She could show it to him. Get his opinion about it. At the very least he might know if she'd translated it correctly.

It was a risk. She didn't want to implicate Gareth in a smuggling scheme. But if she didn't tell Lord Chiverton, she would be following in the footsteps of her father. That was not the kind of marriage she wanted. No secrets. No lies. Elaine would be no better if she started her marriage by keeping secrets from her husband.

"There *is* something on my mind." She removed the note and unfolded it. "I've been trying to figure this letter out."

He took it from her. His eyes ran across the writing, widening as he went. "This is interesting. Where did you get it?"

"Mr. Kemp had it. I don't know where it came from."

"He did, did he? That is even more interesting."

"Why? What do you think it means?"

He shrugged. "It's written in French."

"Yes." She leaned over the letter as he held it. "It's about smuggling, I think. This part here I've figured out. Dragon's head refers to the ruins of Tintagel. The birthplace of Arthur Pendragon."

This brought a splash of surprise to his face.

"The part about the spouts I have no idea. But here, the twelve smocks. I remember something that Gareth—Mr. Kemp—told me about smugglers: that they wear these farm smocks when they are unloading goods from lugger to shore. I believe this means there will be twelve men to move the cargo once it lands at the old dock at Tintagel."

He stared at her. "You are more clever than I gave you credit for. I only wonder if your Mr. Kemp has gotten entangled with spies. These are dangerous times, and our country is crawling with informants for the French."

"No. I don't think so." She pointed to the faint symbol at the bottom of the letter. "That's a smuggler's mark. I'm sure of it."

"Hmm. Nothing gets past you."

He should not be so astonished. Smuggling held a long and inglorious history in Cornwall. It was not so hard for her to work out the letter's subject.

"I still can't figure the three spouts. But I think this is enough to take to the Landguard."

"Indeed. They would be happy to have this information, I'm sure of it. You'll be the heroine of Camelford."

"Perhaps even put an end to the smugglers who have been marauding these parts," she said. "Did you know they've killed five people in as many years. Including my brother, John, and Gareth—Mr. Kemp's—father."

Now that she'd started talking, she couldn't stop. Unburdening herself to Lord Chiverton was like standing in a ray of sun cutting through the dense fog. And like a bird after it warms itself in the glow, she could fly away, so light she had become. No wonder Uncle Charles and Aunt Rose had no secrets between them if this was how it felt.

Now, if only she could discover the whereabouts of Gareth. "Are you sure you have not seen Mr. Kemp at all yesterday or today?" This was the only thing still holding her earthbound.

"I'm sure. Not since the night before last."

If only the letter could point her to his whereabouts.

"No need to hide it," Lord Chiverton said. "I can see you are worried about your friend." He put one hand on her cheek, his thumb smoothing away the creases in her brow. "It suits you that you care about your friends. Kindness looks well on you, my love."

She smiled.

He loved her. And in three days' time, she would be his wife.

He leaned closer. "I hate to see you so distressed, but it feels like providence has brought me to you this gray and secluded morning."

"Why is that?"

The fog pressed in around them, absorbing all other sounds except their own breathing. It was a land of silence and stillness, the mist cloaking them in a world of only her and Lord Chiverton.

He put his hand on the small of her back, drawing her close. "I so rarely get you all to myself. But here you have landed in my arms, just as you have landed in my heart." His eyes fixed on hers, then drifted to her mouth. He lowered his head until his breath tingled her lips. Until his locks of straw-colored hair tickled her skin. Until his lips pressed on hers. Softly at first, then harder.

His hand moved from her cheek to her throat. Pressing. Squeezing. Her eyes flew open. She pushed—pounded against his chest.

CHAPTER TWENTY-ONE

Gareth

Gareth pulled once more against the irons binding his wrists.

"Agh," he groaned. His shoulder was bruised. And very possibly Chiverton had also broken his rib. Thank goodness that man was wealthy enough to afford boots of soft leather. Had he been wearing heavy miner's shoes, it would have been much worse. So that was lucky.

He had no idea how long he'd been chained to this post deep under the Cornish coast. It must be over two days now he'd gone without food or water. Every blink was like wiping sand across his eyes. Every swallow like sawdust. If Chiverton was going to kill him, why did he make such slow work of it?

Of course, he'd prefer to live, mostly for his mother's sake, but his patience with this tethering had ended several hours back. Some water wouldn't be unwelcome either.

Shouting came from somewhere in the tunnels. A woman's voice, from the sound of it, though it was hard to tell because everything echoed, distorted as it bounced its way down the rocky corridors.

A shame he didn't have a hammer and pick or he could look for tin instead of wasting his time slumped against an oak beam. Or copper. Both would fetch a good price.

A single lantern burned above him, hanging on a nail. It was enough to let him see a flash of pale muslin.

"You are a pig!"

Gareth's head jerked up.

Elaine. *No*. By St. Just, no.

She landed hard on the ground beside him, her hair spilling around her. Her eyes red and filled with a fury he'd never seen in her before.

Chiverton stood over them while his lackey roped her to the post beside Gareth. Chiverton's store of iron cuffs must have run dry.

"I'm sorry, my love," Chiverton said, "but I don't think I can trust you out there. I'll keep you here where you'll be safe." He bent forward and cupped her chin. "How about one more kiss before I go?"

He leaned closer.

Gareth jerked against his chains. Blast these fetters. "You didn't offer me a kiss," he rasped, trying to get Chiverton off Elaine. "My pride is deeply injured."

It worked. Chiverton turned on Gareth. "What pride could you possibly have? You are the son of a tin man—a red-mucked laborer without even the sense to accept a lucrative proposal when it is laid at your feet."

Gareth had learned—while Chiverton was beating him with his soft leather boot—that Chiverton had extended an invitation to Gareth's father to join the smuggling ring. Apparently, his father had declined. Chiverton had not taken the rejection lightly, and it had cost Gareth's father his life. Now Gareth was following in his father's footsteps.

"It's your fault she's here," Chiverton said. "Should have kept your red-dirt hands off my strongbox. Then, instead of mingling with the worms in your grave, you'd be attending our wedding." He laughed.

Gareth would have spat on him if he'd had any moisture left to give. It wasn't Elaine's fault he'd taken the letter, so why punish her for it? Unless the letter somehow implicated her. Even so, he was the only one to have seen it. She was no threat.

Chiverton leaned forward and tucked the note into Gareth's waistcoat pocket, patting it a few times as if tucking a beloved child in bed.

Gareth looked at Chiverton, then over at Elaine. How the devil did she get the letter?

"I'm sorry, Gareth," she said. "I didn't know."

"At last, you get what you've been wanting all along, Mr. Kemp. To be with Elaine for the rest of your life." He drew a pistol from his breeches and aimed it at Gareth.

"No!" Elaine screamed at the same moment a shot thundered through the cave.

Gareth clamped his jaws together to keep from yelling. His leg stung like the devil, and a trickle of blood seeped out, making a dark stain on his thigh.

"A little assurance that you won't try anything foolish."

"Or what? You'll shoot me?" His voice sounded like gravel.

Chiverton laughed again, then strode away.

"I hate you," Elaine cried after him. "I hate you with the hatred of a thousand hateful fiends. You are the ugliest, most worthless, most dishonorable man in the world, and I hate you."

Chiverton saluted her without turning his head. Then he was gone around a bend in the cavern, his lackey trotting along behind him.

Elaine turned to Gareth. "Are you hurt?"

They didn't have time enough left for him to enumerate. Besides, she meant only the shot. "I'm fine," he said. "It barely grazed me."

Her eyes hardened. "I hate him."

"Are you sure?" he asked. "Because you sounded a little uncertain."

She pursed her lips at him. A look he'd received many a time from her. Nice to know that amidst threats to her body and soul, she hadn't lost her impertinence.

A bruise of black and purple encircled her neck just above her collarbone. He was going to kill that man.

"Your neck," he said.

"Oh." She swallowed gingerly. "I'll live."

Whether or not she lived had yet to be determined. They had not seen the last of Chiverton. Would that he had never met the man. That was what he got for playing the Good Samaritan. He should have left him and his ridiculous high flyer to rot in the hedgerow.

Now he'd gotten Elaine involved. No. That was not right. She'd gotten herself involved when she'd consented to marry the imbecile. Gareth was merely responsible for putting her neck on the chopping block.

"I'm sorry, Elaine," he said with his dry and raspy voice. "Chiverton is right. This is all my fault."

She shook her head, and her whole body slumped as if her strength had leaked out now that Chiverton was gone and she had no one to yell at. She could yell at him. Heaven knew he deserved it.

"How could any of this be your fault, Gareth? I am a blind fool. A blind and stupid fool. He didn't care for me at all. All he wanted was Havencross because," her voice took on a haughty air, mimicking Chiverton, "it is so well situated for smuggling." She leaned her head back, thumping it on the thick oak beam holding up the wooden supports of the rock ceiling.

"So I gathered."

"I should have known." Her voice shook. "The moment the rumors started in London, I knew that no respectable man would connect himself to me. To my disgraced family. When he asked for my hand, I should have known. I trusted him, I gave him my heart, and he was a deceiver all along."

"Did you, Elaine? Did you give him your heart?" From what he'd seen of their association, there hadn't been much exchanging of hearts. He'd seen civility, cordiality, affection even, but nothing like the giving of a heart to the keeping of another.

She shrugged her shoulders and turned away.

He glanced down at the letter tucked into his waistcoat. "What I don't understand is the letter. How did it fall back into his hands?"

She looked over at him, her face still beautiful despite the long, drawn look. "Your mother found it. And when you didn't come home, she gave it to me to help find you. She knew I could read French. And like the fool I am, I asked Lord Chiverton's help to decipher it. Because I didn't want there to be secrets between us. No secrets. No lies." She practically spat the words out. "See? Do you see how stupid I am?" A few tears pooled in the corners of her eyes. She tried to wipe them on her shoulder, but with her hands bound she could not reach.

Gareth tugged again on his irons, not caring about the burn in his arms nor the trickle of blood leaking from his leg. None of that caused as much pain as watching Elaine suffer and him utterly useless to help.

"The letter contained hints about a smuggler's drop, but I didn't know what they all meant. So I asked him." She glanced over at Gareth. "The worst of it is I think Lord Chiverton is also responsible for the death of John."

"From five years ago? That doesn't seem likely." Chiverton could not have been operating in these parts that long. Certainly not long enough to be behind John's death. Though it was most certainly Chiverton who was responsible for his father's death. Whether by his own hands or the hands of another, he'd given the order.

"I think it might be." She looked so forlorn. "Gareth, we found a smuggler's brand on one of John's bones. The same mark was also on Chiverton's letter."

"Mark? What mark?" He'd not seen it. Chiverton had taken smuggling in a new direction if he was murdering people and then branding their bones. It was the pirates who committed heinous acts like that. Chiverton would do better to take on piracy. Seemed more his style.

"A chough carrying a lantern. It was on a rib bone. And on his letter, though it was . . . very . . . faint."

Her eyes had locked onto the letter protruding from his waistcoat pocket as if he had a powder keg strapped to his chest. He bent his head forward to see what had captivated her attention. He moaned with the pain, his ribs burning. From his angle and with his hands bound behind him, he couldn't get a full view.

"What it is?"

She smiled. "It's nothing."

She'd always been a terrible liar. "Elaine. When has deceiving me ever worked for you?"

She pursed her lips again. "I was surprised that Lord Chiverton left the letter with you, that's all. I thought he would keep it. What is a spout, do you think?"

"Nice try." She'd not divert him so easily. He pressed his chin to his chest and studied the letter again. There was something off about it. It was bigger and darker, as if yellowed by time. "This is not the same note I found in Chiverton's phaeton."

Something flashed in her eyes. "Really," she said, her voice pitched a few octaves higher than normal. "I want to know what a spout is. In the smuggler's note, it mentioned *three spouts mark the spot*. That's the only part I couldn't figure out."

He leaned his head back, resting it on the beam. He was still losing blood, and the effects were taking their toll. He couldn't pass out though. Not until he saw Elaine safely out of this mess.

"A spout is a smuggler's lantern fashioned so that no light can be seen from the side, but only from straight on. A guide for the ship still at sea." He sighed. "Now, what do you know about this letter in my pocket?"

She looked away. "Nothing. How should I know anything about Lord Chiverton and his dealings?"

He didn't have the strength to press further. Chiverton's shot was doing more damage than he'd thought.

"Gareth? What's wrong?" She looked down at his leg. "You said it was just a graze."

"I'm fine." He gave her his most charming smile.

"I daresay you're not very good at lying either." She pulled against her bindings, leaning as far as she could to see his leg.

He twisted, grunting as the musket ball lit every nerve on fire. He managed to turn his thigh just enough that she could see the red stain leeching away his life.

She gasped. "Gareth, you're bleeding."

"Really? I hadn't noticed. I suppose I should have known that would happen after your lover shot me." Immediately he regretted his words. He didn't want to spend his last hours of life bitter at her. "I'm sorry." He cautiously lowered his leg so it rested on the floor. "I didn't mean that." He would give anything if Elaine could make it out of here. But unless he could stop the bleeding, he wouldn't be around long enough to help.

Elaine was silent for a long time. Too long.

"Elowen?"

"Gareth," she said in small voice. "I have something I need to tell you. Something I've never told anyone." But she didn't continue. She gazed off at the wall of black rock shimmering with seeping moisture.

He closed his eyes, waiting, his energy draining.

"It is my fault John was killed," she said at last, so softly he barely heard it.

What a ridiculous thing to say. "But—"

"Shh. Please. Just listen."

He nodded. He would have made the motion of locking his lips except for the inconvenience of having his hands fettered.

"I sent John on an errand. He didn't want to go, but I begged and pleaded, and he finally consented. It was late—long past dark and a storm about. He rode off on his horse, even though the errand was not so far. He thought if he hurried on horseback he could beat the weather."

"But he never came home," Gareth finished.

He remembered only too well how John Cardinham's horse had been found wandering the fields of Havencross with no rider. The search had ensued with every person Mr. Cardinham could get his hands on out day and night looking for his son. Finally, they had to assume him dead. A few weeks later, the Cardinhams packed their trunks and fled to London, never to be seen again—until they fled back home. Quite a bit of fleeing for one family.

Coming only days after Elaine rejected him, it had been one of the lowest points in his life, to lose both his closest friends.

"It's not your fault," he said.

"Hush," she chastised him again. "How is it you cannot simply listen?"

"Sorry."

"I know Lord Chiverton had something to do with John's death because the errand I sent him on was to deliver a letter. The letter that is now stuffed into your waistcoat pocket."

He looked down again. "What is in this letter that could possibly warrant John's death?"

Elaine shook her head. "Nothing. Nothing at all. He must have been in the wrong place at the wrong time. He must not have kept his eyes down."

"So he was killed and tucked away in the cave as a warning to all. A claim about who this coast belonged to."

If Gareth got out of here, he would do whatever it took to rid his home of these pests. Better to do without tea and French brandy and lace from Valenciennes than to live with marauders crawling the coastline.

"Who was the letter for?"

Elaine glanced away. "No one. It doesn't matter now. We should focus on how to escape."

He let it go. She didn't want to talk about it anymore, and he didn't have the energy to press. It was absurd for her to blame herself. No one had given his father a letter, and the same thing had happened to him. The only people responsible were the smugglers. Chiverton and whoever else he had working for him.

He leaned his head back. "I would love to escape. I've been trying for two days, and all it's got me is bloody wrists and a ball in my leg."

She tugged on her bindings. "I've almost . . ." She grunted and pulled until she cried out in pain. Then her eyes roved the cavern, though almost naught was visible in the dim light of the lantern.

When she looked back at him, there was real panic in her eyes. "I think he means to kill us."

Gareth had already come to this conclusion when Chiverton had beaten him in this very cavern. "You'll be fine," he lied. "He wouldn't dare kill a gentleman's daughter from the most prominent family in the area. He just doesn't want you sounding the alarm."

She watched him carefully. He stared right back at her, hoping he could convince her, but she was right when she'd also pointed out that they knew each other too well.

He could barely stay awake. All his strength was leaking out onto the rocky floor. If not for Elaine, he would have succumbed to unconsciousness already. How easy to close his eyes and drift away.

He snapped his eyes open.

"Once they unload the goods and melt back into the countryside," he paused to catch his breath, "you and Chiverton can come to an agreement, and he'll set you free."

"I'm never—" She let out a groan, straining against her bindings, and her hands broke free.

CHAPTER TWENTY-TWO

Elaine

Elaine's wrists were on fire, but she'd done it. She'd gotten out. The man who'd tied her up must have been a little hesitant to bind a woman, for she'd finally been able to work her hands free.

She scooted across the jagged ground to Gareth. His face was whiter than a sheet, and his eyes stared at nothing.

"Gareth." She patted his cheek, and his focus snapped back. "We are leaving this place."

Elaine searched the cave for anything she could use to free him. She found a small rock and hammered at the irons, but they did not give. Her hair had long since come out, and she had no pins to offer so he could pick the lock. But there had to be something. A loose nail. A broken knife. She found nothing.

"Go," he said, his eyes like slits of darkness. "Get out of here."

"Hush. Don't speak." If she could at least stop his bleeding, he'd last long enough for her to find help. She removed a boot and pulled off her stocking.

He watched her with a smirky grin. Head of a household, owner of a mine, and still a boy.

"Stop," she chided. "It's for your wound."

She knelt beside Gareth and wrapped the stocking around the hole in his leg, looping it twice. He gasped when she pulled it tight.

"I'm sorry," she whispered. "We must stop the bleeding." The wound itself was not lethal—assuming it didn't turn septic. It was the slow and steady loss of blood threatening his life.

He was barely conscious as it was. She pressed her hand against his cheek. Cold as the stones around them. She draped her cloak over him and placed a soft kiss on his forehead.

What he really needed was water, but there was none to be found save that which seeped from the rocks. She held her hand to the wall where a slow thread of water trickled back and forth, making its way down the jagged rocks.

She managed to catch a few drops in her cupped hand. He startled when her hand pressed to his lips.

"Here's a swallow of water."

He drank, then she took the remaining moisture and dabbed it across his parched lips.

"Leave," he whispered.

"I cannot leave you." She brushed some matted hair from his forehead.

"Get help. I'll be fine."

If Chiverton returned and found her free, her chance to do Gareth any good was over. If she escaped, perhaps she could find help. Neither prospect seemed right, but one at least gave her a small glimmer of hope.

"I'll be back for you, I promise," she told him.

He gave her one small nod.

"You wait, do you hear me? You wait for me."

He smiled, but he was so weak only one side of his mouth went up.

If he died, she would never forgive him. She would never forgive herself. One more death to add to her growing pile of mistakes. But this time, Lord Chiverton would be made to pay.

Elaine headed down the tunnel—the same one Chiverton had come down. The going was pitch black, and she had to keep her hands out in front to avoid the walls. The corridors turned and split. She paused and listened, trying to decide which way to go. She made her best guess, but it happened time and again until she thought she was going in circles.

She tried to focus on direction, but her mind seemed tied to Gareth. She'd stopped the bleeding, but it would take awhile for him to recover his strength.

The letter. She'd left it in Gareth's pocket. She started back for it, but then halted. It was useless. She would waste valuable time trying to wind her way back to him. She'd get it later, when she returned with the Landguard.

If she had accepted Gareth's offer five years ago, she would have never gone to London and met Lord Chiverton. Never sent John off with that blasted letter, and he would still be alive too.

One wrong choice had set so much in motion, and none of it good. How could she ever have known that by refusing Gareth's hand naught but misfortune would follow?

So many lives ruined. John's, her mother's and father's, hers, and now Gareth's. At the time, it had seemed the right thing to do, no matter her feelings for him. What she wouldn't give now to live that one moment over again.

The echo of voices up ahead gave her pause. She'd been walking the tunnels blindly, one hand on the wall and the other on her head to keep her from hitting it on the low ceiling.

A dim light glowed, winding its way to her from somewhere ahead. Gareth's only chance of surviving depended on whether or not she could get help.

She peered around the bend into a larger chamber that spread out on both sides of an underground stream cutting through the rock. She'd never seen this place before. She'd never come across anything like this near her home. How far from Havencross had they taken her while she was unconscious?

Three men rolled a barrel of spirits along the cavern floor. It clattered loudly along the rocky ground. Two women stood over an open crate, lifting out small packets and securing them to their corsets so they hung down around their legs but would be concealed by their skirts. No one seemed to notice or care that the ladies' legs were in full view of every man in the chamber—least of all the two women. They laughed in soft undertones as they went about their clandestine business.

A stack of smaller barrels labeled "tobacco" lined the wall closest to her. The men disappeared into the tunnel. The women's backs were toward her. In four quick strides, she ducked into the space between the tubs and the wall of the cave.

She was fooling herself to think she could ever make it out without being found. Utterly foolish. But she had to try. It was either die in the cave or die in the attempt. So she inched her way to the end of the stack of contraband.

Another round of thwacks announced the return of the barrel men. A plan quickly formed. As soon as the men pushed the enormous barrel into the chamber, she slipped out into the tunnel they'd just come through, praying with all her might she wouldn't bump headfirst into Lord Chiverton.

Torches burned at intervals along the walls of this part of the cave. Though she was beginning to think the word *cave* did not fully encompass the system of twisting tunnels she found herself in.

More likely, this was an idle mine. In which case, she was probably near the old Tregavern Mine, the only one in the area in disuse. A few miles south of Havencross but still on the coast. Tregavern Mine bordered Squire Stroud's land. If she managed to escape from the underground, she'd head there. He'd be able to send a runner to Mr. Tippet and rouse the rest of the Landguard.

If she escaped.

More voices came echoing down the passage toward her.

She ducked into a side tunnel to get out of the torchlight, withdrawing into the darkness.

The voices grew louder. One was unmistakably Lord Chiverton's. His tall frame flashed into view for a moment as he passed along the main tunnel. He was walking in the direction she'd just come from. It must have been an hour or more since he'd roped her to the post beside Gareth. How much longer till he went to check on his prisoners and found one of them missing?

She was running out of time.

A whisper of cool air blew past her, chilling the back of her neck and rustling her skirts. Outside air was coming in from somewhere behind her. Mines had many shafts and air vents; if she could find one close enough to the surface, she might be able to get out.

She edged along, hurrying as fast as she dared to avoid falling into a shaft. She'd been going only a minute or so when the shouting reached her.

"Sound the alarm!" a man called.

"I want every passage searched," Lord Chiverton called. "Light it up. Find her." He did not sound at all pleased.

She hurried faster, her hands running along the sides, her body bent to protect her head. But not low enough. She smacked into a low ceiling rock.

She pressed her hand to where the swelling was already beginning to grow. No time to waste. The floor sloped upward, a welcome sign that she was climbing toward the surface.

The tunnel opened into a crossroads. In the complete darkness, her other senses awoke. The smell of coppery earth. The taste of the damp and tangy air. And the brush of a breeze across her cheek. A breeze that felt ever so slightly different than the cold bite of the mine.

She turned left just as the faint glow of a torch lit the tunnel behind her.

She ran now, not caring that she might fall to her death down a shaft that sank endlessly into the earth. How did Gareth stand it, working in the depths? Eternal darkness. Nothing but faceless rocks in every direction. And yet it was from these depths that the tin and copper came, providing wealth and livelihood to the people of Cornwall.

The hand she'd been trailing along the roof of the cave suddenly hit nothing. She stopped and looked up. Darkness, but different from the rock.

This was the black of a moonless night. The stars were not visible, but their light gave the cloud covering the softest glow. A ventilation shaft. How far up it went, she could not tell. But if she made it to the top, she would be out of the mine and free.

She lifted her skirts, petticoat and all, and tucked them into the bust of her corset. If anyone found her like this, she'd wish she really was dead.

Pushing off the wall, she wedged herself into the shaft. It was hard to be sure, but the sky seemed almost within her reach. It had been a long time since she'd scaled the sides of a mine shaft. Many times her father had scolded her for behaving like a boy. What would he think of her now?

Pressing her body on one side and her legs on the other, she started up. Her foot slipped, and she crashed to the floor, her breath pushed from her body. She gasped a few times, then struggled to her feet, retucking her dress. The voices were getting closer, louder.

She tried again, working her way up slowly, by inches. Light now made its way down the tunnel. This was her last chance. With a few more heaves, she reached the top. If the shaft had been any longer, she never would have made it.

She pulled herself out onto the wet grass of the heath. It must have been raining while she'd been down there. She lay on her back, resting her aching legs.

The fog had lifted, but the night was still dark and the clouds hung low, threatening more rain. No matter the inky night—it signified nothing compared to the pitch black she'd just left behind.

A man's voice rose up through the shaft.

She jumped to her feet, smoothing her frock down to cover her legs. She spun in a circle to get her bearings, but the only thing she was certain of was the sea to the west. It was enough. She headed inland, hoping to recognize her surroundings or find someone to help her. A farmhouse, perhaps. Or a village.

She ran, glancing over her shoulder to make sure she kept the sea to her back. And to watch for lights that might be following her.

The things Lord Chiverton might do to Gareth now that she was gone . . . Elaine shuddered. She half hoped Gareth would be unconscious. Then perhaps he might not suffer more.

A dark figure rose up in front of her. Elaine dove into the heather, keeping flat on the ground. Motionless.

But it was only a stone standing straight up out of the earth. She slowly stood and walked toward it. The old market cross. She'd guessed right. Tregavern Mine.

She turned her direction northward, toward Squire Stroud's house. A mile or two up the lane, it was the closest dwelling where she could get help. She wished she'd chosen a black dress that morning to blend into the night. Especially when shouts began to reach her coming from outside the mine. They'd abandoned the search of the caverns and had taken it topside.

Lord Chiverton's smugglers knew this part of the land better than she did. They made a living of hiding themselves or their goods in every nook and cranny. All she was sure of was that the road turning northward from the market cross would take her right to New Tor House, the home of Squire Stroud. Keeping to the road was risky, but it was also the quickest way to help and safety.

Her years in London had left her soft. Already she was gasping for breath, her lungs and legs burning. But Gareth was waiting for her.

And so she ran. Her arms pumping and her skirts flying around her legs. Her stockingless foot blistered as it rubbed in her shoe. Her breath came hard, and she cursed the damp of Cornwall that saturated the air. When she thought her lungs would burst, she slowed until she could run again.

Squire Stroud's home loomed ahead. Tall and whitewashed, New Tor stood out stark against the night. She hurried up the drive and banged on the door. If anyone was in close pursuit, they would surely hear her frantic knocks.

After several minutes of pounding, the door opened. It wasn't a servant. It was the squire himself. Fully dressed, with the buttons of his waistcoat stretching to almost bursting. His bald head reflected the glow of the candle he held.

"Miss Cardinham?" The shock on his face only deepened the blue of his eyes. "How did you get here?"

She crossed the threshold without being invited. Until she was inside with the door bolted behind her, Lord Chiverton might reach out with his talons and grasp her.

"I apologize for coming so late." In truth, she had no idea what time it was. She paused to catch her breath, bending forward and dragging in a few rasps of air. "And for my state." Red and black stains covered her dress. A rip in the hem exposed her leg up to the knee, and it was not even the leg with the stocking. Naught she could do about it now.

"How did you get here?" he asked again.

"I've come from Tregavern Mine. There are smugglers there moving cargo." She panted as she spoke. "Lord Chiverton leads them, and they have Gareth

Kemp held captive. You must help me." Another pause to rake in some air. "We must send a man to rouse the Landguard. There's no time to lose. Mr. Kemp's life depends on it."

Squire Stroud closed the door. He smiled at her with his gentle eyes and round face. "Come in. Goodness me, your head is bleeding." He handed her a handkerchief.

She dabbed at her forehead, the linen coming away with a large stain of red. Must have happened when she hit her head.

"Come, come, child." He motioned to the sitting room. "You are safe here."

CHAPTER TWENTY-THREE

Gareth

Chiverton sat on a crate in front of Gareth. In one hand he held a burning torch, in the other his pistol.

Elaine's makeshift bandaging had stopped the bleeding. He'd wandered in and out of consciousness for a while, until the shouting had roused him.

If Elaine made it outside the cave, they'd be hard-pressed to catch her. She could run like a rabbit, that girl. That was really all that mattered to him—that Elaine made it safely away.

As for himself, he was a dead man.

"Where is Miss Cardinham?" Chiverton asked. His face was calm and composed as always, but now Gareth understood the fire burning just behind the velvet brown of his eyes.

"I don't know," Gareth said, his voice dry and raspy. His mouth lined with wool. Very dry wool.

"How did she get out?" Chiverton asked, toying with the flintlock of the pistol.

Gareth may not have been at his most clearheaded state when Elaine had escaped her ropes, but he'd been lucid enough. "She pried her hands out. As I've already said."

The back of Chiverton's hand lashed across his face. "Tell me where she is."

The good news was that after being shot in the leg, he had no blood left to wet his cheek.

"Give me some water, and I'll tell you what I know."

Another swipe of Chiverton's hand stung his face. "Tell me what you know, and I'll spare your life."

Not much of a bargaining chip. His life was already forfeit. He had no doubt of that. Chiverton had killed his father for knowing only a fraction of what he now knew.

Gareth laughed. A dry, cracked laugh that sounded like stones being dragged across a floor.

Chiverton stared at him, then tucked the pistol into the waistband of his breeches and left. He returned a minute later with a tin cup. Perhaps even tin from Gareth's own mine. Or maybe the cup Miss Tippet had seen in Wickfern's General Store. Or maybe he'd died hours ago and this was the devil's version of hell.

Chiverton held the cup to Gareth's mouth, tipping it too fast. Gareth had to gulp it down or risk losing it.

After draining the cup, he licked his lips and tasted blood. Interesting. Apparently he *did* have some left to give.

"I think she ran away," Gareth told Chiverton.

Any diversion would help Elaine. The more time Chiverton wasted slapping Gareth across the face, the farther away Elaine could get.

"Where did she run to?"

"I cannot say. She did not tell me."

"You lie," Chiverton said as he prepared his hand for another backlash. "She wouldn't leave you here."

Gareth quickly responded. "I'm telling the truth." He looked right into Chiverton's eyes. "I swear to you I do not know where she is. I was barely conscious. I only know that Miss Cardinham managed to loosen her ropes, then she was free." He leaned his head back against the wooden beam. "Spare me or kill me, it will not make a difference. I've given you the truth."

Chiverton watched him intently. "I believe you," he finally said. "Where do you *think* she might have gone? Your best guess."

Even if he knew that, he would never say. But he could draw out the conversation to keep Chiverton occupied. "That would depend on where we are now." He had a guess, but he'd been knocked senseless during the transportation, waking up only in this one room.

The oaken beams led him to believe he was in part of a mine rather than a cave. Not Polkreath, of that he was sure. Perhaps Long Cross or Tregavern. They were the closest. Tregavern was no longer used, so that would seem the most likely. Maybe even Dunmore, but that was farther inland, and smugglers clung to the sea.

"Let's test your knowledge of the land where you were born and raised, Cornishman. You claim to know this area better than anyone, so I tell you what. You figure out where we are, and I'll let you live."

Re Just. Why was Chiverton such a fool? One can only make the same threat a certain number of times before it ceases to be threatening. Chiverton had crossed that threshold long ago.

He should get on with it already. Gareth did not fear death. His father would be there waiting for him. And John. It was for his mother he wanted to live. She would suffer most if his life ended here. And Elaine. He would endure all Chiverton's lashings if he could be with her one last time. Tell her how he still felt.

Gareth kept to his purpose. There was nothing more he could do, save stall Chiverton and play his mindless game.

"Well," Gareth said, his voice growing stronger. "By the timber work, we are in a mine. The color of the rock speaks more toward tin than copper. That you are here with your gang of free traders would indicate a mine that is idle. I guess Tregavern. Six miles south of Havencross, along the coast. Half a mile west-southwest from the old market cross of St. Gavern. And two miles south of"—he almost said Squire Stroud's, but if Elaine had figured out her location as well, that was the first place she'd go—"Treligga crossroads."

Chiverton caught his pause and grinned. "You mean two miles south of New Tor."

Blast. That was what he got for being a braggart. Gareth shook his head. "She wouldn't go there." Now he was the one who sounded like a fool.

Chiverton's grin twisted into something Gareth could picture on the devil himself. "I hope she does go to the squire. In fact, I'm counting on it."

Then Chiverton's pistol came down hard on Gareth's head.

CHAPTER TWENTY-FOUR

Elaine

"Come and sit by the fire." Squire Stroud pushed a velvet-covered chair closer to the hearth. "I'll call for tea."

Tea? Had he not heard a word she'd spoken? "Squire, I thank you, but there is no time for tea. Mr. Kemp's life is in grave danger. We must get help immediately."

In a matter of hours, the smuggled goods would be distributed and the mine emptied of all trace they'd ever been there, including Gareth.

"Calm yourself, child." He tried again to get her to sit. "Help will be here soon. You've nothing to fear."

Had he already sent word to the Landguard? When? She'd been with him since he opened the door. And come to think of it, where was his staff? Certainly the squire at least kept a few servants. She'd not laid eyes on a housekeep or a footman. The house sounded unnaturally empty. He'd said he'd call for tea, so there must be someone here to call.

Perhaps the old man had less income than she'd thought. Or perhaps they were all in their beds.

Or perhaps she'd made another monumental mistake.

She glanced at the door. "Maybe it would be better if I borrowed a horse and rode myself. If help is already on the way, I could ride home and not trouble you. I'm sure my father is already searching for me."

In a few steps, he was standing right in front of her, his hand wrapping tightly around her upper arm. "Miss Cardinham, I do wish you'd sit." He steered her toward the chair and pushed her down. "Sit before you collapse." He smiled. "Help is on the way. Take a moment to compose yourself, and I will get you something to calm your nerves."

He turned and left the room through the door opposite the fireplace. She jumped out of the chair.

He was with them. The squire was one of them.

She turned the knob on the door. Locked. There was no other way out of the room. A bank of small windows lined one wall. Only one opened, and it was far too small for her to fit through. Not even her head would go through. She spun around and stared at the door as if it could give her all the answers.

She'd heard gentlemen joke in more than one drawing room in London that the entire population of Cornwall was involved in smuggling in one way or another. That was proving to be far too close to the truth.

The squire was in a perfect position to work the operation. To organize the land runners and distribute the goods. He could have planned it all while Lord Chiverton funded the schemes from the comforts of London. Until he came to Cornwall and got his hands dirty.

She didn't know everything about the smuggling rings, but she did know the one cardinal rule. The gentleman paying for the smuggling never got mixed up with those doing the smuggling. Only one man, the operator—in this case Squire Stroud—could know the identity of the investor, Lord Chiverton.

Lord Chiverton had made a mistake. He'd been caught red-handed with that letter, the one addressed to *T. S.*—Thomas Stroud.

No matter how this night ended, that mistake would eventually catch up with him. Squire Stroud would not be able to cover up the disappearance of two more people. Miss Tippet's father would track them down, though probably not soon enough.

She searched the room for any kind of weapon. The squire had been gone a long time. He could be back at any moment. The room was empty of all but the barest of furnishings. A few candles burned in sconces along the wall. She could set fire to the drapes, but that seemed counterproductive to survival. The squire might open the door and let her out, or he might not.

Elaine tried the window again. It was no use, but the cool air felt good, so she left it open. She dug through the drawers of a small chest in the corner.

"Mum?"

She spun around. The door was still closed.

"Mum?" Someone whispered through the open window. It sounded like a child.

She peered out and then down on the tops of two heads. One with hair the color of autumn leaves and the other white as first cream.

"Williams?"

"'E's coming, miss," Willy White-Top said, keeping his voice barely audible.

"The squire?"

"Nay. The other one. From London."

Lord Chiverton. Her suspicions had been correct. These boys were part of a smuggling gang—the squire's gang. They were starting them young these days. The lads probably had no other choice but to submit.

"Can you get me out of here?"

Sandy Will shook his head.

"Sorry, mum," Willy White-Top said. "We don't 'ave a key. But 'ere's this." He jabbed his elbow into Sandy Will.

Sandy Will reached up as high as he could. In his hand was a knife. A fishing knife. The kind used by the fishermen to quickly gut the fish, with a long and slender blade curving to a point.

She stretched her arm out the window as far as she could, but the knife was just out of reach. She pressed harder against the pane.

The thunder of a horse at top speed grew louder and louder.

"'E's coming!" Sandy Will dropped the knife in his panic.

Willy White-Top searched the darkness below the window. Elaine could not see exactly what they were doing, but the horse was getting closer by the moment.

"You can do it," she said, trying to sound as calm as if she was inviting them to come back and play a round of cricket.

Willy White-Top found the knife and held it out again. Trying to reach her groping fingers. At last, she made contact, and the knife was in her hand.

"Thank you," she whispered out the window.

Willy White-Top was already gone, but Sandy Will whispered back, "Sorry we taked yer brother's bone."

His red hair disappeared into the night the same moment a great beast of a horse skidded into the courtyard.

The knife was a small one, dull, and speckled with rust but far better than nothing. She scrambled to hide it even as she heard the front door fly open.

She slipped it into her stays, praying it wouldn't stab her in her own heart, then threw herself back into the chair. She took one deep breath to keep her heart from sounding the alarm.

A key clicked in the lock, and the squire came in. "As promised. Your betrothed is here to take you home."

Squire Stroud must know his ruse did not fool her in the least. She'd already explained to him Lord Chiverton's part in the smuggling ring and the kidnapping of herself and Gareth. For him to come in addressing her as if he was trying to help her showed remarkable audacity.

Lord Chiverton came in on the squire's heels, rushing forward and taking her into his arms. "My love, I've been worried to death. Thank you for keeping her safe, Squire."

The squire bowed as far as his girth would allow, then left the room.

"For whom was that show?" she asked. "Do you think I haven't figured it out yet?"

He smiled the smile that had won her heart only a few months before; now it raised the bile in her throat. "I have been worried, you know. Very worried."

"Worried I'd ruin your plans?"

He ran the back of his fingers along her cheek, and she swatted his hand away.

"Do you know, I think I love you like this even more than the quiet girl from the country lost in the world of London."

How dare he speak of love. How dare he even speak to her as if he hadn't had her tied up no more than a few hours ago.

"How is Gareth?"

"I don't know what you mean." He rested his arm around her. "Come, my love. I'll help you home."

Elaine twisted away. "Stop it. Stop the charade right now. We both know you are not taking me home."

"Of course I am. Your father will be so relieved to have you home and safely away from those smugglers. Such unsavory people to have in your neighborhood. Something really should be done about that. Lucky for you, your handsome husband has rescued you. We are still engaged, after all. What would society say if our engagement was broken? The rumors I started about your father are nothing compared to the mess I could so easily stir up about you. Or your mother."

Elaine glared at him. "It was you? But—How did you know?"

"I keep eyes on all the important people in my life. I was fairly certain I'd won you over, but a little extra assurance always comes in handy. How much easier to convince you to marry me when no one else would take you. Such a sad girl missing her brother."

"You killed John." She dove at him, ready to claw his eyes out.

He caught her, restraining her. "Calm down. I did no such thing. That was the squire's doing long before I came along. I only met Stroud three years ago, at the races in Newmarket."

She shuddered to think back on how Squire Stroud had sat with his merry blue eyes in her drawing room only a few days ago accusing Gareth of John's death. What an actor he was, almost as good as Lord Chiverton himself.

Lord Chiverton may have been innocent of killing John, but three years was plenty of time for Mr. Kemp. "But you did kill Gareth's father."

His silence confirmed it. She hated him even more, if that were possible. "You are mistaken if you think for one moment—"

"And we must think of the younger Mr. Kemp. You wouldn't want any harm to come to him."

"You're threatening me?"

"Of course not. You are perfectly safe."

But he was threatening Gareth. He had more up his sleeve, this demon from Chiverton. "What do you want?"

"What I've always wanted: Havencross. I will establish the biggest smuggling ring in all of Cornwall. You have no idea the money it will bring."

"Do you not already have enough money?"

He stroked her hair, and she pulled her head away. "My dear, there is no such thing as enough money. I'll be the wealthiest man in England. And it won't be from sitting and doing nothing. It will be through daring and adventure."

He was out of his mind. Mad beyond reason. She repeated her first question. "What do you want from me?"

"Simple." He smiled, and she wanted to slap it off his face. "You marry me as planned, and Kemp lives. You make any slip at all, and the Cornishman dies."

A plan that would only work if he kept Gareth locked up indefinitely, his neck under a guillotine ready to fall the moment Elaine made a wrong move.

The truth settled into her heart with the softness of an axe. Gareth would rather die than live like that—than to have her live like that.

She'd set off for London looking for love, silencing the warning that she'd already found the one man who loved her completely. One mistake. One. And all this. If anyone deserved to die, it was her and no one else.

Lord Chiverton would never be able to make such an arrangement work. Never. He was lying to her. All he needed was enough time and leverage to secure the marriage and Havencross. Then neither Elaine nor Gareth would be needed.

But she had leverage of her own. She would agree to Chiverton's scheme. Not because she was going to go through with the marriage but to give her time to get Gareth out. Just a little more time—that was all she wanted.

"Very well then, my *love*." She spat the word at him. "I accept your terms. But I require one condition."

His eyebrows went up. Whether because she'd agreed to his absurd threat or because she was setting a requirement, she did not know or care.

"I want to see him one last time. I cannot accept until I know beyond doubt he is alive."

Chiverton considered for a moment, then grinned. "We have an agreement." Before she could stop him, he leaned in and kissed her mouth. "Sealed with a kiss. Isn't this wonderful? Already our marriage is off to a good start."

Years ago, Elaine suffered a violent sickness. She spent days bent over the chamber pot, unable to eat or drink anything as it all ended up in the pot. That was nothing compared to the vileness that consumed her now.

He gave three sharp knocks on the sitting room door.

Squire Stroud swung it open.

"She wants to see him."

The squire nodded. "Almost ready."

Lord Chiverton slipped out, and the door lock clicked shut. She was trapped here alone again. Better alone than with that odious man.

She waited a few minutes to be sure no one was coming back—at least not immediately—then hurried over to the window.

"Williams," she called in a loud whisper.

Her only answer was the squeaking of crickets and the croak of a frog.

"Get help," she uttered into the night. "My father or Mr. Tippet. Or tell Mr. Winkleigh; he will believe you." Those were about all the names she trusted.

The crickets made no promises, nor did the frog offer his assistance. Some branches rustled off to her left, probably a cat hunting for mice under cover of dark.

"What are you doing?"

She spun around. Lord Chiverton crossed the room in an instant and peered out the window. She hoped he had better luck than she had. She'd not found at all what she was looking for.

"I was hot from the fire. I needed some air."

He looked at her, then back into the night. "Hmm," was all he said.

She pursed her lips at him. "Worried I might have an accomplice hiding out there?"

He said nothing.

"Let me assure you, if I did, I'd be long gone by now."

He held up a small brown turnip bag.

"Are you going to the garden?"

"It's for you. If this is going to be a long-term arrangement, best if you don't know the location. We have, of course, removed him from the mine."

She snatched it out of his hand. If she had to wear a hood, she would put it on herself.

"I really do admire this new side of you. Had I known how beautiful you are when fired up, I would have angered you long ago."

She jerked the bag over her head, the sooner to get him out of her sight.

He tied something around her neck, securing the sack in place.

"Are you satisfied now?" she mumbled through the dusty canvas.

"Surprisingly satisfied. Let's go."

With his arm gripping her tightly, he ushered her from the squire's sitting-room prison. She came without protest, high stepping to keep herself from tripping. Her free hand pressed along the knife she had concealed in her bodice.

Lord Chiverton led her out the front door and across a patch of gravel. A second hand wrapped around her other arm, and Lord Chiverton let go.

There was a creaking sound, like leather rubbing on leather, and then the chinking of metal. He must have mounted his horse. A moment later, the hand from her arm wrapped around her waist and hoisted her up. Her feet lifted from the ground, and she landed on something softer than she'd expected. Lord Chiverton's lap.

"Hold on tight, love," he whispered in her ear. "I fear this ride will be a long one. I don't want to lose you now that we are finally getting to know each other."

CHAPTER TWENTY-FIVE

Gareth

THE IRON BARS CLANGED SHUT behind Gareth. At least he wasn't in wrist cuffs, trapped inside a mine anymore. He was in a proper prison. Something had changed Chiverton's plans if he now found himself in a cell instead of floating facedown out at sea.

A man tossed him a water bladder and half a loaf of bread.

Now they were feeding him?

Elaine must have done something to change Chiverton's circumstances.

He rolled onto his back, taking a moment for the pain to subside. Every breath was torture, and the musket ball lodged in his leg burned like the dickens.

He unstopped the bladder and drank. The water was stale and gritty, but he'd have drunk mud if they'd offered it. The bread was still warm and delicious. Wherever he was, they had a great cook and a terrible well.

He had no idea how long he'd traveled to get to this new location. The new lumps on his head affirmed they'd not wanted him awake for his journey. He could be anywhere in Cornwall. He listened for sounds of the sea or birds or a night owl—anything to indicate the passage of time or distance, but his cell was silent.

He washed down the bread with the last of the water. His stomach tightened and groaned after so long without food. Even such a small meal did wonders for his body though, relieving his weak and wobbly muscles.

The cell was empty save himself; no bench carved into the stones, no three-legged stool, no straw. Three walls of stone and one of iron—like the prisons of old. He sat on the ground. At least they'd left a lantern burning, though it had been ill-trimmed, and the light flickered like flashes of weak lightning.

Elaine's stocking was doing the trick to stop the blood. His strength slowly returned. The shooting pain in his leg died down to a dull ache. There had been quite the commotion when Chiverton had found out she was gone.

Gareth couldn't pull his thoughts away from her and what she might have done to secure his life—at least for the moment. He still had that letter stuffed into his waistcoat. Now that his hands were free, there just might be enough light to read it.

It was old and yellowed, folded and sealed with the Cardinham seal, though it had long since been broken. On the front, he found his name.

He leaned against the bars to get closer to the sputtering light and unfolded it. The ink was faded and stained but still legible.

My Dearest Gareth,

My hands are shaking like leaves in a gale as I write. I worry you shan't be able to read this. I hope I am not too late.

I've done nothing but think these last two days, pacing my room until my father made me either tell him what is the matter or go outside. I took my pacing to the garden.

I don't know how I shall tell you what is on my mind, or should I say in my heart, for I think you must despise me now. For certain, I despise myself because I fear I have made a mistake.

My Aunt Rose and Uncle Charles are here. It has been six months since her accident, and the doctors tell her she will never walk again. She is confined to her bath chair and the mercy of her husband.

I see how Uncle Charles looks at her, and though she is scarred and broken, his love is unchanged. Grown more, perhaps. It is this kind of love I crave for my own marriage.

When I refused you, all I could think of was what my father, what people, would think if I connected myself to a person with such disparity between our situations. I did not take the time to consider. As I have worn a path through to the dirt, I realize that it does not matter. What is a moment of reproach compared to a life with a man I love?

It signifies nothing to me, the censure of others, if my heart is yours. And it is entirely yours. So here I offer it to you, if you still want it. You may break it, and that would be fair. You asked me to be your queen, and I want nothing more than for you to be my king. You told me you loved me. That I was the fairest in the land. If that love is even half as much as my love for you, I hope you can forgive me.

I will give this note to John immediately and beg him to deliver it tonight before my courage fails. I shall not be well until I hear from you.

I am now, as always, your
Elowen.

Someone cleared their throat in front of him. He looked up, his eyes not quite ready to focus on something so far from where his mind was. But it was Elaine and, behind her, Chiverton, smirking.

He cared not at all about Chiverton. It was Elaine, her eyes going from him to the letter and back to him. It was clear by the horror on her face that she'd hoped he would never read it in the course of his entire lifetime.

"Why didn't you tell me?" he asked. At last he understood. This was the letter that had gotten John killed. This had put him in the path of the smugglers. It had cost him his life. And Elaine felt fully responsible for it. "You could have told me. After."

She shook her head. "Everything changed. I was no longer the second child, the daughter. I was the only child and heir to Havencross."

She knelt on the floor before him, where he sat leaning against the bars. She clutched her chest. Her hair was a tangle of coppery straw. The bruise on her neck had darkened to deep blue.

"How could I? Don't you see? It was my fault John went missing. Mine. I ruined everything. My friendship with you. My brother's life. My parents' happiness. All of it. I had to get away. But I only made it worse. Look at us."

"At least we would have had each other." How much of their sorrow would have been spared by that. All this time passed, and he thought she did not love him.

"Do you think I haven't regretted every hour of every day since I did not accept your offer? If I had listened to my heart in the first place, we would now be sitting in front of the fire with our children at our feet."

Gareth looked down, shaking his head. "We could still have been there, if only you had told me."

To keep silent like that, it was unthinkable. She had hurt him immensely when she'd brushed him away. But to leave him without a word, without a hope, while all the time loving him?

"Every time I looked at you, all I could see was John's face. That he was gone because of me." She scooted closer to his iron cage. "I'm sorry, Gareth. I shall not ask forgiveness. I know it is beyond forgiving."

He folded the letter and tucked it back into his waistcoat, wincing with the pain of it. He did not know what to say. Part of him wanted to reach through the bars and hold her. Part of him wanted her out of his sight.

But out of sight meant back into the hands of Chiverton and the smugglers. The same gang responsible for killing his father and John. The ones Chiverton now funded. He must have come across this letter somewhere, stripped from John's body after his death by the men who'd attacked him.

"Where did you get this?" he asked Chiverton.

"My man had it saved in his stash. Notes such as these become valuable when the moment is right." Chiverton leaned against the stone wall, arms folded. "He showed it to me the moment I set my sights on Havencross. When I began courting the lovely Elowen."

Elaine gasped. "You've known all along?"

Chiverton nodded. "Let me assure you, it's been quite entertaining."

"Why give it to me now?" Gareth asked. There had to be some master plan in all of this somewhere.

Chiverton shrugged. "I suppose, especially now that I didn't get the chance to kill you, I still want to see you suffer." He tipped his head to the side as if pondering life's great mysteries. "Sometimes more painful than what is happening at the moment are thoughts about what might have been."

Gareth hated that man. What had Elaine said? The hatred of a thousand hateful fiends. Only more. And yet he was right. This pain was ten times worse.

"While we are having this moment of truth, I must apologize. I lied," Chiverton said. "Turns out you won't be able to spend the rest of your life with the woman you love. I do beg your pardon."

Gareth's gaze whipped back to Elaine. "What have you done?" What had she traded for his life? What hideous agreement had she entered into? "Elaine, don't be foolish. Think about what you are doing."

She smiled at him. "I have thought very carefully about what I am doing. And I believe this is everyone's best chance at surviving."

She looked right into Gareth's eyes. "Find me," she whispered as silently as an owl on the wing. Then her eyes went to the floor.

"There you have it." Chiverton pulled her to her feet and offered her some sort of sack. "Come, my love. We have a wedding to prepare."

Elaine put the sack over her head, and Chiverton secured it with a short length of cording. He led her up the narrow stairs and out of sight. A door creaked open, then clanged shut.

Chiverton had an impressive amount of arrogance to allow Elaine's visit. Hopefully he had gotten his fill of deranged joy seeing them there, both suffering. If Chiverton believed Elaine would still marry him so he could get his claws on Havencross, he'd better think again. She would never go through with it.

At least, Gareth hoped. Apparently he didn't know Elaine as well as he'd thought. This letter proved it.

He scooted closer to the light, careful not to put weight on his bad leg, and held her letter out.

She loved him. Or at least she had five years ago. So many times he had thought about going to her. The nights he'd lain awake in bed, talking himself out of climbing the wall to her window. He could have written a letter of his own. Instead, he severed all ties and moved on.

Except that he hadn't moved on. This letter in his hand was the biggest reminder of all that he was stuck in exactly the same place he'd been five years ago when she'd taken his heart away with her to London.

That blackguard Chiverton was right. Not even the musket ball festering in his leg was as painful as what might have been.

He slammed his hands against the iron bars.

Something rattled on the floor just outside his cell. Nestled up against the bottom cross rail, a metal object caught the light of the sputtering lantern. A fisherman's knife, exactly where she'd been kneeling. He slipped his hand through the bars and grasped the handle, pulling it carefully in.

Clever girl. She *had* given him his best chance at surviving. She didn't have to marry Chiverton. She only had to play along long enough for him to get himself out. She still had two days before the wedding. Once Gareth was free, they could expose Chiverton for the scoundrel he was.

He tested the blade. Not the sharpest of knives but good and sturdy. She knew exactly what she was doing. "Thank you, Elowen."

He spat on the blade and scraped it along a rock, narrowing the point a little more, until he could slip it into the lock.

With a grunt, he kneeled on his bad leg in front of the door. Pressing his ear against it, he slowly inserted the tip of the fishing knife. Long and thin with a curved tip, it was perfect for this task. Wherever did she find it?

He worked the knife until one of the tumblers caught. Then another. And another. The lock clicked open.

The door creaked as he pushed it. He waited a few moments, but no one came to check on him. He lifted the lantern off its peg and climbed the stairs, gritting his teeth every time he put pressure on his bad leg. He and Mrs. Beaford were two of a kind. Perhaps she had an extra bath chair.

At the top of the stone stairs, he came to another door. This lock was trickier, but he got it after several long minutes. He waited again, listening for sounds of movement or conversation. All was silent.

Anything could be on the other side of this door, from a single guard to a camp full of smugglers. He set the lantern down to have both hands free should he need them to fight, the fishing knife still clutched in his grip. He cracked open the door, not knowing whether to expect night or day.

No light came through. Either it was night, or he was still underground. The air smelled fresh, not like the musty damp of the air in the cell. He put out the lamp. No need to signal to the world that the prisoner had escaped.

Gareth crept out, pressing against the wall to stay hidden. He was outside; he could see the moon and the stars glowing faintly behind a barrier of clouds. He kept the knife at the ready to fend off the guard, but there was none. Rather insulting that Chiverton expected so little from him that he didn't even post a guard. Gareth's manhood was called into question.

Then again, this was only a band of local smugglers, after all. Not Napoleon's army. They specialized in the hiding of contraband, not the keeping of prisoners. If there were goods to be moved this night, all hands would be needed for that.

He took a few steps, limping and holding his ribs. When he turned around, he almost laughed out loud. He was at New Tor. No wonder the squire had put forth so little effort into tracking down his father's killer. It was him—or one of his men.

Gareth cursed them and their children and their grandchildren's children. He would see the squire hanged. Justice at last for his father—and for John. The squire had most certainly been involved in that murder as well. That was how he'd come into possession of Elaine's letter and then passed it on to Chiverton.

Tonight would be the end of it. Chiverton, Stroud, and the whole gang of them.

But first to find Elaine. Chiverton claimed he was taking her home, but he wouldn't really risk taking her back to her house bruised and battered as she was. Not to mention stockingless.

She could be inside the squire's house. Perhaps he had another secret prison. Then again, maybe Chiverton had indeed taken her home. He was extremely good at playing the part of the elegant beau, the gentleman from London here to court his future bride. And his arrogance knew no limits, so perhaps he thought he would get away with it.

Gareth made a slow circle around New Tor but found no sign of Elaine or anyone being home. The squire's house was all dark. A safety precaution, no doubt. No one wanted light glowing in the window when there might be king's men about. Smuggling was dark work. Face to the wall, and all that. If Elaine was in there, Gareth would never be able to tell without going inside.

The knife she had given him had saved his life, but it was not enough to take on more than one or two men. Chiverton, he knew from personal experience, was armed. Gareth's leg wound put the odds even less in his favor. Better to ride to Havencross and rally some men.

Gareth limped off toward the squire's stables. The squire never rode; he traveled only in his oversized curricle. No horse would survive the man on his back. But even a carriage horse would be ten times faster than walking on his maimed leg.

He found what he was looking for—a stout mare sleeping in a straw-filled stall. The only animal in the stable, making his choice easy. She blew her hot breath in his face but stayed quiet while he fitted an ancient bridle over her ears. The saddle was clearly meant for another mount, but there was nothing he could do about it.

The moon behind the clouds cast an eerie glow across the land, turning everything it touched into silver.

He led the animal to a mounting block and dragged himself up.

Havencross was several miles away. Much closer was Camelford, but he didn't know who he could trust there. He had to think, but his head was foggy and muddled. Elaine had been gone a long time, most of the night, it seemed. Surely the Cardinham household was out looking for her. Most of the parish should be out looking for her.

Chiverton must have some kind of plan to explain away her absence. How he found her wandering the heath. How he saved her from the dangerous smugglers. He was an earl. They would believe every word and praise his name from now till kingdom come. All hail the glorious Chiverton.

Gareth shook his head, reining in his thoughts. He mustn't let his hatred for Chiverton cloud his judgment, not if he meant to find Elaine. She would not sit quietly and wait, knowing the truth about Chiverton. More likely, that blackguard had her tucked away somewhere in the Cornish underbelly.

Gareth's escape would be discovered at any moment. He must find her quickly—before Chiverton could spirit her away to Gretna Green, if they weren't already on their way there now.

Gareth's head tipped forward, and he nearly fell off the horse. He'd not make it to Havencross in this state. But if he died trying, at least Elaine would be free. Or at least free of his part in her dilemma. She would still be at the mercy of a maggot. He gripped the reins tighter and urged his horse on.

CHAPTER TWENTY-SIX
Gareth

HE NEARED CAMELFORD SQUARE AND veered off on the road toward Havencross.

"Mr. Kemp?" a man called, approaching him on horseback. In the darkness, all Gareth could make out was a silhouette. It wasn't Chiverton—not enough arrogance. It sounded like John. But that was impossible. Unless, of course, Gareth was dead.

It was not beyond the realm of possibility that he'd fallen off his beast in the fields and now lay dying and this was all an illusion playing out in his mind.

"What are you doing?" It wasn't John. It was his father, Mr. Cardinham.

Cardinham rode up to him. "Goodness, Kemp. You look like death."

This neither confirmed nor denied the possibility that it was all in fact one big nightmare brought on by loss of blood and the very real possibility that he was already in purgatory in the next life. Or maybe his purgatory had come early.

"Mr. Kemp?" Cardinham moved his mount even closer and reached out, taking hold of Gareth's animal's bridle. "What happened to you?"

"I'm looking for Elaine," he said.

Mr. Cardinham's eyes narrowed. "At the devil's hour?"

"She must not marry Chiverton." This was what mattered most. He reached for the threads drifting in and out of his mind, but they eluded him. There was more to say, but he could not think of it.

"Sir," Cardinham said, "I don't believe that's any of your business." He reached into his coat pocket and pulled out a flask. "You're injured. I'm on my way to Dr. Woodbury even now. Mrs. Cardinham's sister has taken a turn for the worst. You'd best come with me."

Cardinham unstopped the lid and handed Gareth the tin flask. It had the Cardinham symbol etched on the front. Gareth put it to his lips and tossed down a gulp. Then another. Then another. The liquid burned as it went down, coating his belly with the fire of Hades. But the sting did wonders to clear his mind. He took one more swallow, then handed it back.

"I can't," Gareth said. "There is no time. I must ask, do you know where Miss Cardinham is? I believe she is in danger."

Mr. Cardinham eyed him through slits for a moment, taking in his disheveled hair, his complete lack of appropriate attire, the woman's stocking stained red, keeping his life from leaking out. "She stayed the night with Miss Tippet."

"Miss Tippet?" This proved his suspicions about Mr. Tippet and the Landguard. What better place to keep her hidden away. It was a clever excuse on Chiverton's part. "How do you know?"

"Not that it's any of your concern, but she walked into Camelford yesterday and didn't make it home before the weather closed in. She sent us word that rather than trouble with a carriage, she'd stay with her friend overnight. You know how girls are."

Gareth had little knowledge of how *girls* were, but he knew how Elaine was. It would take nothing short of a typhoon to deter her.

"Does it seem like Miss Cardinham to let weather keep her from home?"

Cardinham shook his head. "No, I suppose not. But she and Miss Tippet are friends."

"Sir," Gareth said. "Chiverton is not what he seems. He is involved deeply in the gang responsible for John's and my father's death." Gareth pointed at his leg. "It was he who shot me."

"Don't be ridiculous. Chiverton is not even from these parts."

Chiverton had everybody fooled. "I'm telling you he is involved. I know this of a certainty. I beg you to believe me. He is the man financing the smuggling, and now he has come to Cornwall to be closer at hand. He does not care about Elaine; he only wants Havencross for its location."

At last, it seemed he was getting through. The man's eyes widened. He released the bridle of Gareth's horse.

"Wait." Gareth kicked his one good heel because he could no longer move his injured leg, urging his horse to come alongside Mr. Cardinham's. "There is more. Squire Stroud is also involved."

At this, Cardinham balked. "Impossible. I know the squire well. He is a friend and magistrate." Cardinham eyed him again. "How do I know you're not the one who's been turned to the smugglers? After all, you're the one out skulking in the middle of the night."

"Are you suggesting I killed my own father?" He'd given Cardinham more credit than that. "You must see how preposterous that sounds. Instead, consider this: Why has nothing been done to find the real murderer? Why has the Landguard accomplished nothing to stop the smuggling? Why has the squire let the matter go on and on unsettled? He reported to me many times that he was doing his utmost, but now I see that he was doing nothing because he was responsible for the killings in the first place."

Cardinham was listening. Gareth could see doubt prowling his brow.

"I was as surprised as you to discover the squire's involvement. But I have just come from his house, where I was a prisoner held captive because I had discovered the truth."

"Perhaps you are right. It does make some sense. But I cannot wholly agree until I see for myself. For tonight, at least, what matters is my daughter."

In this, he was right. Of first importance was Elaine and prying her out of Chiverton's hands. If they found her, Cardinham would see the truth soon enough. But he still had to mention his suspicion of Tippet.

"I believe Miss Cardinham may indeed be at the Landguard office," Gareth said, "but not visiting her friend. Rather, under the watch of Tippet and Lord Chiverton."

"Now you accuse Tippet as well? Come, man. Even you must see how ridiculous this sounds."

"It is a large and well-funded gang of smugglers," Gareth said. "I'm sure there are many more involved than even these."

Cardinham shook his head in disbelief.

Gareth had used up his strength.

Elaine. He must not lose sight of his top priority. He would waste no more time trying to convince her father. "Off to the Landguard, then, but we cannot go barging in unprepared."

"That won't be a problem." Cardinham patted a rifle looped onto his saddle. "I'm not fool enough to ride out without some protection. Besides, he wouldn't dare harm a gentleman."

Meaning, of course, that the life of Gareth and his father were valued less. He hadn't even realized his implication, so naturally had it fallen from his lips.

Cardinham pushed his horse faster. "If Elaine is in trouble, that's all the reason I need." He turned his mount down the lane that led into Camelford.

If she wasn't at Havencross, the Landguard was as good a place to check as any. Chiverton was not fool enough to send a letter to Havencross detailing his hostage's true location. But with the right kind of persuasion, they might still be able to get Tippet to talk.

Free at last only to follow Cardinham back to the door of the wolf.

The Landguard office was situated across the River Camel. As they neared the bridge, a ragged form rose up in front of them. Cardinham's horse reared, but he managed to keep his seat. Gareth pulled on the reins, swinging his mount in a tight circle to keep it from doing the same.

It was Broken Betty. She hissed at the horses, then turned to Cardinham and mumbled something.

Elaine was right. Gareth's Cornish was greatly lacking, for he understood nothing of what she'd said.

"Out of my way," Cardinham grumbled as he maneuvered around her. "I don't have time for this."

The woman reached up with her gnarled hands and grabbed the bridle of Gareth's horse. She had several tattered shawls tied around her shoulders and a face like an ancient seaman. She said something again, but Gareth could not make it out. Perhaps something about Saint Piran.

She said it again, pointing across the fields. "*Mires orth Sans Pyran.*"

Look at Saint Piran. Or so he thought. He didn't have time for this either, but when he tried to move on, she wouldn't let go.

"I'm on urgent business," he told her.

Broken Betty hissed at him, shaking her head and showing the few brackish teeth she had left. "*Sans Pyran,*" she insisted.

"Yes, yes. Saint Piran." Patron saint of Cornwall—or at least patron saint to the tin miners. The church in Camelford was Saint Piran's.

And then it hit him. Chiverton's entire scheme depended on marriage to Elaine. All the banns had been read. Elaine was of age. By law, the ceremony must take place between nine and noon, but what was that if Chiverton or Squire Stroud had steel against the vicar's throat. Records could be falsified. A special license forged.

He should have studied his Cornish better, despite Elaine's teasing. "Uh . . . Miss Cardinham? *Sans Pyran*?"

Broken Betty hissed and spat off the side of the bridge. A great glob that glistened in the eerie light and then plunked into the slow-moving water. Gareth's empty stomach churned.

She let go of his horse, melting back into the night.

"I think I know where she is," Gareth called out to Cardinham, who waited for him on the other side of the river.

"We all do." He motioned at Gareth to cross the bridge. "That's why we're headed to Tippet's place."

Cardinham did not fully understand what he was up against. He had not seen the extent of Chiverton's wrongs and still thought Tippet could help. The truth would hit him hard when Tippet opened his door with his saber drawn.

Gareth couldn't wait that long. If Broken Betty was right—and he couldn't believe he was taking a lunatic's word for it—there was a marriage taking place at this moment. He had no time to waste. "She's at Saint Piran's."

CHAPTER TWENTY-SEVEN

Elaine

"YOU WILL PAY FOR YOUR sins," Elaine whispered at Lord Chiverton as he led her up the aisle. She would have shouted it at him had they not been in the house of God.

He smiled at her. "As a matter of fact, I have already been paid handsomely for my sins, my dear. You shall see how wealthy we will be with our smuggling runs and under-the-table dealings."

Three candles flickered on the altar, barely illuminating a few feet beyond. The entire church was empty of all but three other people shadowed by the candlelight. One was undoubtedly the vicar. And then two witnesses—to make all official.

By the circular outline, one was Squire Stroud. And the other—

"Brixton?"

He grinned at her, a smirky, brazen thing.

"You are dismissed. Don't ever show your face at Havencross again. I daresay you are the worst servant I've ever seen." She turned to Lord Chiverton. "You had a spy in our house all along?"

"I told you I keep eyes on my people. How else was I to know what you were up to?"

She raised her hand to slap him, but he caught her by the arm and held it until they were standing in front of the vicar.

How Mr. Foss could be part of a smuggler's ring and still call himself a man of God, she did not know. It was an abomination to think how many barrels and sacks of goods had been stored in the churchyard or inside the table tombs. Perhaps her own ancestors had shared their resting place with a tub of tobacco or a few yards of lace.

When she had agreed to Lord Chiverton's terms, she'd thought she had three days, time and enough to free Gareth and escape Chiverton's clutches.

She never thought he meant to march her straight to the church this very night. She was still in her ruined dress, with one stocking missing.

This is for Gareth, she reminded herself. She owed him this, at least. Hopefully he'd found the fish knife and made his escape.

The vicar stepped forward, holding a book at the end of his long and pointy nose. "Dearly beloved," he said to the empty pews and the tapestries fluttering in the draft. "We are gathered here in the sight of God."

Elaine nearly laughed. She suspected God had forgotten about this lonely part of Cornwall. How else could He let so much bad happen? And in a moment's time, she would be married to the worst man of them all.

For Gareth.

Once she was assured of his safety, she'd find some way to get out of this. Surely her father would help her.

Chiverton's plan was to leave with her tonight on a honeymoon tour of Europe. At least, that was what the note said that she'd been forced to write—along with one telling her family she'd stayed the night at Miss Tippet's. After a month's absence, what could be done? She might even be carrying his child by then.

Please, dear heaven, anything but that.

The vicar droned on about how marriage was to be taken reverently, discreetly, advisedly, soberly, and in the fear of God. Lord Chiverton may have been able to take such vows lightly, but she could not. When she married, she meant for it to be sincere. A pledge before God of truth and faithfulness. Not this mockery.

Lord Chiverton leaned forward. "Don't worry, my love, I always cry at weddings too." He wiped her cheeks with his thumb.

"I'm only doing this for one reason," she said.

"I know. Believe me. I went about this all the wrong way. I should have used that letter to my advantage long before now. Saved myself weeks of courting. Ah well. Lesson learned."

The door at the back of the nave creaked. Lord Chiverton stared intently into the darkness, his smirk gone and his body on full alert.

"I declare an impediment," came a voice from the shadows. Gareth.

His figure moved slowly, limping toward the center aisle. Bent at an odd angle. He sat on the first pew he came to at the very back of the church.

Gareth had made it. He had escaped. And by some miracle, he had found her.

"I beg your pardon?" the vicar said, looking at Chiverton, then back to Gareth.

"I said, 'I declare an impediment.'"

The vicar's eyes shot back to Lord Chiverton.

"Proceed," the earl said to Mr. Foss.

Lord Chiverton gave Squire Stroud a nod, and he, in turn, jerked his head at Brixton. "See to it."

Brixton stepped off the dais and started down the center of the nave.

Gareth raised a rifle and aimed it at him. Or maybe it was pointed at Lord Chiverton, Elaine could not tell.

"Listen," Gareth said, resting his firearm on the back of the bench in front of him, still keeping it aimed and ready. "I'm tired. I've been bound, starved, jailed, and shot. So let me be plain. If you do not release Miss Cardinham and end this game, I will kill you. If I hang, I hang. I don't think I really care anymore."

Gareth pulled the flintlock back, and the click echoed in the silent church.

But he was only one against four. Elaine had not come willingly to this altar so that he could throw his life away in Saint Piran's church.

"No!" She put her hand on Lord Chiverton's arm. "We have a deal. One which I am prepared to honor."

"Elaine," Gareth said. "Could you just this once not be so stubborn? I don't have the strength for it. Think what you are doing. Chiverton will never allow me to live no matter what you do. Enough of this." He raised the rifle at Lord Chiverton. "Either you release her, or I shoot you. That is my final offer." He laughed. "Or maybe I'll just shoot you anyway. Turnabout and all that."

Gareth was out of his senses. One shot at Lord Chiverton would not put an end to it. What about the squire? The vicar? And Brixton, wavering in the nave, still trying to figure out if he should apprehend Gareth or not? Gareth couldn't take them all down with one ball.

The door to the church creaked again, and two more figures emerged from the dark. Her father and Mr. Tippet.

"Papa!" she cried. She leapt off the dais, but Lord Chiverton caught her.

"Not so fast, my love." He put his arm around her. "You're too late, sir. We are already wedded."

"That's a lie," Gareth said. He was beginning to sound more and more like he'd spent the night in his cups over at The Black Hart Inn rather than as Lord Chiverton's captive. "No vows have been exchanged. No pronouncement of man and wife." He lowered the rifle and lay down on the oak bench of the pew. "No ring," he called out, though Elaine could no longer see him.

The door creaked again, and two of Tippet's men entered.

In a flash, cold steel pressed against her ribs.

"Stay where you are," Lord Chiverton said, "or she gets a ball through her heart."

Her father stopped, putting his arms out, warning Tippet and his men to stand down. Her father stood frozen in the middle of the church, an easy target for any of Lord Chiverton's men. Gareth, at least, was behind a bench.

She could feel the barrel of Lord Chiverton's gun slowly moving. He would never allow himself to be taken so easily. He was going to shoot someone. Her father. Once her father was dead, Havencross would be hers and then his.

"No!" she screamed. But the explosion of gunpowder drowned her out.

She watched her father, waiting for him to fall. But he didn't.

It was Lord Chiverton who fell to his knees.

Elaine twisted away, searching the back of the church for who had fired. Smoke wafted up from Gareth's rifle.

A thick moment of silence clouded the church as they all watched Chiverton press a hand to his bleeding leg. Almost the exact same spot he had shot Gareth.

Then the entire church sprang into action.

Brixton pulled a pistol from somewhere and aimed it at her father. Mr. Tippet leveled his Landguard musket on Brixton.

Lord Chiverton was struggling to his feet, weapon clutched in his hand, cursing.

From the corner of her eye, she saw Squire Stroud make a dash for the chancel door. Mr. Tippet took his aim off Brixton and set it on the squire. There was nothing stopping Brixton from shooting her father.

Elaine grabbed the three-pronged candlestick, dumping the candles onto the stone floor, and hurled it at Brixton with all her might. Two of the candles sputtered out, plunging the little church into near darkness.

She could not see whether she had hit Brixton or not.

A shot rang out. Then another one, followed by the sound of crashing glass. Someone grabbed at her. Lord Chiverton. She spun out of his reach.

"Unhand me," a man yelled from beyond the altar.

Then she heard the vicar's voice. "Not the Ascension window!"

The scuffling and grunting of men filled the church—blind men fighting in the dark for their lives. The clanging of weapon on weapon, weapon on stone. Splintering wood. The sharp tang of gunpowder.

From the light of the single burning candle lying on the floor, she saw Lord Chiverton squint into the darkness, his pistol ready to fire at the first thing that came into his vision.

A hand grabbed her from behind. "Over here." It was Gareth.

He pulled her away from the candle, out of the light that would give her away. They bumped into one of the pews, and Gareth swung her around, crouching with her between two benches.

Another shot fired, followed by a grunt and a thud.

"My father," she said, trying to go to him, but Gareth wouldn't release her.

"Stay down." His arm wrapped firmly around her waist. "He will be fine."

"How can you know that?"

Gareth did not answer.

"Someone get the candles going," Mr. Tippet called. His voice came from the direction where she'd last caught a glimpse of Lord Chiverton.

Another thud followed by a curse. "Brixton, you idiot. That was me," Lord Chiverton moaned.

Gareth's breathing came loud and labored beside her. She looked at him, though she could see nothing in the darkness. He didn't sound well. She reached out, finding first his shoulder, then neck, then cheek. He was hot. And bristly, after going several days unshaven. His hand landed on hers, alighting at once both gently and fierce. He turned his head, pressing a kiss into the palm of her hand.

"Gareth," she whispered.

At last, the speck of light grew bigger. The sounds of fighting faded into groans and gulping breaths.

"Father?" she called, peeking her head above the pew.

"I'm here," he said. It was he who was setting the candles back on the altar, using the one to light the others.

"It is over," Mr. Tippet called loud and clear.

Elaine stood. Her father seemed unhurt. She ran to him, falling into his arms. She'd thought for certain Brixton had shot him. Indeed, he'd probably tried.

Lord Chiverton lay on the ground, face pale. He was cursing Gareth and Elaine and even the Almighty Himself. Mr. Tippet stood over him, motioning for a young man to come forward with a pair of wrist irons.

"Make them good and tight," Gareth called. He was sitting on the bench now, even paler than Lord Chiverton.

"Thank heaven that's over," Squire Stroud said. He pressed his hand over his arm. He must've been hit by a ball. "I've been cajoled into this mess and am desperate to find a way out."

"Save your breath, Squire," her father said.

"He already knows it was you who killed John," Gareth called from his pew. He had lain back down again, only his voice giving him away.

Lord Chiverton laughed.

"Our engagement is over," Elaine said. She couldn't find an insult bad enough for him.

"You really do grow more beautiful the angrier you get, my love." Lord Chiverton winked at her.

That man was pure evil. He would never bring any good to the world. Never. And she'd had enough. She grabbed Lord Chiverton's pistol off the floor and leveled it at his head. The steel was still cold against the palm of her hand. It had not yet been fired. She pulled back the flintlock. Every person in the entire kingdom would be better off without him.

"Miss Cardinham," Mr. Tippet said, his voice calm and steady. "Lower the weapon."

"No." She wrapped both hands around the stock, her knuckles white. "Look what he has done. He killed Mr. Kemp. He tried to kill Gareth. He nearly killed me. He deserves this."

Her father stepped forward, but Mr. Tippet stopped him. "Stay back, sir." He kept his eyes on Elaine. "Let the law deal with him. The Crown will see justice done."

She shook her head. He was an earl. The whole affair would be one big joke. "He will go to the House of Lords," she said, "and he will smile and flatter and lick their boots. They will slap his hand, and he will go free. How is that justice?"

Even if they did hang him, it would not be justice for her brother. She swung the firearm at Squire Stroud. "Perhaps I should take revenge for John instead." None of these evil men deserved to live.

"Elowen," Gareth said, his voice weaker than ever. "Look around you."

One of the beautiful stained-glass windows was shattered. Night air poured in, flickering the candles. Saint Piran's church was in ruin. Brixton lay sprawled across a broken pew. Dead. And a member of the Landguard lay unmoving not far from him. Gareth was right. There had been enough death. And she would not waste any more of her life on Lord Chiverton.

She gently released the flintlock and handed the pistol to Mr. Tippet.

"Get him out of here," her father said, tugging Elaine away from Lord Chiverton.

Mr. Tippet locked the irons around Lord Chiverton. One of his Landguard did the same to Squire Stroud.

"Where's the vicar?" Elaine asked.

"Did you want to shoot him too?" Lord Chiverton asked.

She did not even give him a glance.

"We caught him trying to make a run for it," one Landguard said.

"I'm sorry I ever doubted you, Mr. Tippet," Gareth called, but his voice barely reached them.

"Perhaps you'd better see to Mr. Kemp," her father told her. "And get my rifle out of his hands. I'm not sure about his wits just now."

While they escorted Lord Chiverton and Squire Stroud out, Elaine walked down the rows until she came to Gareth. He was lying on his back on the wooden bench with his eyes closed, gripping her father's gun across his chest.

Elaine put her hand on his, removing the firearm from his grasp.

His eyes opened to half slits. "Not sure I should hand this over to you."

"Nonsense. I'm perfectly fine."

"Now you are." He released the gun. "It doesn't have a shot left anyway, so I suppose we're all safe a little longer."

"I wouldn't have really shot him." At least, she didn't think so. "I just wanted to scare him. I wanted him to feel, even for a moment, what it must have been like for your father. For John."

Elaine set the gun to the side and knelt on the pew in front of him, reaching over the back of the wooden bench to stroke his matted hair away from his face. A touch of color returned to his cheeks as he lay there, finally getting the rest he needed. "I do have one favor I'll be asking."

"What is it?" he mumbled. He was fading quickly.

"I need my stocking back."

He laughed once. He placed his hand over hers. "I'm keeping it for my treasure."

His hand went limp, but he was only asleep. Elaine could feel his heartbeat through his thin shirt, steady and strong.

"The carriage will be here soon," her father said. "We'll take him back to Havencross. We sent someone from Tippet's place over to Dr. Woodbury. He should already be on his way there for Rose."

She nodded. Her father sat beside her on the bench. She turned forward, leaving Gareth asleep on the pew behind her.

"I thought he was a good man," she said. "How could I have been so blind?"

"He played his part well. We all thought he was good. And generous for taking you in after . . ." He stopped without mentioning London. It seemed insignificant now. And absurd the way they avoided any mention of it like it was a plague.

In truth, it was a plague. A sickness they'd let seep into their family. A plague of indifference. Detachment. If she'd told her parents about John and the letter, about Gareth's offer, things might have been different. If they'd relied on each other instead of each going alone, perhaps London could have been avoided altogether.

"What did happen in London, Father?"

He sank lower onto the bench, leaning forward to rest his elbows on his knees. He looked up at the altar and the figure of Christ looming over it. The first rays of morning lit the stained-glass window.

"I already told you. And it was the truth. I met a woman unhappy in her own marriage. She listened to me, confided in me, and it comforted me. That is all."

"But why could you not confide in Mother? She needed comfort too."

He shrugged. "You are right to be angry with me, Elaine. I have wronged you and especially your mother. I knew it then, and I know it now." He sighed heavily. "Who can say why we falter, why we fall. I am weak, I suppose. Vulnerable. Not like you. You are the strong one. Look what you have done this night, what you were willing to do to save Kemp."

She turned and looked at Gareth. "What did Gareth tell you?"

"Everything. Chiverton's involvement. The squire. His suspicion of Mr. Tippet. Though Tippet turned out to be clean. I am surprised about the vicar though."

"And the letter?"

"What letter?"

So Gareth hadn't mentioned John and the letter.

She could not sit here with the eyes of God upon her and blame her father for dividing the family while she herself held most of the blame. She must speak. If ever there was to be healing again in her family—in her heart—she must tell her father what she had done. If she held on to this any longer, it would drag her down and drown her forever. "I'm not strong at all, Father. In truth, I am the reason we have fallen apart. Not you."

He turned to her with eyes wide. "Why do you say so?"

She was ready now, at last, to tell all. To carve open her soul and lay bare her secret. She opened her mouth to speak, but the words would not come.

There was no language written or spoken to tell her father she was responsible for the death of his son. Her brother. The heir. That she was the rift in the family. He could not see into her heart, the blackness that consumed it, eating away until it was like the petals of a winter rose clinging to the stem. One small tap and they all fall to the ground.

"She blames herself for John's death." Gareth had woken up. Or, more likely, he'd been lying there listening all along. His voice was soft and tired but strong enough to be heard. "She wrote me a letter and asked John to bring it to me. The night was dark and squally, but John loved her, so he obliged."

"And that was the night he never came home." Her father finished the story. They all knew what had happened from there—the smugglers, Squire Stroud. The cave.

Her father watched her, but she could not tell if it was anger or sorrow that shadowed his face. She hoped it was anger, for that would be easier. It was what she deserved.

"I'm so sorry, Papa. I didn't know," she whispered. "I didn't know."

"Why did you not tell us? You should have told us."

She lowered her face into her hands. She had ruined everyone's lives. "Do you not think I wouldn't give my very life to go back and change it? I am sick. Broken in my mind and in my heart." She thumped on her chest, her tears flowing freely. One mistake on top of another. And all of it for ruin. "I have done so wrong."

Her father handed her a handkerchief; she'd long since lost her reticule.

He put his arms around her. "You cannot blame yourself. I was wrong to say that." He held her for a moment while she dried her eyes.

"When I went to Lady Forton's, I knew it was wrong. With every step, I knew I should turn back. But I didn't. I was weak and foolish. But you, Elaine, you cannot carry the burden for John's death. It was something you could never have predicted."

She nodded. She'd heard his words. Now if only she could believe them.

"How many times do you think John snuck out of the house to go to Lowentop?"

A faint puff of laughter came from the pew behind her.

"Gareth came calling with pebbles at John's window, and your brother would climb down the corner stones like a cat, and they'd be gone. None of us knew what evil was lurking. It could have happened at any time. You cannot blame yourself."

Her father looked back at Gareth. "What was in this letter that was so important?"

Gareth grinned. "Urgent news, sir. Urgent news."

Elaine turned around. "Go back to sleep, Mr. Kemp. You are not fit to be awake."

Gareth only smiled bigger.

Mr. Tippet called to them from the door. "Your carriage is here, sir."

"Thank you, Mr. Tippet."

Her father and Mr. Tippet helped Gareth up and hobbled him to the door.

"I thought you were part of the smuggler's ring," Gareth said to Mr. Tippet, "because you didn't put any effort into finding my father's murderer. Thought you were a blasted turncoat with a handsome daughter. Wouldn't you agree, Cardinham?"

"Gareth, hush." Elaine rapped him gently on the back of his head. "I'm so sorry, Mr. Tippet. He's lost a lot of blood, and I don't think he's had anything to eat or drink in several days. He's not himself."

"He had a good bit to drink from my flask," her father said. "I think that might be part of the problem."

They got Gareth into the carriage, and Elaine climbed in and sat beside him. By the time they crossed the bridge out of town, he was asleep again, leaning on her shoulder.

CHAPTER TWENTY-EIGHT

Elaine

ELAINE SAT AT THE WINDOW, looking out over the heath toward the cliffs and the sea. Sheep grazed in the field while the choughs followed along behind, feasting on the insects.

Gareth slept in the bed. His mother had been here with him all day yesterday, but the doctor assured her he was in no danger and she should go home and get some rest so she'd have the strength to nurse him in the days to come. That was what had finally convinced her to leave.

Below the window, Elaine's father and mother walked the garden. Her father seemed determined to right his wrong. And so did Elaine, if that was at all possible.

She stood and turned to find Gareth staring at her.

"You're awake."

He grinned. "I am if I have your permission. You must tell me if I'm fit to be awake."

"You should be thanking me. You have no idea the nonsense falling from your lips." She crossed the room and poured him a glass of water.

His eyes at last were clear and bright. His cheeks tinged with the color of fieldwork and sun. His hair clean from the blood and grime of Lord Chiverton's hand.

He drained the cup. "What did I say?"

"Well, first of all, you practically told Mr. Tippet you wanted to marry his daughter. Did you know her name is Ambrosia?"

He snorted. "Yes. I know. That is a serious obstacle. Fetch me my writing desk. I'll send word immediately that the wedding is off unless she can produce a more suitable name."

"You are incorrigible." She sat on the edge of his bed and leaned forward, turning his head to the side. "Let me check this wound."

His eyes were on hers as she lifted the bandage wrapped around his head. Her face burned with the intensity of his gaze.

"You are so beautiful. The fairest living or yet that ever lived." He was quoting King Arthur again.

"Hush."

"Except for one thing."

"Oh, and what's that?"

Without warning, he reached up and pulled out her hair pin. She'd put it up herself this morning, a quick and simple knot. Gareth had loosed it all, her copper hair tumbling down her back.

"That's better."

"Gareth Kemp." She snatched the pin out of his hand. "You have no right." She glanced at the door. "Someone might come in." She'd left the door ajar, and anyone could appear at any moment. A servant, her father. "What would they think?"

"Do you know, I don't care. There is something about having your life threatened repeatedly that makes you realize how silly all this nonsense is." He sat up and shifted the pillows behind his back for support. "Elowen Cardinham, I've waited five years for you to come back to me. I don't care who might come in."

La, he was brazen this morning. Still, his words spread warmth through her body. She had waited too, though she had not known it until recently.

"If you had not left me that knife, you would be married to that blackguard and I would be dead."

"He promised not to hurt you if I married him. He was to keep you alive so I would bend to his will." If anything would have happened to Gareth, she would have bolted like a dog at the racetrack.

"How long did you really think that arrangement would last?"

She shrugged her shoulders. "I only needed it to last long enough for you to find the knife and break out. I am not such a fool, Mr. Kemp. I knew the moment our marriage was official he would end you. And probably my father as well."

"No. Indeed you are no fool. But I do wish you'd have put a little more thought into what might have happened to you."

Elaine replaced the wrappings on his head. "It was my fault we were in that mess, so I should have been the one to pay for it. I thought only of you."

He reached up and put his hand on the side of her cheek, cradling her head while his thumb brushed across her lips. He pulled her close, then hesitated. She supposed he wanted to give her a chance to refuse.

How could she though, when every inch of her yearned to be closer? All the years of lost chances with him fell away. Her eyes went to his lips, and that was all he needed. He pressed his mouth on hers, holding her with a strength that lit her blood on fire.

Then he let go. "Mr. Cardinham."

Elaine's heart stopped completely. She jumped up and away, wiping her mouth, crossing the breadth of the floor in two steps.

But the room was empty. The door had not moved. And Gareth was holding his chest, laughing.

Oh! That man. "You should be punished for that, Mr. Kemp."

"I am already punished." He moaned. "By the new pounding in my head."

He deserved no less. She'd nearly had an attack of apoplexy.

"I'll fetch the doctor. He wanted to be informed the moment you awoke."

"Wait," he said. "I think we have some unfinished business I should like to clear up before we are interrupted."

She folded her arms from her corner of the room. "What business?"

"Please." He patted the bed again. "I'm sorry I teased you. I did not think I'd find myself alive after the squire's dungeon. And this morning I wake to both life and you. You must forgive me for feeling a little lighthearted."

He did look remorseful, sitting there in the bed with a strip of gauze wrapped around his head. Only days before, she had feared he might not survive the cave, then the squire's house. She could not stay mad at him.

She sat again on the edge of his bed.

"I assume by the way you threw yourself at me just now that you no longer hate me. Am I wrong in that?"

"Mr. Kemp. I nearly married a vile man for you." How could he doubt?

"Yes, but you also nearly married him when he wasn't so vile."

That was true. But so much had changed that she could hardly think upon her folly without hating herself for it. She had done well at deceiving herself into believing she cared for Lord Chiverton, but she could see now all that had mattered was that he would take her away from her past.

"I heard you talking to your aunt at the castle ruins," he said, "about finding your own Camelot. We've made up many stories over the years, you and I and John, about the adventures of King Arthur and his knights. About Gwenevere." He gave a little laugh, probably thinking of the time Elaine had found her and then lost her in Merlin's Cave.

"We have, indeed," she said.

"Elaine, I understand now why you left Havencross to hide in London. But my life is here. The mine. My mother. Lowentop. All I lack is you to make my Camelot complete. But I do not want to tie you to a place where you cannot be happy."

She stood and walked back to the window. When they left London just a short month ago, suffering the entire journey in that carriage of silence, she'd dreaded returning to the scene of her greatest mistakes, had worried that every rock and hedge would carry memories of John and Gareth. The two men she'd loved and lost all in one wretched decision.

She had been right. John was here, in the creaky floors of Havencross, in the castle ruins, in Gareth. Memories around every corner. This was what Lord Chiverton was meant to save her from.

She would have found out soon enough that life with him was no Camelot.

She loved this country. She loved the barren heath and the honeyed cliffs. The weather that brought new changes every hour. The thrift that covered the coastline in a blanket of deep pink and the rare orchids blooming in the meadows.

The ancient people who lived here had left their mark on the land. Tristan and Isolde. Uther and Igraine. Arthur and Gwenevere. The earth whispered their mysteries to her in the quiet morning mist.

London was never quiet. Horses and carriages clanked up and down the cobbled roads day and night. Coal pumped smoke into the air from chimneys and factories. The sky was a ceiling of gray, trapping the stink from the refuse until it suffocated.

Havencross was filled with memories, both good and bad. But it was part of her blood, and when she was away, her veins ran thin.

"Elowen?" Gareth said from his bed. He had a worried look on his face. "I do not wish to force your hand."

She returned to her seat on the bed beside him. "You do not force my hand. I give it freely and happily. Though it may be difficult at times, I belong here." She brushed her hand across his cheek. "But know this. Havencross is not my Camelot, Gareth Kemp. My Camelot is you. It has always been you."

He leaned back into his pillows with a smile on his face. "At least we have one reason to be grateful for Edmund Crawley, Earl of Chiverton."

"Goodness. Why?"

"If he had not been so vile, I might have lost you to him forever." He took her hand in his, stroking the back of it.

He was too good for her. "I made a mess of things. How can you ever forgive me?"

"Elowen, I forgave you the moment you left the cave that day five years ago." He held her hand tighter. "That is not to say it has been easy. There were days when my anger, my grief consumed me. And when I read your letter, I cannot tell you my disappointment for our lost time together. But even then I forgave you. Because I love you. That is what love means."

Like how her uncle loved her aunt. And how Arthur loved his Gwenevere.

She had no right to his affection after all she'd done. She did not deserve a man like Gareth. She deserved Lord Chiverton. A liar and a thief. A murderer. For she was all those things too, in a way. Yet Gareth reached up, stroking her cheek as if wanting her now more than ever.

She would try from this day forward to never hurt him again. No secrets. No lies. She believed him when he said it would not always be easy, but she could imagine few things worse than what they'd already been through.

"I'm inclined to think the legend has it backward," she said.

"What are you talking about?"

"It is you who is the most valiant and fairest living or yet that ever lived."

Gareth wagged his eyebrows. "It is true," he said. "Miss Tippet was just telling me so the other day. She is always so kind, you know."

She pulled her hand away. "Be serious."

But he just laughed.

She stood again. The whole house was quiet. She checked on her parents out the window. They were still in the garden. She could see them between the bank of lavender and hawthorns. It seemed her father was making progress because her mother's arm rested on his.

Dr. Woodbury had given her aunt a draft that had helped clear her lungs, but it made her very tired. She was sound asleep, and Uncle Charles was undoubtedly at her side.

"Come back," Gareth said. "I promise to be serious." He patted the bed again where her indentation still formed a hollow on top of the blanket. "I'll talk of nothing but boring, practical things."

She pursed her lips at him simply because she knew he hated it.

"I find that after five years of wanting, now that I have you, I cannot do without."

"Fine," she said. "But only because I feel sorry that you got shot."

"I can live with that."

She sat on the bed beside him, but the moment she did, he pulled her in. Not for a kiss but until her head rested in the curve of his neck and her body was tucked tightly inside his arm.

"Gareth!" Not that she did not enjoy the way he held her like he would never let go, but it was altogether inappropriate. "Someone will see us. Hasn't our family had enough scandal?"

His hold only tightened. "You are right, of course. Just one minute and I promise I will not bother you again until after we are wed."

"Wed? You have not even asked me yet."

"Yes, I did. How have you already forgot?"

That was five years ago. She curled her feet up onto the bed. "One minute." She closed her eyes because she could not imagine a more perfect place in all the world.

When she'd first come back from London and gone down to the cave, she had pleaded with Merlin to take her back in time that she might undo her mistake of refusing Gareth's offer.

Now here she was with Gareth, his offer of marriage renewed. She had not gone back in time, but it was close. Better than she had dared hope for.

"Hear me now," he whispered. "We will not dwell on the past. It cannot be changed. John would not want you to feel burdened. He would want you to be happy. He would want us to be happy. Let us look to the future. Yes?"

"Yes," she said. "I will try." John would want them both to be happy. And speaking of John . . . "Gareth, how did you find me that day in the cave with John's remains?"

He cringed a little. "I think it best if you don't ask that question."

This only made her more curious. "Tell me."

"I was led there . . . by a woman in a green dress and long, dark hair. She beckoned me from the cave's opening in the cliff walls."

Elaine leaned up and stared right into his face. "Gwenevere? Are you in earnest? Why did you not tell me?"

"I did not tell you at first because there was other business at hand. Then I did not tell you because I was angry with you; you were marrying another man. Then I did not tell you because there was no time."

Just when she thought everything was at last in the open, he'd been keeping this. "It's all right," she said. "I forgive you, because that is what love means."

He laughed out loud, pulling her back until she was settled beside him again. "The Lady Gwenevere seems to be looking out for you."

"Do you really think it was her?"

"Who else could it be?"

Indeed. No one else would have known where to find her brother. At least, no one willing to show her. Merlin must have sent her. For Gwenevere had played her part perfectly to bring her and Gareth back together.

Gareth released her. "Your minute is up. Now go and fetch me some breakfast because I'm starving."

"Perhaps just one more minute, if you don't mind."

His arm tightened around her again. "I don't mind at all."

Elaine put on her bonnet and shawl and walked out the back door to the edge of the cliffs. Gareth had gone home a week ago. He'd stayed only long enough to arrange the marriage details with her father. After all that had happened, her father welcomed the idea of Gareth Kemp. Her mother too. For when she told her about him, her knitting needles kept on at a natural, even pace. A calm and steady minuet rather than her frantic jig.

Of course, Elaine had been over to Lowentop every day since. Mrs. Kemp had hugged her until she felt light-headed from lack of breath. Gareth was recovering quickly, already up and about. Tossing all the pieces of Lord Chiverton's phaeton into the yard and burning them to ash.

The breeze blew as it always did coming off the sea. Her hair, unpinned yet for the day, fluttered out behind her. She stretched out her hands, each holding an end of the shawl. The blue silk billowed out behind her like a sail in the wind. It was the same shawl she'd loaned to Gwenevere down in the cave.

It had been a long time since Elaine had felt so light. If the winds picked up, she might very well fly.

Squire Stroud was on his way to Bodmin to face trial. Lord Chiverton would go before the House of Lords. Brixton and the man from the Landguard were being laid to rest. But these were thoughts she'd rather not contemplate. *We will not dwell on the past*, Gareth had said. And she'd promised to try.

"Miss Elowen Cardinham."

She grinned. Only one person in the world called her by her Cornish name. She turned to greet Gareth just as a gust blew up from the cliffs. It caught her shawl and swirled it up into the sky, the cloth coming to rest on the far side of a hawthorn tree.

"Mr. Kemp," she said, walking toward where he waited with arms outstretched. She hurried, the sooner to be in them.

He closed his arms around her, pulling her in tighter than ever. His broken rib must be mending.

"How are you feeling?" she asked.

"Better now. Infinitely better." He did look very well, his dark hair mussed by the wind and his eyes the color of the golden sun as it passed through the silver-clouded sky.

"I'm glad to hear it. For I've promised to take Aunt Rose on a stroll around the gardens. Perhaps you'd like to accompany us?" Her aunt was also feeling a great deal recovered. Uncle Charles had said she would be fine, and he'd been right.

"It would be my pleasure," he said. He took her hand, following along as she went to recover her shawl.

But her shawl was not on the ground. It had landed on top of a low rock wall. And on top of it lay a circlet of gold, very much like the one that had been on Gwenevere's head.

Elaine glanced around, but there was no one to be seen. Nothing but the wind tugging at her gown and whistling through the hawthorn leaves.

"What is this?" she asked as if Gareth might have an explanation.

"I cannot say." He also searched the heath.

She lifted the circlet. It was heavier than it looked. Real gold, with an emerald in the center. "Gareth, I think this belongs to Gwenevere."

Gareth took it from her, examined it, then handed it back. "She must mean for you to have it."

Perhaps. For nothing thus far concerning the mysterious woman had seemed an accident.

She put the circlet on her head and gave a little curtsy to Gareth.

"It suits you well. After all," he said, "you are the fairest in the land." He leaned close, kissing her cheek and then her lips. "But don't tell Gwenevere I said that," he whispered into the curve of her neck. "Or Miss Tippet."

Elaine laughed. "It's not too late to change your mind."

Gareth gave her one more kiss. "On the contrary, 'tis far too late."

She wrapped her shawl around her shoulders, and they started back toward Havencross.

Gareth held out his arm, and she looped her hand tightly around it. She was here at last, where she'd wanted to be all along. A different path would have been easier, but nothing about this moment could be better.

The crashing of waves faded as they crossed the heath. The weathered stones of Havencross waited in the distance. She leaned her head against his shoulder.

What a twisting, wretched road that had led her home, but how welcome the rest now that it was over. And she had a new path now, one she would walk with Gareth at her side. Her heart at last at peace. Queen of her own beautiful Camelot.

A FEW WORDS AND WHAT THEY MEAN

bal maiden—*Bal* is the Cornish word for *mine*. Bal maidens were young women and girls employed to work above ground at the mines, usually hammering ore into smaller pieces. Their workdays were long and grueling year-round, even in the most extreme weather conditions.

brambles—The common blackberry.

chough—(Rhymes with ruff.) A member of the crow family, these birds have a black body, a slender, down-curved reddish beak, and reddish legs. Once common in Cornwall, they are now rare.

devil's hour—The hour between 3:00 and 4:00 a.m., when spirits and demons are most likely to be out and about. A period of bad luck.

dredgy ore—Inferior ore.

duw genes—"Good-bye" in Cornish.

fairings—A Cornish biscuit (cookie) made with ginger and other spices, similar to a ginger snap.

free traders—Another term for smugglers.

hevva cake—(Heavy cake.) A thin, dense cake made of flour, lard or butter, sugar, and dried currants. A crisscross pattern is often scored along the top to represent fishing nets.

Landguard—Mounted customs officers sent to patrol areas of heavy smuggling. There were usually not nearly enough Landguard officials to do much damage to the smuggling gangs. Underpaid and persecuted by smugglers, many of the Landguard turned to smuggling themselves.

lugger—A small sailing ship with two or three masts. Very popular with smugglers.

meur ras—"Thank you" in Cornish.

moorstone—Granite, the prevalent stone of the Cornish moors.

pasty—(Rhymes with "nasty" but is actually quite delicious.) A meat pie usually consisting of beef, potatoes, onions, and turnips baked in a pastry, like a turnover. Very popular with the miners, as they were easily transportable. Many of the mines contained arsenic and other toxic minerals. The miners would hold the pasty by the thick crust to keep from transferring these minerals from their hands to their food, then discard the crust.

pilchard—A small silvery fish in the herring family. Heavily fished off the Cornish coast.

piskey—One of the fairy folk—a pixie. Sometimes considered mischievous, sometimes lucky.

revenuers—Customs officials whose job was to collect the import taxes and prevent the smuggling of goods.

stargazy pie—A traditional Cornish dish made of baked whole pilchards, eggs, and onions. It is placed in a dish and covered with a crust, like a pot pie. The pilchards are placed so that the fish heads are all poking out above the crust, as if gazing at the sky.

tetty-rattle—Cornish stew made with potatoes—"tetty" refers to potatoes.

wreckers—Men who plundered wrecked ships along the coast.

AUTHOR'S NOTE

(Caution: Spoilers Ahead!)

SHOW ME A CORNISHMAN, AND I'll show you a smuggler.

Perhaps not far from the truth during the eighteenth and early nineteenth century in Cornwall. I did not exaggerate the number and diversity of people involved in smuggling at that time. Some were heavily involved, like those in my story, and some simply followed Kipling's advice and turned a blind eye.

Watch the wall, my darling, while the gentlemen go by.

The more I researched, the more astonished I became at the scope of smuggling operations in Cornwall. To some, they were villains; to others, heroes. But they affected the lives of everyone.

It wasn't until the middle of the nineteenth century that Britain's free-trade policy finally made large-scale smuggling a memory.

My husband and I traveled to Cornwall to research this book (and to celebrate our anniversary). We fell in love with the rocky cliffs and the tiny narrow roads with hedges twice the height of a person. I've never seen anything like it. I reached out of our car window and picked wild blackberries from the hedges when we had to slow down for oncoming cars.

While there, we listened to BBC Radio Cornwall and heard a very interesting discussion about the Chiverton Cross Roundabout in Truro. Apparently, the roundabout had recently been overhauled in a multimillion-pound improvement project. But it seems the people of Cornwall were not happy with the results.

For over an hour, they called in to the radio show and complained about the number of accidents at the new Chiverton roundabout. It kept going on and on, people talking about the utter mess and confusion at this place—especially during high-traffic times. They hated it. And that is how Lord Chiverton got his name.

I was especially excited to see the ruins of Tintagel again. I hadn't been there since I was eight. The Arthurian legend holds a special place in my heart (because, apparently, I'm an incurable romantic), and I wanted to put a few references to it in this book as a backdrop. What a beautiful place, standing on the tiny headland with the wind spinning whispers of Arthur and Gwenevere all around me.

Cornwall is an amazing place, and I hope through this book I was able to capture at least a small snippet of its magic.

For more on Cornwall and the inspirations behind *Havencross*, see my Pinterest page: www.pinterest.com/juliedaines.

ACKNOWLEDGMENTS

I MUST START BY THANKING my husband for taking me back to England to experience Cornwall. For waiting patiently while I covered every inch of the Tintagel ruins and for going deep into the tin mine with me. He is the best! I didn't even mind that he fell asleep in the passenger seat and made me drive all the way from our house in St. Ives to Bodmin Moor—and back. I got to listen to Jamaica Inn while driving to the actual Jamaica Inn.

Thanks again to Samantha Millburn for taking my gibberish and helping turn it into a book that (hopefully) makes sense. I have so much gratitude for all the folks at Covenant who use their talents and skills to make my books lovely. They are all wonderful people!

Special thanks to my beta readers. Your honesty is brutal but appreciated more than you know. Tiffany, as always, cheers to you for starting everything and being beta-reader supreme. Michelle, for taking the time even with newborn number four. And, Rachel, I can't wait to return the favor!

My final shout out is to Stuart, Brady, Jacob, and Maren. I'm not sure they consider me a "real" author yet, but that's okay. I'm just happy to be their mom.

ABOUT THE AUTHOR

Julie Daines was born in Concord, Massachusetts, and was raised in Utah. She spent eighteen months living in London, where she studied and fell in love with English literature, sticky toffee pudding, and the mysterious guy who ran the kebab store around the corner.

She loves reading, writing, and watching movies—anything that transports her to another world. She picks Captain Wentworth over Mr. Darcy, firmly believes in second breakfast, and never leaves home without her verveine.